The Heather  to
The Hawkesbury

Sheila Hunter

Pacific Wanderland Publication
3 Avoca Valley Way
Kincumber NSW 2251
Email: spowter@bigpond.net.au
(02) 4368 6723
www.sheilahunter.com.au

Available from Amazon.com, CreateSpace
and other retail outlets
Also available on Kindle and other devices.

1st Edition Printed, 2015 Amazon ISBN 1533473641
2nd Edition, Digital 2016 ASIN: B01A21JYWQ
3rd Edition Large Print 2017 Amazon ISBN 533473641

4th Edition published in Australia in 2018 by Pacific Wanderland P/L© 2018 Sara Powter,
ISBN-13: 978-0-9945782-2-8

A catalogue record for this
book is available from the
National Library of Australia

Cover Painting is by Joseph Lycett (engraver)
English c.1775–1828, worked in Australia 1814–22
View of Windsor, Upon the River Hawkesbury, New South Wales 1824
plate no. 15 in Views in Australia published by J. Souter, London.
Hand-coloured aquatint 23.5 x 33.0 cm. State Library of Victoria, Melbourne (30328102131561/16)

Cover Photo insert and right, (edited) is both Of and Owned by,
Deb Cox and family.
Taken at Old Sydney Town, Somersby, NSW in 1980's

Cover design by Sara Powter and internal layout by Jenny Cowan
Printed in Australia by McPhersons

The Heather
to
The Hawkesbury

Sheila Hunter

Co-Winner of 1999
NSW Premiers Senior Citizens Award

Editor's Note:-

The background to this story is gleaned from the authors own family history. Her Ancestors came from the Isle of Skye during the Highland Clearances and Potato Famine and were themselves Macdonald's who arrived in Melbourne Victoria on one of the Highland and Island Emigrations Society Ships.

Sheila's Macdonalds did not come to NSW nor were they farmers, they went to the Victorian goldfields and became storekeepers and undertakers. Her husband's family were also "Bounty Immigrants" as they were called and came from various parts of Scotland and Ireland. The McLeans came from the Isle of Mull, the Gibson's from Northern Ireland, but there were other families and they had very similar backgrounds to the characters in the story except most of them were totally illiterate to written English at least! They spoke nothing but Gaelic and had little or no manners of any known sort, let alone personal hygiene! They would use the same containers for both cooking and for 'bodily functions' during the nights! They never washed either themselves or their clothing. They must have been very unpleasant to be around and yet it was these same people who settled the Northern areas of New South Wales and felled the trees, started the dairies and farmed the fertile flood plains around all the northern rivers.

This story follows a different class, a middle class of immigrants, educated and clean, far different from the majority of Highland settlers, but all had the same Highland Tenacity!

Sara Powter

Dedication

To our family -
who come before and prepared the way for us today!

and to my children -
who have yet to travel the path that was made for them!

Let us learn from each other.

Sheila Hunter
1924-2002
© Sara Powter 2014

That future generations might know and those yet unborn:
that they in turn might teach it to their children;
So that they might put their confidence in God:
and not forget His works but keep His commandments.

Psalm 78 v 6 , 7 NRSV the Bible

NAMES AND AGES ON SCOTTISH FAMILIES
ON DEPARTURE FROM SKYE

Murdoch (42) & Mary (41) MACDONALD
5 children: Malcolm (14), Duncan (12), Catherine (10),
Mary Ann (5) & John (4)

Alec (38) & Margaret (Meg)(38) FRASER
(Mary's friend Meg was Murdoch's cousin)
6 children: Ian (14), Jennet (Janet)(12), Elizabeth (Effie)(10),
Jamie (8), Kate (6) & Eliza (4)

Caroline (Caro) (33) & Alistair (42) MACLEOD
(Murdoch Macdonald's Sister)
3 children: Donald (16), Ann (10), Jane (8)

Elspeth (35) & Fergus (40) MACKENZIE
(Mary Macdonald's brother)
4 children: Hamish (14), Sara (12), Alison (10), & Susannah (6)

(see end for further Family Trees)

CONTENTS

viii

Musing: *Prologue*

"I think Australia is going to the dogs and if we don't watch out there'll be no Australia to live in."

"Bill, give it a go!" Every generation has said that the next is worse than the last."

I sat listening to my two brothers and it made me think about our country. I wonder what our forbears thought of this place when they came here. I imagine that the men would have taken it better than the women. I don't know, though ... when I think of old Aunt Jane and what a tough old girl she is. Eighty seven and her mind is still very sharp. I should really write a lot of her stories down before she goes and before I forget. I really must do it.

"Sally, wake up, there's something boiling over on the stove."

I roused myself and hurried to the kitchen.

"Bill, I've just thought up a new project for myself'"

"Not another one, dear," laughed Bill, "what is it this time?"

"Well, you and Chris started it, when you were talking about how this generation is letting Australia run down"

"What are you going to do? Start a new political party?"

"No, Bill, I am not! I'm going to write a book and tell the people what went into making this wonderful land of ours. You know our young are pitifully ignorant of what our grandfathers did. Our own people came here about a hundred and thirty years ago and I'll bet there is a story or two in their doings. I must ask Aunt Jane if I can go through all that stuff in her old cedar chest"

"Go to it, girl, you may as well give it a try."

"Right - good for the Macdonalds!"

CHAPTER 1: *Hopes and Plans*

Murdoch quickly looked out from his dry shelter, braced himself and went into the cold rain. He leaned into the wind and carefully picked his way down the road in the dark. It was very cold, but he smiled to himself and lightened his step as he went.

In a deep corner of his heart there lurked a doubt. "Well" he muttered to himself, "the decision is made, we cannot turn back now."

Mary looked at the wet figure as he stood dripping just inside the door.

"The word has come, my Mary, we are on our way."

In the dim light of the cottage Murdoch Macdonald saw his wife stiffen and pale. She sat down quickly, took a breath and smiled bravely at the man, seeing suppressed excitement in his eyes.

"Tell me about it!" was all she said.

"The Laird received the papers today and The Society has booked passages for the four families. We all go together. Praise the Lord! You will be fortunate in having your brother and my sister with us, love, and the Frasers, too. Many have had to travel with strangers, but we will be a family party."

"How long have we, Murdoch? Where do we go?"

"Wait, Lass, until I get my wet things off and we'll warm by the fire and I'll tell you."

During his brief absence in their sleeping quarters Mary was able to still her churning thoughts and was sitting waiting by the fire when he returned.

He placed some papers in her hands and said, "These tell us that we leave on June 11th by steamer to Liverpool and there we stay in the Government depot until the ship, the *Mistress Azure*, sails to take us to Australia. So we have two months to prepare for it. The Laird has told me what to do and how to pack our things.

Lady Macdonald, too said she would like to talk to you four lassies so she can help you plan the packing and what clothes you are to take. We must take some food with us on the voyage and things for cooking and eating. Life will be hard for some months, lass, but I'm sure it will be worth it in the end."

"Oh, Murdoch, it is all so strange to think of. We won't know how to manage"

"Yes, we will Lass, the Laird will help us four men to plan and Lady Macdonald will help you mothers to decide about our families. Aye, but it is grand to think about."

Mary studied the faraway-look on his rugged face. She was faint of heart. It was almost unthinkable, this life of the future. The Colonies - strange, hot, barbarous places they seemed. How could she face leaving this green land she knew so well. Deep down she knew that it was inevitable, the plans were made, but there was always a little hope that something would stop them from leaving. She realised that Murdoch was looking at her. He leaned over and took her hand.

"Mary, my darling, don't look like that. I'll be with you all the time, I'll not leave you. We must look beyond our own desires. There is nothing now here for us in our Islands. Since the Clearances there is nothing for a farmer in Skye. Our boys Malcolm, Duncan and John what of them? And Fergus, Alistair's and Alec's children, and our two fine lassies Catherine and wee Maryann? We must make a new life for them. We'll work hard and soon have farms of our own. It is possible in the new lands, but not here in Scotland, not here on Skye. If I have to cross the world to set you up I will do it, but I'll need you by me Mary. I cannot do anything without you. I'll look after you, I promise, and I will build you such a grand house, one with stairs, and we will call it "Duntulm" after the old castle, only this one will be our new castle."

Did ever a woman have such a man? How could you resist such an appeal? Mary kissed him sweetly and said, "Come, my adventurer, come and have your supper, and you shall tell me more as you eat it."

***

The Laird sat in his big leather chair, staring at the bright flames, one hand idly fondling the satin ear of his favourite hound, beside him. He turned as the door opened and smiled as his wife, a tall dark Highland woman like so many of her Scottish sisters.

"Well, how did you get on, Colin?" she asked, sitting in the opposite chair stretching her feet to the warmth.

The Laird sighed. "Murdoch has just left with the papers, dear. I am sure they will be a good group. In a way, I am sorry to lose them, or at least sorry the Macdonalds and the MacLeods are going but Fergus MacKenzie is a bit of a risk. I daresay I should not have sponsored him as he is so ill and Alec Fraser is a positive risk, but I'll be happy because Skye is well rid of him."

"Should you do so, then? The Highland and Island Society would not thank you for sending anyone who has a dubious character."

"I've considered it well, my dear, and Murdoch Macdonald and Alistair MacLeod guarantee they will keep him in line. I sponsored Fergus because he is a good man, he is Mary Macdonald's brother, and Murdoch feels assured that the voyage to the Antipodes will cure his chest complaint. I hope so."

"You'll be sorry to see Alistair go, won't you?" asked Lady Macdonald.

"Yes, it is a sad thing that we lose such men as Alistair, but there is no place for him here. The education his father gave his children is wasted here. I would say that Alistair could have done very well academically, but what chance has he? He was born in the wrong class. It will be interesting to see how he makes out in New South Wales."

"Well, I couldn't imagine that he would find much use for his book learning, there will be surely little opportunity, except for teaching his own children. What does he intend doing, Colin?"

"They all intend farming. Perhaps not Fergus, if he ever does reach Australia. I think he will end up being a clerk or something. Alistair tells me that he has quite an aptitude for reckoning. It may be useful to him. He also tells me that Alec Fraser is hopeless but that Alec's wife Margaret is almost as quick as Fergus MacKenzie. She is a good lass, maybe she will help keep Alec straight."

"Do you think our people will find a better life in the colonies? It all seems so far away and strange."

The Laird looked over to his wife and smiled, thinking of the difference between her life and that of the destitute farmers on his estates. He said, "I have often wondered what I am doing sending these people to such an unknown place as Australia, Fiona, but what have they here? Very little prospect of seeing their families grow up healthy and useful. Think of Alistair and his family trying to fit into the cottage with his parents and others, too. Murdoch is all right as he hasn't had to share with his family, so far, but he would if he stayed. He would have to share with his brother when he marries. There is no other place for him. And there is no work for the young ones. Fergus is still home with his family and what a squeeze that must be. Alec Fraser is a problem to all but for Margarets' sake several relatives have taken them for a spell. At least, Fiona, they have a chance of getting work in Australia and often a cottage goes with the job on a farm. The life will be very healthy and I believe farm workers can get jobs easily now that gold fever has taken the land. Apparently a great number of shepherds and farmers have gone to the gold fields. I don't suppose I blame them but I am thankful that the Highland and Island Immigration Society tries to tie them down with a promise-to keep away from the 'diggings' as they call the gold fields."

"We wish them well, Colin. After all we have heard that the McCuan's are settled well there, so I daresay it can be done."

***

The sun burst through the door as Mary opened it. She pulled her shawl around her as she stepped out into the sparkling crisp morning. What a glorious spring day!

"Dear Lord," she said, looking up to the sky above, Why do you give us such a beautiful day? Why can't it still be raining? I want the sky to cry, just as I'm crying inside me."

Standing on a rise she looked across the green sodden fields to the scattered houses on the slopes to the sea. A rare day indeed and the memory of it to remain with her all her life. Turning she looked at the misty purple Cuillans[1] in the distance. Taking a deep breath of the pure cold air, she turned again to find her husband and eldest son Malcolm standing at the door.

"Ay, it is a grand sight, love, one that we'll carry with us when we go. Come, we'll tell the children of our plans. Malcolm has been telling the young ones that we're off on our adventures and I'm sure that think that we are going today."

As Mary passed him he gave her a quick squeeze and a big smile. Malcolm plying them with questions as they prepared their oatmeal.

"Now Mary, I think it would be good if you, Caroline, Elspeth and Margaret could see Lady Macdonald quickly and you plan our packing and we men will speak to the Laird about transport, money and the rest."

The potato famine of 1836-7 was bad in Ireland and just as devastating in the Western Isles of Scotland. Then a second which began in 1847, caused even more heartbreak for the people, as the population of the places like Skye had increased to more than the area could hold. There were 26,000 in Skye alone and so many people were starving that the government sent in shiploads of oatmeal and potatoes to the affected areas to help their plight. The idea of immigration then was accepted as one of the unpleasant necessities, and it was at this time that the Highland and Island Immigration Society was formed by the Clan Chiefs.

As well, there was much pressure for the people to leave their homeland, for many of the clan chiefs, the Lairds, had to sell land, mostly to southerners who wished to run sheep on their new land and fence the farmlands, and as a consequence wished to clear the land of unwanted tenant farmers.

Many tragic stories of the way these carried 'clearances' were out were fresh in the minds of the Macdonalds. People who had been lifelong neighbours had been forced to go on the road to find shelter and a new life of sorts, for their old, their young and themselves.

[1] Cuillans - the Main mountains in Isle of Skye

Murdoch and his brothers-in-law and friends were being backed by the Highland and Island Society to voyage to Sydney Town and so begin a new life there or in the country beyond it. This society was made up of clan chiefs, including Lord Macdonald, and other concerned men, who paid the passage for selected people to leave their families and start afresh. The emigrants being asked to pay this back after settlement.

The people in Skye travelled little, for really there was nowhere to go except to visit a close neighbour. The thought of leaving their island was a challenging one, but to travel across the world to an unknown land was a thought so frightening that it almost could not be imagined.

The Skye farmer was a tough man. He had to be to cope with the wild cold land he farmed. The woman, too, was tough, but maybe was not the adventurous person her man might be. He had to be brave and strong to tackle the huge job of transporting the whole family through an experience like the one that Murdoch was contemplating. She would always stay by his side.

At least, they would not be alone. Murdoch's good friend, Mary's brother, Fergus, his wife and four children; Murdoch's sister Caroline and her husband Alistair MacLeod and their three children; and Alec and Margaret Fraser with their six children, would make up the group with Murdoch and Mary's own five bairns[2].

The boys went with Murdoch to cut and stack peats and Mary busied herself with her usual farm chores with the three younger children about her, thankful that their chatter kept her mind occupied. Every now and then, ten year old Catherine would put in a question and Mary answered these as she could. She sent them all with a message to her mother, as she finished her work, telling them to stay there until she had visited their Aunts Caroline and Elspeth up the hill.

Before she could leave the house her two sisters-in-law arrived in great excitement.

"Mary, what do you think of it all? Aren't you thrilled that word

2 Bairns - the word for Children in Scotland

has come at last? I wanted to come earlier but the cow has just calved and Alistair needed me."

"Oh, Caroline, I do suppose I'm excited, too, but I'm frightened as hell."

"Yes, I am too," joined in Elspeth. "Now that we really are going I wonder if I truly want to."

"But we'll all be together and we will have Margaret too" said Caroline.

"There's no doubt about you Macdonalds, you will try anything. Caroline, you are so like Murdoch. I am sure he is not afraid and I seem to be filled with thoughts of all the things that can go wrong."

"Mary, you know you don't want to stay here. What is there for us? We are hard workers" Caroline said eagerly," and we know we will do well if that's what is needed. I for one am very tired of working for very little and want the chance of getting my children into the sun. I don't want them to get sick like Fergus. How is he this morning, Elspeth?"

"Pleased that we have the word" she replied, "He does feel he is a burden though, and wonders whether we ought to go. I do pray he gets better soon. It would be wonderful to see him in full strength again. I think your mother is pleased to see us go, if only to get Fergus well again, Mary."

"Yes, I think she is holding on to that thought and weighing it up against our leaving. What will we do without our mothers? We have always had them near by." Mary cried.

"We'll just pray that we can stay together and help each other. Aren't we fortunate that we can do that, as far as the colony, anyway" said Elspeth, "and then we will just have to leave it to the Lord to take care of the rest."

"Yes" said Caroline, "He will be with us wherever we are. Did you know that Macleod's are having a 'ceildh'[3] tonight? Everyone wants to hear about our news, so most of our friends will be there."

"I suppose there will be many 'ceildhs' in the time we have left. Do you remember when Murdoch's cousin went away, there were many" mused Mary. "I wonder if they'll be others to have 'ceildhs'

[3] Ceildh - Scottish social gathering with food, dancing & music

in Australia with us. We must never let the children forget our dances, poems and songs."

"Lassies there is one thing that concerns me and I feel that I must speak about it." Caroline looked seriously at her sisters-in-law, "it is one thing to take Fergus along, sick and all that he is, but we love him so that we'll not find him a burden even if he cannot work for a long time, but can we really cope with Alec Fraser? I know we are fond of Margaret, but truly, I think she has such a lot to manage with her six bairns, being an unruly lot at the best of times and I feel sure that you'll agree that Alec Fraser is not an asset."

"Don't fret, Caroline, Murdoch and I have talked about Alec a lot. I know he is a shiftless man, but Murdoch feels that he can keep him on the right road. We'll all do it for Margaret's sake. She is so dear and we can help make her burden lighter." Mary assured them.

Chapter 2: *Preparation*

There had been a great deal of preparation for months, many hours spent weaving, spinning and sewing, boxes made for packing, food prepared for the journey, but even though much had been done there was still little time in those last two months for sitting by and being idle. There were the normal farm chores to do for the farm, that would be taken over by a new tenant and Murdoch wanted it left in good order. This was some consolation to Mary and Murdoch, as their poor little piece of farmland would remain to be used by Murdoch's younger brother Angus and thus make his life a little more secure. Poor though the farm was, it was more than Angus had now. It was a case of move out and make room for others.

Mary spent as much time with her mother as possible. They both knew that their parting would be the part of it all.

"We'll not talk of it, "suggested Margaret MacKenzie, at first, "We'll just speak of our time together." But they found this impossible as this journey was the all consuming thought in each of them.

So they just talked and talked, of their fears and their hopes, deeply realising that soon they would see each other no more.

"I'm so glad you are all going together, lassie. You'll be able to look after the others. Do tell me how Fergus progresses. I know he will be better when he gets into a warmer land."

"I think he is better already," said Mary, "just thinking about it seems to have given him vitality. I do feel he has improved. He does seem to be coughing less than he did. It will be good to arrive in spring in New South Wales. We will really be having one very long summer and the Laird told Murdoch that the voyage could be mostly warm. He said that it is the best time of the year to go." She fell to musing. "Mother, how can it be springtime there and autumn here. What a strange place it must be. I wonder what the ship will be like?

I wonder how we shall manage food, sleeping, oh, Mother, I wonder so much. It is like walking to a cliff and stepping over, not knowing how far you are going to fall."

"Have faith, my daughter, the Lord will take care of you. Without this assurance I could not let you and Fergus go, and my grandchildren. It will be a big hole in your father's and my life, but we mustn't dwell on that. We will know that you are secure and that the children will have the prospect of a good future. It will be hard on you and Murdoch for you will shoulder a great deal of the burden, but Caroline and Elspeth will help you and Murdoch will have Alistair and I am sure Fergus will help when he can. Please God he gets better quickly."

"Yes, Mother, and I will write as often as I can and tell you how he is. I am sure we will make out all right. It's just not knowing what is in front of us."

***

On most of the lengthening evenings after supper, Murdoch and Mary would take the children walking, just walking around their homeland. This rugged, green island that was so much part of them. They would walk over the meadows, through the soggy peat, up into the hills, the children running like young calves, jumping the babbling burns, hiding in the clean fragrant heather, or perhaps turning seaward to sit on the cliffs to watch the gulls and seahawks, an otter playing on the shore, or just sitting and breathing it all in. They didn't seem to want anyone else, which was strange. They just wanted to absorb all that was around them so they could take of it what they could to this strange new land that someday may mean to them what this one did now. That was too impossible to think about, right now they only wanted this.

One such evening, almost at dusk, as they sat looking out to sea, a voice sounded behind them, and coming up to them on the hilltop.

"I see you people come here often. I watch you so close. I think I know what you feel, for I felt it when I left here to go to college."

"Oh, Mr Macleod, sometimes we feel we are going to prison or something like that," cried Mary as she watched the Rev David Macleod walk up to them.

"Not so bad as that, Mary," laughed Murdoch, "but we do feel as though we cannot get our fill."

"'Tis a grand view indeed Murdoch, and to my mind none better but there may be some in the parts where you are going. My cousin Hugh tells me Australia is a truly grand country. And I would say just right for people like yourselves."

"That's kind of you, sir. We pray that we make a job of it, with God's help."

"What will the church be like in Australia, Mr MacLeod?" was Mary's query.

"Well, the places are so scattered that you may have to make your own, Mary. It will much depend on where you go. Where ever you go the Lord will be with you, you'll not be lonely, He will be at your side. Do you have any plans Murdoch?"

"I do know that we'll not go to the goldfields, Mr Macleod. I'll not take my family there, even if the Highland and Island Society would allow us to. We did hear that so many men are leaving their farms that there would be places the plenty. So we'll go to Sydney and try to get places through there."

"I believe you are right. I've heard that Melbourne resembles a madhouse, so I would keep away from there. My cousin Hugh told me that a hard-working man can earn such wages that they can soon buy their own farm. You'd like that Murdoch."

"Aye", I would. It's something that would never happen here, Mr Macleod. It is a great dream we have. I would dearly love to set Mary up in a nice wee house and with the boys to work hard on a farm that was ours. Think of it, Mary love, just think. I hope to get a job as a shepherd or a farmhand and work to save our money. The boys, too will work for that. I hope Mary need not.

"There is a great deal of land for a hard worker there and the Government is only too anxious to help those who are willing to pioneer new country. Murdoch, we' miss you in Skye. We all look to you as a leader. When the Society started sending people to the colonies, I'm sure the Laird didn't want to ship people like you out, or Alistair or Fergus. They would truly like you to stay and perhaps rid us only of the shiftless ones. And talking of shiftless ones, you'll need to keep your eye on Alec Fraser. You've taken on something there, man. I daresay he will listen to you, particularly as it is only under your care that the Society is taking him. He is a lucky fellow to have you in charge. I do feel that it will gave the children their only chance to be in your care. But as I say, we'll miss you."

"It is kind of you to say so, Mr Macleod. We find it hard to go, but we can all see that there is little for our children and theirs if we stay, and the prospect of getting on is very tempting. Don't worry about Alec. We'll manage him, and hope to keep him in line if only for Margaret's sake. But he is a very likeable fellow."

"I know that, and I hope it works out well. The Laird was telling me the other day that he almost envies you somewhat. He would like to do the same for his bairns, but thankfully he is a true clan chief and his people come first and he will stay here no matter how hard it is"

"Aye, he told me this himself. He is a grand father to us all."

"Look at those young ones, not a care in the world." Macleod pointed with his stick at the young Macdonald's rolling in the heather like puppies. Tiny John sitting by watching his brothers and sisters in their frolic. Chuckling he went off down the hill.

"Remember it all, lass," said Murdoch, "remember it all so you can tell our young ones. Malcolm and Duncan and even Catherine will remember some, but absorb it all so you can tell wee Maryann and John, for they'll not know it at all. Just look at the sparkle of the water, the deep red purple of the heather, and the bog myrtle there amongst it, our purple mountains oh, what a sight. The green grass but I suppose they have that in Australia."

"Oh, Murdoch, you sound like a poet."

"I feel I could write and write lots of poetry about this, but the words don't really tell what I feel. We'll miss this land of ours, Mary.

But, come, we must take the children home. Tomorrow will soon come and more peats are to be cut for Angus."

Collecting the children they wandered back to their home. Mary put the two little ones to bed while the oldest ones sat at the fire with Murdoch, who knocked the peats together to boil water for their bed time drink. They plied him with questions about their new life, Catherine listening with amazement at the answers her father gave the boys. It was all so strange. She just couldn't take it in, so she let her eyes wander round the inside of their house, looking at all the things she knew so well. Soon they would be packed up and taken, where? It was a bit frightening to think about. This dear house, so closely did they live together, even sharing it with their cow. She could hear the cow lipping her food in the trough. "I suppose Uncle Angus will like to live here with her." the sleepy girl thought.

Chapter 3: *Setting Out*

The ship was coming at noon and so the four families had to have all their possessions at the waterfront ready to be ferried out by boat. Hugh Macleod, who owned the rowing boat had luggage piled up in boatloads so they could be handled easily. As soon as the steamer came round the point they shoved Hughie's boat out and quickly loaded her.

At last all the gear was aboard and old Hughie was on his way back for the passengers. The Frasers went first and then the MacLeods, the MacKenzies and the Macdonalds. The boys full of excitement and the girls also eager, but more conscious of the poignant moment that their parents were experiencing. The men saluted their beloved parents and covered their emotions by organising the loading of the children.

Mary and Elspeth frantically farewelled their mothers and as each was handed a small child they climbed into the boat. They sat side by side on the broad seat, not speaking. Their faces tense, white and pinched, determined not to shed tears and clutching their burdens until Maryann in Elspeth's arms said, "Aunty, you hurt." They tried to relax but sat looking back at their beloved isle, the homeland that they would never see again, and at their wonderful parents, the centre of their lives until now.

A feeling of panic welled up in Mary, and then the tears came. "Mother, oh Mother," she sobbed. "How can I leave you? Oh Mother."

"Mary," came the deep gentle voice of her husband, behind her, "bear up, Lass, take it all in, and don't miss a bit of that sight. Open you eyes and take it all in."

With a sobbing sigh, Mary wiped her eyes. "Yes, Murdoch, you're right. I mustn't lose one moment of what we have left. Look, Elspeth, look at that beautiful land."

God was very kind for it was a rare sunny day. Not often was it so calm and blue. They drank in the beauty before them. The green bareness of the fields running from the sparkling sea up to the blue and purple mountains Cuillans were there ever such mountains as these? breathed Mary.

The houses, some white, dotted through the emerald fields and the smaller white dots of the sheep that had been the cause of the clearing of the farms.

"Breathe it up, lassies, and have your last look. We're here."

With a struggle, they got themselves and the children aboard the steamship, and said their last farewells to old Hughie.

"God be with you, my lads and lassies" he said, "we'll miss you sore indeed."

"And you, Hughie, thanks for all you've done."

They watched their last link with Skye row himself back to their waiting loved ones on the shore. The steamer blew its whistle and hauled up its anchor and nosed out to sea.

"Fergus, are you all right?" cried Elspeth, catching sight of her husband's white face. "Oh, Murdoch, quick."

"Heh, man, grab hold of me and sit down. Here, sit on the luggage and don't move until we get settled in." Murdoch lowered Fergus to the bags of clothing and soon his colour came back.

"I'm all right now, friend, but will stay a moment if you don't mind. I wonder where Alistair and Alec are?"

"Here now, Fergus, just seeing to our quarters," said Alistair, coming up on deck." Soon I will show you where to go. You stay there Fergus and I'll get the women and children settled first."

Now that the voyage had begun they stood and looked around them. The noise and smell of the coaster was something that they could not have believed. They soon settled into their quarters but there was room only for the women and girls, the men would have to make do on the deck. Queer and cramped they thought it, but felt they could manage as it would only be a matter of days before they would be in Liverpool and then their really big voyage would begin.

The children were anxious to explore and it was with difficulty that the adults were able to curb the curiosity of the young. The little ones were only content to stay by their mothers as it was all so strange and noisy.

"Noise, noise, will it ever stop?" said Mary. "The worst noise we've ever heard was the sound of our storms, but this just goes on and on."

"They tell me you get used to it, but I find that hard to believe", encouraged Elspeth. "Maybe the sailing ship will be better. I don't think it could be any worse".

As quickly as they could they put their travelling things away and went up on deck to see the last of their island.

"What great fortune the weather is so good. The sea is calm and I feel sure we'll not suffer from seasickness, Mary." Murdoch turned to see his brother-in-law behind him. "Fergus, should you be here lad? You maybe should be abed."

"No, I'll not miss the last glimpse, man. I daresay I'll not see our land again."

"It will be there for hours yet. It is a big island and I think we'll have it for quite some time."

They could still see it, or what they thought was Skye when they went for their evening meal. It became quite mixed with other isles and mountains that it was hard to be sure but while they could, they looked.

All through the days that lay ahead the families watched the coastline, new to them as none had left their homeland shores before. The women were mostly concerned with keeping track of the children, who rapidly became used to the new life and so roamed as they were permitted, or not at times. The older children had a great sense of responsibility and so watched over the younger ones. The parents spent most of the time together, glad of their closeness to each other in this unknown adventure. They were sorry for smaller groups of people and even lone ones, picked up from various ports on the way south. They stayed apart wanting only their own company, frightened of too many new things to come.

They called in at Glasgow, their first experience of a big bustling city, but did not disembark as it was all too big, dirty and noisy to attract them. They stayed aboard and soon they were in Liverpool.

Chapter 4: *Embarkation*

Liverpool, a foreign city, a foreign land, a foreign tongue. The first they saw of it was the forest of masts of the overseas vessels. They seemed endless, but at last they arrived at the wharf and Murdoch took charge again.

"Alistair and Alec are staying aboard until I get you settled into the Government depot. Fergus will come with us."

The Government depots were large buildings built to house emigrants while they awaited embarkation.

As the four women entered the building they were amazed and horrified at finding one very large room. Just two long shelves along each side divided every four feet by a partition two feet high, with a mattress on each shelf. There must have been three hundred people in the room. The place was clean enough, but what crowding! Mary emitted a groan and hid her face in Johnny's coat as she clutched him tightly. "Oh, Murdoch, we surely don't have to stay here, do we?"

"Aye" said a voice nearby. Mary turned and found herself facing a wee bent man in a faded kilt. "Aye, lass, this is the only accommodation to be had. It's not so bad today, but until yesterday it was terrible. Thank our Lord, eight hundred people sailed then."

"I've never seen so many people in one room."

"I daresay you haven't, madam, but they tell me it's worse on the ship."

"Oh, no," breathed Mary.

They were taken to some unoccupied sections and the women tried to settle into it while Murdoch went back to the ship for their luggage and the other men.

For two days they lived in these quarters with little to do but sit together and mind the children. Murdoch, Alistair and Alec spent most of the time seeing the agent and arranging the shipping of their luggage.

Fortunately their ship, the *Mistress Azure*, was due to sail on the third day after their arrival. Many of the people in the depot were envious of the Macdonald party as some had been awaiting a ship for some time.

Mary could not believe any ship could be as bad as this. No privacy, just people, people. Children screaming and the stench of unwashed bodies everywhere. She found too, that it was very hard to understand the speech of those around her. She knew they spoke the English tongue, but it often seemed impossible to believe this. What a blessing they were not alone

It was a job to keep the young ones out of mischief. Fergus and the older boys were trying to amuse the younger ones, leaving only the very small for the mothers to cope with.

Small Johnnie was such a worry too, as he seemed hot and fretful, surely he wasn't sickening!

At least the food was very good at the depot and the women were content to procure large quantities of food for their families, some of it quite strange to them, but the boys enjoyed it all immensely.

Even years later the memory of the next day didn't fade. To Mary it was a nightmare. They were able to get aboard the ship fairly early in the day. The women, laden with hand luggage and the smallest children, staggered up the gangway. They saw that some people had big wooden boxes to store their gear, but many, as did the Macdonalds, carried a great deal item by item. There seemed to be a constant stream of pots, pans, mugs, plates, shovels and tools of all kinds. Cows, pigs, sheep and hens, all taken aboard and as much food as the people could manage. Basic food was supplied to passengers, but most, like the Macdonalds, brought more.

They had many eggs stored in fat, and bacon, potatoes and other vegetables and, of course, oatmeal for porridge and cakes.

Mary was quite wrong, the ship was much worse than the depot. There were hundreds of people below decks, but where the depot was light and clean, the room they were taken to was very dark and it smelled evilly.

This time there were two shelves running along each side of the ship, one upon the other. Each section four feet wide with a small board separating each bunk. There was a long table running down the centre, with seats on either side. This was where the passengers ate, cooked and generally spent their hours.

Mary took all this in and turned turtle and headed for the deck. "I won't stay, Murdoch, I can't stay. Where can I put the children? How can I look after them there? How could we spend four months in that? Please Murdoch, say we'll go home, please." With this she burst into tears, clutching the whimpering, hot John, and sat hard on a large coil of rope, with the children and a frantic Murdoch around her.

"Mary," Murdoch said sharply, "pull yourself together, lass." He waited for the sobs to stop and after a time she raised a tearful face to him with pleading in her eyes. Murdoch cut in sharply. "It's no good, lass. We cannot go back and you know it." As she appeared to want to succumb to tears again, he sat beside her and put his arm about her.

"Lassie, there's no turning back. We've committed ourselves. I realise it's terrible down there. I realise that so much depends on you. I realise that it is a big risk to have the children down in that dark hole, but love, look past this, look at the end of the journey. A new start, a new home, a chance for the children that they'd never get at home." He gave her a quick squeeze and said "Mary, my love, we've been through a lot together. We've laughed together, loved together, worked together and near starved together. And now look at our children. It's for them we'll go through this, to give them a chance where they will grow free and healthy. The colony is young and so are we.

Let us look at this journey as an end and then we can start a new beginning in New South Wales. We're not the first to be taking this voyage and the people before us weathered it, so we must too. Dry your eyes and let us settle into this next home of ours. The others will wonder where we are."

So once more descending to the sleeping area, they found Alistair looking for them.

"We're in great luck," he greeted them, been able to get the area at the end for all of us and so we can put curtains up and have a great deal more privacy than if we were a centre section."

And so the voyage began.

Chapter 5: *At Sea*

The first day at sea was blue and calm. They settled in amazingly quickly and things looked somewhat better, but on the second night out Johnny appeared to be really ill. The surgeon, Mr. Harris, came to see him and several others who were ill and gravely "hm'd" and "ha'd". "He certainly has a fever, but what, at this time, I do not know. Just give him drinks and we will see what he is like tomorrow."

Tomorrow turned out to be just one more day that Mary did not want to remember and indeed for several days after it as well. During the night they ran into a severe storm and they all found what a ship can do in rough weather.

As the ship tossed, people and belongings went everywhere. Most were seasick and it was an impossible task to tend those who needed it. There were not enough water closets for so many sick people and no way to clean up until the storm was over. Indeed at times the ship rolled so much that it was difficult to move out of the bunks anyway.

Murdoch was very seasick and Mary too, but she had to put it aside as she was constantly tending young John. The others too, were sick except Alec and surprisingly, Fergus. All the children were sick but the older boys and Catherine recovered quickly and were a great help to their parents.

Surgeon Harris struggled around the ship seeing to as many as the poor man could manage. There was little he could do to help any of them and Johnny worried him constantly. The small boy was very hot and at times quite delirious.

The storm raged for three days and then gradually began to subside. Mr. Harris said they ought to have sailed through it, but it seemed to stay with the ship for an interminable time.

The Scottish people discovered what sort of people their fellow passengers were at this time, Many were filthy, foul-mouthed folk and Murdoch and the other men tried to protect their families from them as much as was possible.

During the severe weather the hatches had been closed and this made the stench of countless unwashed bodies and the general smell of the quarters even worse as so many had been seasick. What a relief it was on the day the hatches were opened. The ship was still moving a great deal but the rain had stopped and the waves had stopped breaking over the hatches. So at last some good clean air was felt through the dark quarters.

It was as well that the early emigrants were not as tall as the modern Australian. There was little headroom between decks, for the deck above was only six feet four and from this protruded many heavy beams. So it was cramped to say the least. The noise of many booted feet on the wooden decking above and the constant buzz of conversation, laughter and arguments so close at hand was hard for the Highland people to take. Mary had found the noise on the coastal steamer annoying and intrusive, but it was nothing like these horrible, personal, persistent, intrusive noises.

At last they could go on deck in the fresh air. The cooks were again able to set their stoves going and tea and hot food was cooked and served on the deck. It was quite cold above but as many as were able dressed themselves and their families in warm clothing. It was difficult to manage eighteen children. The mothers sat on the deck in a circle with the little ones amongst them and the fathers took the older children in hand, trying to keep them occupied and interested.

Malcolm and Duncan Macdonald, Hamish MacKenzie, Donald MacLeod and Ian Fraser were the oldest boys in the group. Three were fourteen, Donald thirteen and Duncan was twelve.

They were thrilled to stand on the tilted deck with their fathers holding onto the rail, watching the waves tear by. To look up into the rigging and see the stretched sails on the masts. They felt the cold salt air and to breathe cleanly again. Oh, what a thrill! Sickness was forgotten for a time.

Mary had taken Johnny to a sheltered place for a short while. He was still very sick and only his little face was to be seen in his woollen wraps, a pale little wisp of a fellow. As long as she could she stayed near the stair where the air was fresher. She knew now he would get better, but he was still far from well and unless the weather improved and allowed a more normal life on deck she feared for him.

Chapter 6: *Life On Board*

As they sailed south the days became warmer and they were soon to experience their first real heat.

The heat brought a change in their lives. Surgeon Harris suggested that as many men and boys who wished could sleep on deck. This allowed the women and girls to have more sleeping room and although there was more noise from the deck above, on the whole it was quieter in the quarters at night. If it rained there would be a scatter below but they were fortunate that the weather was kind for a lengthy period.

It was during this time too that the men often bathed on deck and the women were able to strip and wash - both themselves and their clothes.

Unfortunately, some did not make use of the ablutions and remained in their filthiness, some for the, entire journey. These people did not make pleasant travelling companions and indeed, the whole company soon sorted itself into groups. Those who tried to make the best of the bad conditions and those who seemed to delight in making everything difficult. These latter were mostly those who remained dirty, were quarrelsome and obstructive in every way possible.

The folk from Skye were among those who made the best of it all. All emigrants travelling below decks were divided into 'messes'. The 'mess' captain rations were issued to a 'mess' and he was deputed to receive the ration and apportion it out to last the stated time. The men took it in turn to act as 'mess' captain, going on deck at meal times to receive the meat, soup and other victuals set aside for the meal. They at all times, tried to shield their families from any of the unpleasantness experienced in the quarters. It was usual for one of the party to remain on guard of their possessions, for thieving seemed to be second nature to some of their companions.

Mary noticed that the health of all improved as the voyage progressed, even little Johnny was an active little fellow once more. Fergus seemed to thrive on sea travel. She was proud of the way he was able now to share the tasks with the other men. Perhaps consumption would not be a reality after all. What a letter she could write to her Mother! She chuckled as she thought of his organising prowess. He had all the rations worked out a fraction. By now he knew exactly how much each person would eat and how to make the ration last the time. He had worked out a roster for all the jobs and all were included except the children under six, who were dubbed "the bairns". One of the mothers and often two were allotted the task of bairn-minding. This way allowed task time and free time. At times it was difficult to keep all the children occupied and when tempers flared, Fergus would have everyone, out on deck if possible, doing exercises and drill. Many of their neighbours laughed but the Skye children were less trouble and a greater help than those who were just allowed to run wild, as many were.

It was not only the emigrant children who at times ran free but those of the cabin class who would play truant at times.

Murdoch was involved in an incident with one such lad on a day where the sea was rather bouncy. He was standing on the sloping deck, bracing himself against the movement of the ship, breathing in the fresh sea air. He heard a shrill voice above him on the poop deck calling,

"Come down Master Hugh, come down quick." Murdoch couldn't see the child spoken to at first, then to his horror, saw a small boy heading up the rigging. He was just about to rush after him when the ship lurched and the small truant was plucked from the ropes. Murdoch rushed forward and caught the child neatly, just saving him from going overboard. The nursemaid was just in time to see the rescue and called in a sobbing voice, "You naughty boy Master Hugh, you nearly went over."

Murdoch ran up the steps to the poop deck and put the lad down. A little white face looked up to him and said, "I nearly went over, didn't I?"

"You did that, young master. I think you knew that it was a silly thing to do."

"Yes, I suppose so, but the seamen look so grand running up the ropes and I thought I'd try. It is a bit scary up there."

"Master Hugh, you will get me into such trouble with your adventures," the nursemaid said, pushing the lad's cap on his head.

"What will your Papa say? You must thank this man - do please tell me your name. Yes, thank him properly."

"My name is Macdonald. There's no need for thanks. I've young ones of my own and I know how active they can be."

Hugh took off his cap and solemnly shook hands with Murdoch saying "I really am sorry Mr. Macdonald, that I was naughty and I am sorry to you, too, Annie, for giving you such a fright." Murdoch left them.

Later that day Hugh's father sought Murdoch out. "John Trent, merchant of Sydney Town," he introduced himself. "I am grateful, Macdonald, for your quick action this morning. I believe my son Hugh would have gone over the side if it hadn't been for you. I thank you."

"It was good that I was there to catch him, sir. I just happened to be in the right place at that time."

"Well, Mrs. Trent and I are in your debt. I do hope Hugh thanked you as he should."

"He did that, Mr. Trent, and he felt badly that he'd disobeyed his nurse. I do not think he'll try that caper again. I'm sure he was quite frightened."

"Are you off to get your fortune at the diggings Macdonald?"

"Why no, sir, I'll not take my family there. I hear that they are pretty rough places. No sir, I am a farmer and I want to make my fortune, if God wills, on the land."

"What part of Scotland do you come from?"

"From Skye, in the Western Isles."

"I believe things are not good for the Highlanders at the moment.

"They are not, sir. In many places conditions are severe. We've not been so very badly off, but some of the folk are literally starving."

"Why so, man?"

"Well sir, our potato crops have been bad for some time to begin with and then the closures have been very hard to bear."

"What are the closures?"

"Well, when the potatoes failed and the seasons bad, year upon year, the Lairds were hit badly too and many of the Lairds found that the only thing to do was to sell some land and save their people. Many rich southerners bought up land, finding that our land is good for sheep. They could only keep the sheep if they enclosed the pastures. The crofters or farmers had always farmed their land in the traditional manner, small holdings and sharing grazing for their cows. Since the southern landlords have come they find the crofters a nuisance and try, and do, get rid of them so that they can run their sheep. Many folk have had their houses ruthlessly torn down and been turned out onto the roads to wander. Some lairds have done a great deal to help their folk but some have let their people down in a bad way."

"The laird being your clan chief, I take it?"

"Yes. On Skye the Laird of the MacLeods - 'The McLeod' we term him - sold his castle to feed his people. Our Laird, the Macdonald, paid our passages rather than see us starve."

"A grand gesture."

"Some of the lairds formed a society called the Highland and Island Society to assist people to emigrate. They arrange the passage and assist us with the payment. There are rules we must keep but this is not so hard as we do not wish to go to the diggings."

"Where are you going?"

"Sydney, sir, and we hope to keep together if possible. You see, we are rather a large party. Four families. My wife and five children, my sister, my brother-in-law and my cousin's families."

"Are you all farmers then?"

"Yes, we have been, but Fergus MacKenzie, my wife Mary's brother, has been ill with chest trouble and the Laird has had him working with his agent on book work and he did very well according to the Macdonald. So Fergus may seek a position in commerce. My sister's husband, Alistair MacLeod, is keen to farm and also my cousin Margaret's husband, Alec Fraser - but I fancy Alec is rather tempted with gold. We have eighteen children between us and so are rather a large group. "

"I will help you if I can, Macdonald. I'm no farmer but have farming friends. You should have no trouble getting places as so many are going out to the diggings and leaving their jobs. I am a merchant and have lived in the colony most of my life and so will be glad to advise you if I can."

"I would be sincerely grateful if we could discuss the colony, sir. We are pitifully ignorant of what is before us. I will ask, too, that you may speak to the other men for we are all full of questions."

"I have two friends aboard, too, they are farmers. You may care to speak to them also. William Forrest and Charles Parry, both have properties on the Hawkesbury River west of Sydney and should be helpful to you. I will speak to them."

"'Thank you, sir, we'd be most grateful."

"We must arrange further talks, then." Then, extending his hand, Mr. Trent took Murdoch's in his and said, "Again I thank you," then ran up the steps to the upper deck.

Chapter 7: *Heat and Cabin Fever*

As the days passed the weather turned hot and sultry and shade was a scarce commodity. There was little to do but sit where you could watch the flying fish sail past the ship as it cut through the waves. Occasionally someone would shout, "Whale" or "Porpoises" and those interested would crowd to the rails peering out at them. Anything to break the monotony of the endless, blue, hot days. It was the time when tempers flared and it was prudent for the groups to remain aloof. Keeping the children occupied was a large task. The older ones quickly got into mischief if allowed and was too hot for energetic games. Fergus still organised drill but found that early in the morning was the best time for this.

Twice there came the call of "Ship ahoy" and one of these vessels pulled alongside to take on mail for England and some back to the colony.

On the thirty seventh day out from Liverpool rang "Land ahead" and there was a rush to the deck rails. The coast of Brazil was seen in the distance. It was a tantalizing thing to see the distant land and know there would be no landing. As the sea had remained calm throughout the heat they were content to know that their voyage was progressing and that their goal was not this land.

Even the cabin passengers found the heat a trial and many of the ladles and gentlemen were seen seeking shade and respite from the sun. One lady had a favourite place where she would sit and watch the people below her. She would always have a pleasant smile for anyone who looked up in her direction.

John Trent moved up beside her. "In your favourite place again, my dear?"

She smiled up at him. "Yes, John, I do find all the people fascinating. So many people. I think so much about them. I wonder where they came from and what they want to find in the colony and whether they will find it?"

"Well Emma, you've seen something of the successes and failures of the colonists."

"I know John. I've not seen them quite like this. Some must come from the slums in cities and seem to take the crowded conditions well. They just carry on as ever. These seem to me to be the ones who will find the country life of the colony so hard and will certainly want to stay in Sydney Town. Then there are those who do not seem to be able to handle the mass of people and yet I feel that these are the true pioneers who won't mind the isolation of the Australian bush."

"It will be interesting to see how some of them fare."

"I fancy, John, that that is your Scottish group." Emma indicated very carefully the large Macdonald group. "Since Mr Macdonald saved Hugh from going overboard I have watched them carefully. Could I meet them, please? The women seem to be very pleasant."

John carefully studied the group under Mrs. Trent's scrutiny. "You could be correct my dear, although I do not see Macdonald."

"One of the men has just gone below so perhaps he will return."

Murdoch appeared as she spoke carrying a cloth. He and Alistair tied each corner of the cloth to the ropes to make more shade. The women gratefully moved under it with the smallest children.

"Macdonald, would you please come up," John Trent called down to the deck below.

Murdoch came up the steps and was introduced to Mrs. Trent who beamed upon him and gave him her thanks for rescuing her son.

"I take it that is your family, Macdonald. Would you take us below to meet them please" asked John.

"It would be an honour, Mr. Trent"

Mrs. Trent led the way and Murdoch introduced his new friends to the family. Malcolm and the older boys were asked to take the children aside and care for them while the adults spoke.

Very quickly the men surrounded John Trent and plied him with questions and Emma sat under the shade with the four Scottish lassies who were shy at first, but she quickly drew them out and soon they too asked about the life ahead of them. This new country was to be so different. Fancy a winter that had no snow and things that grew all year round, and trees that kept their leaves.

Chapter 8: *Sickness and a storm*

As the weeks went by the weather grew cold. The sea remained kind and there was much time to learn from the Trent's a deal of the type of life led in the colony. John Trent introduced the Scottish group to his friend William Forrest, a farmer who lived west of Sydney near the Blue Mountains, and also Charles Parry from the same area. Both these men were farmers and they proved a great source of information to the men from Skye. Farming in the colony seemed to bear no resemblance at all to the farming that the four men had left behind in Skye, where winter conditions were hard and the life ahead seemed to be one long summer. They were most anxious to know if anyone would employ them as the conditions seemed so different, but Forrest and Parry assured them that they would soon get into the way of things. They'd had word since their arrival in England that many farms were bereft of labour as many farm hands had left secure jobs to seek their fortunes at the diggings. They were sorry not to be able to offer any positions to the Scots as they hoped that their farms were still fully manned. They did spend quite a deal of time speaking to Murdoch, Alistair and Alec and the men found a wealth of knowledge coming their way.

In the meantime John Trent and Fergus MacKenzie had found a great deal in common. Although Fergus was completely ignorant of city life, he was very taken with the thought of entering commercial life. He had very little capital indeed and so thoughts of buying into business was never thought of, but he did hope to enter a shop as an assistant and start from there.

John Trent said nothing about assisting him, but watched and listened carefully and wondered whether he should offer Fergus a start. He was unhurried about it all and was pleased to note that Fergus showed no signs of expecting assistance in any way. In fact, all three Australians found the Scottish folk very independent and asked no quarter. They had been brought up in a hard climate, a hard country and hard work was the only thing that brought results in their view. Alec Fraser was the only one who showed any interest in the diggings, but he was shy about putting his tentative questions. Murdoch and Alistair were quick to change the subject if it was touched on. Alistair particularly was abrupt and had small tolerance of any 'silly notions', as he called them.

As the cold increased, life out of doors lessened and most hours were now spent below decks. Even when the sea roughened, few people suffered any ill effects for the passengers had their "sea legs". That is, until one night the ship started tossing, the wind began to scream through the rigging and once more hatches were battened and the air below became fetid and hot. The ship was at this time in the cold and infamous Roaring Forties, where ships took this route for extra speed. The trouble was that when one got into a freezing storm in these latitudes, one stayed with it a long while. Late in August there was snow on the deck. From below you could hear the sailors slip on the frozen deck. It was a terrible time for all concerned. Food was short for those brave enough and able enough to want it. Many were sick and unable to control themselves, so the stench itself brought on sickness.

As ever it was John who gave most concern to Mary and Murdoch. He had never recovered fully from his previous illness and he had found the tropic heat enervating. Mary had been thanking God for improvement in his health and appetite when they ran into the storm.

The storm raged incessantly, day & night, day & night. People moaned and vomited, children cried, whimpered and vomited. Life below decks was appalling.

All things come to an end, even storms, and after two full weeks they sailed out of it, or the storm left them. They didn't care which, all they knew was that the world regained some normalcy. They found that during this 'limbo' time, when everyone just lived for themselves, that several people had died and four babies born. One of these had died as it was premature.

It was heaven to feel the fresh air again as hatches were removed and mopping up began. What a mess! What a shambles! Even those who were well had not been able to move much as they were thrown off their feet continually. Several old people had broken limbs, in fact, it was amazing that anyone escaped injury.

When the stoves were lit on deck and tea was served, everyone agreed that there had never been a better drink. 'Ambrosia' some said, 'nectar' from others. "Hot, clean tea, a great drink."

Johnnie was a sad little fellow. He'd lost a great deal of weight and again his eyes seemed enormous. All he wanted to do was lie in Mary's arms and suck his fingers. It was an effort to make him eat anything at all. But the other children soon made up for all the meals they had missed.

Even though the storm had passed, it was far too cold to resume life on deck and so they had to carry on in the dark room with all the other hundreds of souls, intent on seeing to their own needs first.

Life improved as time went on, there was a slight feeling of warmth and then one day the sun shone and there was a movement to go on deck.

Mary wrapped Johnnie in warm clothes and took him into a sheltered nook to watch the others play and run about the older children wildly excited at the freedom of the decks again.

By mid September the weather was quite spring-like and it was felt that the long journey was coming to an end.

One evening after the children were abed, Mary and Murdoch stood speaking to the Trent's and Mr. Forrest.

"We wonder" said Murdoch, "whether we imagine it. But we feel we can smell something different in the air."

"It's Australia". "It's eucalyptus". "It's gum leaves" said the three Australians. They laughed at the astounded looks. William Forrest explained. "It is true, you can smell the land. It is really a pungent smell and after all this sea air, you can pick it up easily."

"You may, sir, but I must admit we are used to pungent smells. I am so glad you do not share our accommodation, for we do have pungent smells. I do agree anyway, that Australia has an agreeable smell. It makes our new life seem so close." As he said this his arm stole around Mary's waist. His Mary was very quiet about their new life. He felt a fear and lack of enthusiasm for all that was ahead of them. At this moment he could see she had a frozen look, one that he rather feared. When she looked like this he felt she was far from him. Perhaps she was. Perhaps she was in Skye again. Murdoch was fortunate that he accepted whatever came, he didn't fret about what he didn't have. He wanted the best for his family and he felt that they'd made the right step to get it. For Mary it was different. She felt the hardships badly. She was a proud, upright lass and it had hurt her badly to have to let her loved ones share this horrid polluted life of the last months. Well, if this Australia was as big and empty as they had heard, she would be able to nestle her flock under her wings again without interference. If only they knew what was before them. If only they had a place to go to. Oh well, he would leave it all to the Lord, He had never let them down.

Murdoch realised that John Trent had addressed him.

"I don't think you're listening Macdonald."

"Sorry, Mr. Trent, I was day-dreaming, wondering what is before us."

"We were saying just now that Forrest and I would be willing to give the men of your party references. Even though we've known you such a short while, it may help you."

"Thank you, sir, very much indeed. I am sure it will assist greatly. The others will be most grateful too."

"We'll see that you will have them before we dock in Sydney."

"If you will excuse us, we will tell them. Goodnight Mrs. Trent, Mr. Trent, Mr. Parry. Come Mary." He took her hand as she also said goodnight and led her below.

"He seems a very upright fellow Will doesn't he."

"Yes, he does. In fact, they all are. I'm willing to believe that they are workers."

"I do have a feeling that Mrs. Macdonald is not as happy as her husband though," put in Emma Trent.

"Mrs. Macdonald seems a very fine woman, Emma."

"Oh, I'm not denying that. In fact I have become very fond of her. I am sorry she will not be living in Sydney. I would like to follow her life. I am saying that she has a deep unhappiness in her. I think she mistrusts this life she is about to enter. The circles under her large blue eyes are getting larger. This tells me of many sleepless nights, I am thinking."

"Perhaps her small child keeps her awake, Emma," put in William Forrest.

"He certainly is a worry to her. No, I do not think that Mary Macdonald is accepting of this new life as the others in the party."

"I hope for her sake she becomes reconciled to it, my dear. I do feel New South Wales has a lot to offer a newcomer." John took her hand. "Your people came when life in the Colony was very grim and they came to terms with it."

"Yes, I know dear, and I think she will too, but I have a feeling that she will be badly hurt by it all before that. The men have it a lot easier than the women. I have lived in the Colony all my life, but I have never had to live in a farm house with the bare essentials and have snakes and spiders and all sorts of creepy things running all over me. I would hate it and I am sure Mrs. Macdonald is a sensitive soul and will hate it too. I have compassion for her."

The men laughed at the dainty figure, both unable to picture the pretty creature coping with snakes and things.

"I hope you will never have to cope with snakes and spiders and live in a farm house, not while you are in my care, my dear. I don't think you need be concerned about Mrs. Macdonald. I am sure she is a very strong person."

"Oh, I am sure she is, you know that is not what I meant."

"Well, if you are fortunate they will settle in a district where you can keep in touch."

"Yes, if they go out to the Hawkesbury you may be able to give me news of them, William."

"I might be able to do that, Emma. In the meantime I do think we should dress for dinner." They went to their cabins.

A few days later there was a cry of "land ahead". Such excitement there was. People crowded on every available piece of deck and peered ahead. Hardly discernible, the land strip gradually grew, but very slowly, There was a scurry of packing and sorting for most of the passengers were disembarking at Melbourne and as they saw Cape Otway to the north, they knew their journey was nearing the end.

The ship passed through the Rip into the large Port Phillip Bay and then the land could be clearly seen. For hours the Scottish folk sat watching their new homeland. As they were going on to Sydney they had no packing to do and were glad to be out of the accommodation and let those who were leaving have the space to pack.

Elspeth said, "Well Mary, here it is, this new land. What does it hold for us, will we be happy or will it hold tears?"

"I imagine there will be many tears mixed with the laughter, Ellie. I can laugh now at myself. You remember what a fuss I made on seeing the ship. Now I don't want to leave it and take the next step. I would never have believed I could feel so."

"Surely our new life won't be as bad as this has been. It's just the unknown that's so frightening."

"What! Oh what! is before us?" said Margaret Fraser. "I pray we'll be close. I don't think I could bear it if we were far away."

"Alistair doesn't mind if we are," put in Caroline MacLeod. "He thinks we ought to be separated so we can grow into true Australians. He said we'll stay too Scottish if we live nearby."

"Oh, Caroline, We must be together, it would be terrible to lose touch. I didn't know Alistair thought that way. I'm sure Murdoch wants us all close," cried Mary.

"You know Alistair, Mary. He says little, but when he makes his mind up you can't move him."

"Don't worry about it now lassies," said the cheerful Margaret. "Just trust in the Lord, He will see us right. We have at least another week of this."

In Melbourne port there was so much activity that they were content to sit in the shade on a beautiful late September day and watch it all. The children stayed close, for if they didn't, they got in someone's way. All day long boats came alongside and one after another of the passengers left with possessions piled high. So many had no idea where their future would be. Many women were saddened because the plans of coming to farm in the new land were forgotten as their husbands were infected with the gold fever. Many men were willing to risk all, including small capital and their families in order to join the rush. All expected to amass fortunes quickly, but the wives not so sure. Murdoch, Alistair and Fergus were untouched by it all, but Alec soaked any information up that he could and had said many times quietly to Margaret that he'd like to try for his fortune this way. It was just as well he had promised Murdoch to stay with him for he was sorely tempted to head for Ballarat with his family. Murdoch tried to keep a firm hand on his friend, for he knew his thoughts better than Alec gave him credit.

The women said tearful farewells to a few of their fellow voyagers but were intensely relieved to see several go who had been a constant source of trouble.

Fergus had been on duty in the quarters watching that someone didn't "mistakenly" pack their goods. He came back on deck, laughing as he sat down, saying, "Well, I think the last of the rogues have gone and we can breathe easy. I had quite a tussle to keep your big cooking pot, Meg. Luckily I saw old Smith slip it into his bag. He wanted to fight me for it, and dropped his bag in the scuffle and everything in it spilled out. You should have seen Willie Thomas' face when his father's clock fell out, and Edwin Davis found the spoons his wife lost weeks ago. So we tipped his bag right up and you should have seen what we found. There was not one thing that belonged to Smith. So Willie took him by the collar and the seat of his pants and shoved him over the side into the boat with his family. He's now cursing us all the way to Melbourne."

"If that's what you found in one bag, I wonder what has been packed in others. It is good to see the last of them, and the Browns too", put in Murdoch.

"It should be quiet now, with most of the folk gone. We should be able to spread out now" said Fergus. "It looks so different, let's go and see."

They gazed at their quarters and saw such an unfamiliar sight. The few who were left were spreading their possessions around in greater comfort than they had experienced all the voyage.

"The children can share differently now," said Mary. "Johnnie, would you like to sleep with Jamie in a bed of your own?"

"Oh yes, Mother, but I want to be near you."

"You will be, my son, you can sleep right next to me with just the curtain between us and Jamie will be right next to Aunt Margaret."

"That will be fun, Mother. Can I talk to you through the curtain?"

"Yes, Sonnie, you can pull it aside and have little talks to me when you wake in the morning."

They were all light-hearted as they re-arranged their things.

"Mamma" said Catherine, "I know the ship has stopped, but every now and then I feel that it is moving. What a funny feeling."

"Yes. I was speaking to Mrs. Trent about it and she said that we may feel it a lot when we go ashore in Sydney. But it will pass quickly. I suppose we have our sea legs now and we will have to get our land legs again."

The ship sailed the next day and as they were heading once more through Port Phillip, John Trent came below and said, "Macdonald, I wonder if you and the other men would care to come to our cabin. We wish to speak to you."

"Right, sir, I will find them and come straight away."

Trent went up the stairs and as he disappeared, Mary tuned to Murdoch. "What do you think this means, Murd?"

"I wonder too, lass. Well, I'll soon find out I daresay. I'd better find the others. Come on. Mary."

Murdoch found the men pointing out some aborigines to the children. They could see them quite clearly and they were a fascinating sight to people who had never seen dark skins before. Murdoch broke in and gave the message from Mr. Trent and leaving their families, the men went below to the first class cabins. They had never been in this part of the ship before. All the varnished wood and fittings made the men feel as though they were in another world. It was all so unlike their quarters.

William Forrest was waiting for them and showed them to a large unoccupied cabin. Charles Parry and John Trent soon joined them.

"Sit down, men," John Trent said. "We have all had mail in

Melbourne and we find that the labour situation is worse than we had last heard and we are now in a position to offer you work."

The Scotsmen murmured delightedly.

"I have been moved for some weeks to offer a position to Fergus, but did not think I would have an opening, so thought I would wait until we berthed in Sydney before mentioning anything. However, I find that I have lost my head clerk and feel now that I can tell you what is in my mind. I want to expand, opening branches in provincial towns, and I would like to take you on Fergus, as a clerk at first, because you are inexperienced and then train you in buying and selling. How does that appeal, man?"

"It appeals greatly, Mr. Trent, and I am truly grateful for the opportunity. I will try not to let you down, sir. It is more than I ever dreamed."

"I am sure we will deal well together, Fergus. I have not chosen you for your ability, for you've none of that yet, but I feel that we will work well together. I am a hard master, but you will learn well under me."

"I can vouch for that" broke in William Forrest. "You could not have better."

"Thank you, Mr. Trent," said Fergus. "I can only say that I am overwhelmed."

"Now it is my turn, John," said Forrest. "We too have had mail and both Charles and I have lost men from our farms. Charles will be happy to offer you, MacLeod, a job with him."

"Yes, now I can offer you a job and hope you will accept it. There will be a house of course, and so will be able to house your family."

"And I would like to offer positions to you and Fraser, Macdonald. How does that sound?"

"It sounds grand, sir," said Murdoch and Alec in unison.

"Aye", said Alistair, "it does that. Thank you, sir."

They then got down to discussing their futures with their new bosses. After some time, John Trent broke in. "I think we ought to leave it at that for the time being. You must be keen to share the news with your wives and I suggest you do this. We will have time to discuss this further during the next week of our journey before

45

we reach Sydney. There will be much you will want to know and also the ladies will wish to speak to my wife about their new lives.

The northerners stood up and Murdoch, as spokesman, said, "Gentlemen, I speak for the others when I praise God for our meeting with you. It has been beyond our expectations to get work before we even land in New South Wales. We thank you for your confidence in us. I can say here, sirs, that I can truly vouch for my friends ability to work. We do thank you, and 'good day' to you all.

"Thank you Aye, we do," and "Thank you sirs" put in the others and they left the cabin.

On reaching the deck Alec grabbed Murdoch and whooped with joy, then tried to dance with Fergus. Murdoch laughed and the dour Alistair just stood there with a large grin on his face. They hurried below and each clasped their wives and hugged them with glee. Their families gathered around them and they shared their news. The whole party was simply delighted.

"It takes such a lot of the mystery out of our arrival," put in Margaret.

"We'll be close." said Caroline.

"We'll not be living far away," Murdoch pointed out, "but Fergus and Elspeth will be furthest away. We will be happy to know that you are well settled and are not too distant."

"What do we do when we arrive in Sydney?" asked Mary. "Did you find that out, Murdoch?"

"No, love, not yet. Mr Trent knew we wanted to share the news with you and suggested that we talk later during the rest of the voyage."

This is what they did, too. Fergus and Elspeth were delighted to find that there was a house for them in Sydney, near the warehouse that would be Fergus' new work place. Mr. Trent suggested that tents would be put up in the yard of the house until the other families could move to their houses on the farms. Mr. Forrest suggested that the women and children stay in Sydney until Murdoch, Alistair and Alec got their belongings moved. The women were most anxious to know what their new homes were like and on hearing their descriptions, were quite dubious about them.

Timber cottages seemed very frail things to shield their loved ones from the weather. Emma Trent assured them that the material was usual in most areas. She had been interested to hear about the construction, the warmth and security of the stone thatched crofts that the newcomers had come from. She assured the women that they would soon accustom themselves to their new dwellings and would see the benefits of the lightness and design of the cottages.

Much of this last week of travel was spent learning about and speaking of their futures and so the time went very quickly. The coast was visible all the way and soon they came to Port Jackson. The ship turned west between the heads to sail up the beautiful harbour that was the gateway to their new land.

Now it was their turn to hustle and bustle to pack their belongings. Everyone in clean clothes, but children rebelling in their tight best clothes and bonnets and hats. The party bid farewell to the ship, the place they had hated on sight, but seemed now to be an old friend, a place of security. Each had a rather empty feeling inside, a wonder of what was ahead of them.

A last farewell to their friends in disembarking in Sydney. They climbed into the boats that were ready to take them ashore. At last, land after four months.

Chapter 9: *First Sights*

There was Sydney before them.

A gathering of houses, large and small, clustered along the shores and the hills above.

The day was one of those blue-gold days that Sydney does often produce, especially in the October warmth. The newcomers seemed to feel that it was the only kind of weather that Australia had, as the sunshine had followed them all the way since Melbourne. But they were not thinking about the weather, they were too busy with their thoughts. Each one was silently taking in the scene before them. Disappointment rose in their hearts as the unprepossessing wharves and their scruffy-looking work parties came into view. A jumble of thoughts rose to the surface in each.

"What is before us?"

"How will we fit into such a strange-looking place?"

"Will the children be well in all this heat and dust?"

They were certainly fortunate that John Trent had taken them under his wing. He suggested that they remain on board until he could get their accommodation settled. So, by the time they came ashore wagons were waiting to transport them to Fergus' new home.

The children gathered in the centre of the wagons while their parents sat on the edge silently taking in all the activity around them.

Some of the houses were quite small and squalid, but they could see large residences beyond these and as they drove through the town they saw the business centre and many lovely carriages carrying smart ladies and gentlemen. As they drew near the Haymarket they were upset to see so many dirty beggar children. Mary shuddered on seeing them and drew John and Mary Ann close to her. A mother's natural instinct was to keep her children

49

away from dirt and disease and she hoped that hers would not have to mix with such as these.

They drew up to a terrace of stone houses, whereupon Fergus took a key from his pocket and opened the door of Number 32. He turned to Elspeth and said, "Welcome to our new home, love. I do hope you and the bairns will be happy here."

Elspeth led the women and children into the house. The driver of the wagon said, "I will take the wagon up the lane at the back Mr. MacKenzie and unload through the gate there. Then we will help you put the tents up. The gate opens this side, so would you open it?"

The men followed the women through, curious to see their first English-style house. There was a long passage the length of the house running from the front door to the back and several rooms opened from this to the right. Halfway along the passage it opened out into quite a large living room. There were three bedrooms and a kitchen which was near the back door and a tiny verandah outside.

Hamish opened the back door and called out, "look Mama, you can see right through the house. Isn't it strange?"

As he looked, the men arrived at the high back gate. He ran down to draw the bolt and let them in. They unloaded huge bundles of canvas and soon the new settlers were learning to put up a tent. None had ever seen a tent before and so were quite surprised to find what a great shelter they were.

The women were wandering about the house settling where each could sleep and how they could feed such a large hungry group of people. Soon they were settled in and beds made on mattresses that Mr. Trent had sent from his store.

Two days after their arrival, Murdoch, Alec and Alistair boarded a boat at Darling Harbour[4] and with all their furniture and goods, they steamed to Parramatta. There wagons were waiting for them, Alistair to ride with the driver on Mr. Parry's wagon and Murdoch and Alec on Mr. Forrests'. They went along together for most of the way until they came to a crossroads in the bush where Mr. Parry's wagon turned south and Alec and Murdoch waved to a silent and dour Alistair as he disappeared through the trees.

[4] named in 1826 after Gov. Ralph Darling

The two plied the driver with incessant questions, their eyes trying to take everything in. They could now see the source of the pungent smell they had experienced at sea. Such strange grey foliage. It all looked so dry and dusty. Alec reached up and plucked some leaves from the overhanging trees. "Rub them in your hands and smell them," said Michael Flynn, the Irish driver.

"We're having a dry spring and the trees are dusty, but the rain soon washes them clean. Not that they are ever really green, not like the green in Ireland."

"Nor in Scotland," put in Alec.

"What's that?" asked Murdoch, pointing to some pretty animals back from the road.

"These are wallabies, and there are bigger ones called kangaroos, some stand as tall as a man." replied Mick. "Watch them go."

Murdoch and Alec watched, stunned, as the animals hopped away.

"Do they always hop like that or is there something wrong with them?"

"Yes, they hop like that all the time. There are plenty of them about and you will get used to them. They are good to eat too."

"Are they savage?"

"No," laughed Mick, "they aren't savage at all. In fact, they are very nice animals and make good pets. But they don't like dogs and if one attacks them they can sit on that great big tail of theirs and rip a dog to pieces."

"They have faces like deer. Do they taste like it?" asked Murdoch.

"Well as I haven't eaten deer I can't say" put in Mick, "they are good to eat in a stew. You usually eat the tail."

They passed farms with large houses and smaller wooden cottages, each man curious to see the type of house that they might expect theirs to be. Mr. Forrest warned them that the houses would be small. They looked such dusty little abodes, not at all like the stone houses at home. They couldn't help being disappointed at their appearance.

After many hours they came to the town of Riverbend, a group of houses along a dusty road, a church, a hotel and a store.

Murdoch hoped it would be a friendly town, but it certainly was a strange-looking one.

Half a mile further on the wagon stopped in front of a timber cottage.

"This is your new home, Alec," said Mick, as he pulled the horses up at the gate.

Alec looked at the house that looked like so many they had seen. The garden was very pretty and he knew Margaret would revel in that. He pushed the front door open and was pleased to see several rooms, but saw that it would be a tight squeeze for his eight folk.

Mick came up behind Alec. "How many young'uns have you, mate?"

"Six," said Alec. "Two boys and four girls."

"Well, you'll find that some will want to sleep out here. The biguns will, anyhow. Come out here."

He led the way through one of the bedrooms to a verandah that ran the length of the house.

"I grew up in this house. Me Dad and Mother lived here for years. So I know how good it is to sleep here."

"Ay, it would be," said Alec. "Ian and the others will like this."

"Come on, let's get the stuff unloaded," said Mick, and they went back to the wagon to find Murdoch already untying the ropes holding Alec's furniture and goods. They carried the loads in and soon Alec was left in the cottage to start unpacking.

Mick pointed to another cottage on a rise among some trees and said, "We'll he up there, that's Macdonald's house. Come up the driveway and ask at the stables."

Murdoch waved to Alec with a smile and climbed up beside Mick. Along the road a short distance they turned in to a long tree-lined driveway that curved gently, running past a large pond where birds were massed. They drew up beside a lovely two-storied house. Murdoch had never seen anything lovelier. There were creepers covering a wide verandah which ran around the house. Whoever planted the garden was an artist, for the whole place was a blaze of colour.

As they approached the house, Mick pulled up as a very pretty woman came down the steps, followed by Mr. Forrest who greeted Murdoch and asked Mick if they had had a good trip. He turned to his wife and said, "Our new farmer, my dear. Murdoch Macdonald from Skye, of your land."

Mrs. Forrest cried delightedly, "From Scotland? Welcome to 'Forrest Park', Mr. Macdonald."

She extended her hand to him. He detected a faint burr in her pleasant voice.

"Thank you, Mrs. Forrest. Would you be coming from Scotland?"

"Yes, I do," she laughed. "We must talk about it all. I come from Mull."

"Carry on to the cottage with Mick, Murdoch. He'll look after you until I can show you around." William Forrest took his wife's hand and led her into the house.

Mick took the laden wagon round to the commodious stables and drew up, then called out and a man came out to them.

Mick said, "Hello, George. Meet Murdoch Macdonald. This is George Peters, Macdonald. George, will you come and help us unload? We left Alec Fraser at his house and he'll follow us soon."

"G'day," greeted George as he jumped up on the wagon, rolling a cigarette as soon as he was settled.

Murdoch still couldn't see his house as there were so many trees around the homestead, but soon, there it was. Very similar to Alec's, but the garden was a shambles. Weeds everywhere and not a flower to be seen.

Mick saw his disappointment. "The garden ain't much, is it?" Old Fred wasn't much of a gardener, but the house is sound. It don't leak anyway. If your missus is a gardener, she'll soon knock it into shape. Go and look at the house."

Murdoch went through the gate and up the path through the tangled weeds. There was a verandah here too, bigger at the front than Alec's, but the same area along the side. He pictured his children claiming it as theirs. One of the internal walls had been painted white and Murdoch was delighted to see how light and airy it was. He tried to think what Mary would do to it and how soon her stamp would be upon it.

"Come on, Mick, let get onto it."

Soon they were unloaded and Mick suggested returning to the big house. "The Park," he called it. He said that Mrs. King, the cook, would be expecting them for a meal. As Murdoch shut the gate, Alec joined them. He whistled when he saw the mass of weeds.

"A bit of a mess, old son," he said to Murdoch. "I imagined that you would have a garden like ours, and I am so pleased about ours for Margaret."

"Yes, I must admit it is a bit of a disappointment. I must try to clean it before my lass gets here."

"I'll help you man. We can't have her coming to this."

"When it's cleaned up it's not so bad," said Mick. "Mr Forrest has had good fruit trees put into all the farmhouse gardens and the fences are good, so you'll soon see the difference. Mr. Forrest used to make Fred clean it up every now and then. He hates the place being untidy."

Mick took them to the Park kitchen and there he met Mrs. King who was a massive woman. She sat the hungry men down to a large table and served a beautifully cooked meal to them.

"Mrs. Forrest said that you are to eat here until your families come, so be off to yours now Mick."

"Well, don't you be feeding them so much that they cannot work, Mrs. King."

She hunted him off with a large spoon saying, "The cheeky fellow."

They did enjoy their meal and afterwards made off to Murdoch's house and settled down to sleep, their first night on 'Forrest Park'. They were up early the next morning and were soon learning the jobs they were to do.

Murdoch stopped as he worked, stood still and looked around him. What a glorious spring day. Funny that it should be spring when autumn was turning everything gold at home. It all seemed so different. It was different. As he stood he turned and looked. Man, it was grand enough to please any farmer. The pastures were green and lush, sparkling with early morning dew. The cows stood sleek in the sunlight, chewing in their contended way. Across the fields, paddocks they called them here, he looked to the Hawkesbury

River winding along beneath the high Blue Mountains. They were such a lovely clear blue, not like the Cuillans, but again so different. Not really high either, he supposed, but my, they were lovely on this first morning of being a farmer. What a place to have brought his family! What a place for the boys to work in! What a place for his three lassies to blossom in, his lovely Mary and the two little ones. It would gladden a man's heart. It does gladden my heart! He suddenly took his hat off and threw it in the air. "Hooray! ... we are here."

On the following Saturday Murdoch once more travelled the dusty road to Parramatta, with Mick driving the wagon. There was great merriment when he greeted the families again. Alistair was there too, to collect his folk and he and Murdoch were able to exchange news of each other's farms. Alistair had found conditions much as the others had and was as excited as such a dour man could be at the potential he saw in their new land.

With children, the women and the luggage in the wagon, Mick turned the horses towards home. With such a light load, the horses broke into a trot, much to the delight of the children. Malcolm, Duncan and Ian sat beside Mick and asked incessant questions and eagerly looked at every new thing. Murdoch leaned back against the seat talking to Mary and Margaret who eagerly questioned him about everything. Murdoch was telling Margaret about her lovely flowers, breaking off to say, "look children, look at the kangaroos. See Johnnie, Donald through the trees over this side."

Johnnie was so excited as he scrambled over the seat that he fell on his father. "Where, where?" he cried.

Murdoch pointed to the two soft grey animals that stopped to look at them, then they turned and bounded away. The little boy cried with delight.

"There are quite a few of them. They come down to the farm. You often see them in the early morning, and a lot of other things too. The whole place is very busy with birds and other things. They are such strange creatures. I daresay we'll learn a lot about them as we become Australians."

"What is that noise, Father?" asked Duncan. "It goes on and on."

"They tell me they are big insects, son, called cicadas. I've not seen one close, but you see them fly. Look, there's one now."

They all looked about them, wondering what next they would see Mary stole a hesitant hand onto her husband's arm and looked up at him and queried, "You like it all then Murdoch?"

"Yes, lass, I do. I think we have a chance here that we are most fortunate to have."

"But it's not home, Murd," she said wistfully, looking out at the foreign-looking landscape. "Everything looks so grey and dirty and I don't think I have felt really clean since I arrived. It all looks so unfriendly."

"No, we won't feel those clean sea winds of home, but we'll have other things."

"Is Mary's garden full of flowers like mine, Murdoch?"

"No, Meg, it isn't. The people who were in your house were good gardeners-but Fred is a bachelor and didn't go in for flowers. Or vegetables either as far as I can make out. We'll soon have it in Order.

I'm sorry that I didn't have the opportunity of cleaning it up before you came, Mary, but I have been learning my job. I did want to have something done for you."

"Never mind Mother, Duncan and John and I will soon have a garden for you," said Malcolm, "although how you make a garden I don't know, but we will soon learn, wont we, Johnnie?"

"Yes, Malcolm, we will grow pretty flowers for Mama." chimed the little fellow.

Duncan asked, "Can we have potatoes and vegetables and things, Dad, like Mr. Forrest said?"

"Yes, son, we each have an acre of land around our house, with a really good fence around it. Mr. Forrest has had fruit trees planted and they are just finishing flowering, and lass, this means that we will have our own peaches, plums and apricots. There is a grape vine on a frame on the back verandah. It will be great having such things for the children.

"How lovely, Murd. Mrs. Trent told us about the fruit here. I am looking forward to tasting then."

"Do we have fruit trees, too, Murd?" asked Margaret.

"Yes, indeed you have, Meg. We'll not be short of good food for the children. I think we'll see ours grow healthy. Mr. Forrest supplies meat for all his workers and shares anything else he has. I am sure that we have fallen on our feet. We can thank God that He led us to Mr. Forrest."

"If this could only be," said Mary, looking at her children, still pale from the unhealthy conditions on the ship. They were all dark-haired as she and Murdoch were. She knew they had an unhealthy transparency after the crowded and dirty conditions and the very bad food that they'd had. She and the other mothers had reveled in the fresh food they had obtained Sydney. Murdoch already had a red tinge to his face and as she looked at him he smiled down at her. She put her hand up to his cheek.

"I am sunburned," he said. "We'll have to see that the children do not really burn. The boss has warned us about it and until they get used to the hot sun we will have to take care of them. Your brood will suffer, Meg, with their fair skin and hair. Alec looks rather boiled at the moment. He's had to rub oil on his face, for he is quite burned.

"Poor Alec," said Meg.

"It doesn't stop him," said Murdoch. "He's never still. Into everything, and works that hard. I think he wants to have a farm himself, before next week. He is absolutely reveling in it. I think he likes Australia."

"Dear Alec," she replied, "he was ever impatient for what he wants."

"One thing about Alec is that he is not ambitious for himself. He's forever saying, "Meg would love one of those" or "I must buy a pony for the children as soon as I can." He just can't wait to do it all now."

Alistair and Caroline, in their wagon, were behind the dust of the 'Forrest Park' families and soon Mick pulled up so that the families could bid their farewells. There was much sharing of all they had seen and hurried plans for seeing one another at Christmas if they could. Their wagon turned off the road and was soon out of sight. There was now more interest in their surrounds as they felt they were nearing a new phase in their lives. Eventually Riverbend came into view and Murdoch was able to tell about those inhabitants he had met. They silently drove through the town they would soon know so well. Looking to the right-and left they acknowledged a wave or two.

Soon they drew up outside the Fraser cottage and Alec quickly ran down the path to meet them all, holding his wife and as many children as he could close to him.

"Look at them, Mary, you'd think they had been separated for year," chuckled Murdoch. "Well, Meg, what do you think of it?"

"The garden is lovely, Murdoch, as you said. Goodness, will ever learn the names of all those flowers?"

They all went into the house and could see that Alec had burned much midnight oil in putting their things to order.

Meg cried, "Oh Alec, you have worked so hard. Look, there is Mam's vase. Oh Alec!"

Murdoch broke in. "We'll leave you to settle in. I am sure Mary will be anxious to see her house. Come along children."

The Frasers hardly knew that the Macdonalds had left. Everyone was opening doors and looking at everything. It was all so strange.

Murdoch put his arm around Mary as they set off again. "Mary, my dear, your garden is nothing to look at. Alec has done much with their things. I didn't," he said hesitantly, "because I thought you'd prefer to put them away yourself. Oh love, I can see I could have done more."

"Hush dear, you know it will be fine and we can do it all together."

They turned into the long driveway of 'Forrest Park' and were all delighted at the pretty scene ahead.

Alison and William Forrest saw them arrive and came from the house to meet them. Alison liked the look of this tall Highland lass and like Emma Trent she could sense a sadness within her. "A sensitive lassie we have here," she thought, but said, "We'll not keep you, Mrs. Macdonald, as you'll be anxious to see your new home. We must be friends. I look forward to knowing you."

"Why, thank you Mrs. Forrest, that is a kind welcome."

As they neared their home, Murdoch uttered a cry of delight. Mick chuckled and said, "Look. No weeds."

"Alec, I'll be bound." said Murdoch.

"Yes, he got George to help him. He couldn't get you away quickly enough. He wanted to surprise you as he reckons his wife had a nice garden to come to and yours didn't. Nice bloke, Alec."

"Dear" Alec said Mary.

"Just like Alec," put in Murdoch.

They all climbed down and started through the gate, carrying their things to the house.

"I'll be off then, Mac. See you around."

"Thanks so much, Mick."

Alec and George had rid the front garden of the worst of the weeds and had roughly dug over the beds. It was far from perfect, but it did give the place a lived-in look and you could see the fruit trees still with blossom on them. They trooped inside and Mary looked at the house that would be their home for some years. Perhaps forever, she thought.

What a funny, ugly place it seemed. Bare rough boards on the verandah and smoother ones in the house. The floor, walls and everything timber.

"We'll paint it up and make it look nice, lassie. We'll put some mats on the floor and curtains at the windows and soon it will look like home".

"Oh Murdoch, not like home, not a bit like home". She seemed to stifle a sob and then took a deep breath. "Oh Murd, you have unpacked a lot."

"Well, dear, I tried to do enough to start with, but didn't get too far."

Just then there was a scream from Catherine, "Come Father." Murdoch raced through the house and found Catherine looking at a long brown snake on the back verandah. He picked her up quickly and shoved her at Mary.

"It didn't bite you, did it child?"

"No, Father. What is it?"

"I must get it before it hides."

Soon there was a thrashing sound outside and Murdoch was able to tell them that the snake was dead. Malcolm and Duncan had been most in interested spectators and wanted to handle the squirming thing.

"Leave it alone, boys. It can kill you even though it is dead. Leave it absolutely alone. I'll take it away. Catherine, sure you are are not bitten?"

"Yes, Father, I didn't go near it, it looked so horrible but Father, it isn't dead. Look, it is still moving."

"It is dying, dear, and still very dangerous. You must watch out for them all the time. Do not try to kill it yourself, but run away fast and call me."

"Will they chase me?"

"I think not, lassie, but Mr. Forrest will tell us more."

While all this was going on, Mary had stood immobilized with fright gazing at the squirming créature.

"It's all right, Mary. No harm done," said Murdoch casually.

"It's good to see these things early on, so that they can learn to cope with them."

With this, she collapsed in a heap, sobbing "What a horrible thing! What a terrible place! I hate it. Murdoch. I hate it. How many of these things have we all around us? How will I cope? All the dirt the heat, the flies in my mouth, this horrible house, and that noise, does it ever stop?"

"Malcolm, Duncan, come away from that snake. Put a light to the fire and we'll make your mother cup of tea."

Mary took her bonnet off and started to look around her new house. Every now and then a shiver went through her as she thought of the evil-looking animal could have killed her daughter.

Chapter 10: *Settling in*

In a surprisingly short time they settled into their new life. Mary soon had the house in order and the boys were delighted to begin the garden. Their father had instructed them to clean up all the accumulated rubbish of years and bury it in a deep hole. Mr. Forrest said that snakes lived in old timber and rubbish and so the sooner they had it tidied up, the sooner they would rid the place of vermin. The boys were taught how to kill a snake and they were able to put their new-found skill into practice. Soon the whole place looked clean and tidy and with guidance from Mr. Forrest a vegetable garden was started. The fruit was soon setting on the trees and the summer promised good crops for their table. They had a cow to milk and as soon as the fowl pen was finished, they planned to have fowls, then perhaps pigs and all sorts of exciting things.

Very soon after their arrival little Jamie Fraser came down with a severe fever. It was Scarlet Fever and very soon two other Fraser children became ill too. Then Mary Ann Macdonald caught it and then finally Johnnie.

Dr. Kenny came to see the sick ones and Margaret Fraser was thankful that their doctor was such a fine man. He was very concerned about her little daughter Eliza and made frequent visits to see her.

Mary got to know him quite well when Mary Ann became ill and fortunately the little girl recovered quite quickly. When Dr. Kenny saw John he said, "We'll hope this little chap stays clear of this fever, Mrs. Macdonald. He is such a wispy fellow, isn't he?"

They were congratulating themselves that they had kept him free, when one morning he awoke hot and sick and with a sore throat. Soon the telltale scarlet spots appeared and Mary had a very sick little boy on her hands. Alec appeared one evening red-eyed and sad.

"I'll ask for your prayers friends for our wee bairn is in dire need of them. Dr. Kenny thinks she is slipping away."

"Oh man, I am sorry. Please God she is spared. We have our wee one very ill too. He has the illness far worse than Mary Ann did. He's terribly sick he is and not much strength to help him. He has never picked up from that fever he caught in Liverpool."

Eliza died that night and a heavy gloom hung over their homes. Had they come all this way to lose their precious children in this hot, cruel land?

Small John hung between life and death for some days and Dr. Kenny thought that there was no hope for the small elf getting through this scourge. Murdoch was distressed at Mary's appearance too. Her big eyes were bigger than ever, making her a large version of sick Johnnie. She had had many sleepless nights with Mary Ann before the small one became ill and he thought she may give in under the strain, but Mary was as strong as whipcord. She was rarely ill and shrugged off the suggestion that she should let Murdoch take a turn at the bedside. She knew that the little boy had nothing to fall back on. So much sickness in the past few months and in her heart she dreaded that he may join Eliza's resting place in the Riverbend churchyard, but, he did not succumb. Mary seemed to infuse her strength into him and he fought back with amazing courage. They all felt that God had spared him and was given back to them once more. He came through it a white ghost of a mite, but gradually he improved. Mary could once more start to fill out his little frame. All the family helped to look after him, Malcolm carrying him gently in his strong arms and sitting him under the peach tree while he worked in the garden. Duncan would sit beside him, showing him his latest find. Duncan was fast becoming the family naturalist. He was fascinated with all the insects, animals and plants in this new exciting world. He was forever getting into trouble for bringing his new friends into the house. His mother hated all the 'creepy things' as she called them. She couldn't believe that there could be so many different things that wanted to share her house with her. She learned to be somewhat tolerant as her twelve year old son introduced these creatures to her and she sat and watched with fascination the emergence of a hawk moth from its chrysalis. Such a weak, wobbly thing that struggled on too-fine legs, looking wet and crumpled. To watch it crawl up a stick that Duncan had placed for it and watch it pulsate while its body fluids pumped it's wings straight, was a revelation to her. There the plain silky fawn moth sat to dry. It sat there all day and quite often she left her work to look at it. It showed no sign of movement until night time when it fluttered its wings, setting up a faint buzz and it flew off into the night.

This son of hers soon had her dodging the orb spider webs in the garden, making her walk around a tree to leave the web intact, so that the big spider in the centre could remain in situ. He explained that this was the mother spider and that her babies were in a leaf beside the web. He knew she was the mother because he saw her lay the eggs. He thought the little fellow nearby was father. He amazed her with his knowledge of things about him and his ability to observe. She was proud of his prowess. He spent a great deal of his time wandering the farm, making friends quicker than anyone else in the family. His wanderings brought him an assortment of acquaintances and he gathered new ones about the district as he collected his specimens.

Malcolm would work with his father whenever he was allowed and he helped his mother with all the things in the home garden and the farmyard. He was learning to build sheds and shelters for all their animals. They were a hard-working family, loving and caring of one another. Mary watched her family growing into tanned Australians. As the summer wore on their olive skin took kindly to the harsh sun and all looked healthier and fitter than they had ever been. Even little John looked as though he were heading for a stronger childhood.

So different to the tall, slim darker Macdonald children, the Frasers took after Alec in colouring and were all red or fair-haired. Sunburn was quite a problem at first, but Margaret was learning how to live with the fierce summer sun.

Margaret found it hard to believe that she had lost one of her precious brood before the little one had enjoyed much of this new interesting life of theirs. She found herself wandering up to the little grave often. She would sit beside the mound and think of her baby. Alec had no idea how often she paid this visit until he came home, mid afternoon one day to find her gone and Effie, her eldest daughter, told him where she was. He went to the churchyard and sat beside Meg, who was quite dry-eyed.

"Come love," He said, this isn't any good. "Our wee girl isn't here, you know that."

"I know Alec. I know I am being quite silly, but I miss her so and I just cannot get used to the idea. I know she is not here and I think if I come here often enough I will really realise that she won't come back." She sobbed now and he put his arms around her, her head on his shoulder. He took his handkerchief out and handed it to her.

"Here, love, mop up your tears. Nothing will ever take away those few years we had with our wee one. Let us try to think of that and help each other to fill the place she leaves. Remember the others, lass, they need you so much. Come now, we must go back."

So, hand in hand they walked through the gate and back to their waiting children.

Chapter 11: *The First Christmas*

Although they kept in touch, there was no chance for the other families to visit until Christmas when the MacKenzies were able to arrange their first trip to the country.

Fergus had settled in well with the firm of Trent and Co., Importers and Retailers. John Trent found a ready pupil in the Scotsman and was surprised at his quick grasp of city life in trade and commerce. He had expected to lead him along slowly, but Fergus was more than ready to take to his new life in leaps and bounds. His appetite for knowledge was insatiable and he seemed to be forever poking into every corner of the business. When Emma Trent asked her husband how his new protege was shaping, he spoke of Fergus in glowing terms.

"Fergus is very keen to make himself indispensable to me. He seems to want to learn everything at once. He is forever investigating something so he can see how it works. Young Hamish is almost as keen as his father. We will have to put him on the payroll in the New Year, for he is always about the place asking questions and helping where he can. That family can certainly work. I have never seen better."

"And how is Mrs. MacKenzie taking to her new life, John? For a countrywoman this town life must be quite a shock."

"According to Fergus she is taking it very well indeed. They are attending the Scots Kirk and I believe that Mrs. MacKenzie is involved with the work there. She is very concerned for the girl waifs of the town and has already suggested work in that area with a Mrs Yates and Mrs Fishbon in one of Mr Ricky English's houses. I see a bright future for them all."

Fergus was able to take his family on a four day-break to Riverbend. The children were quite excited at this adventure and eagerly looked at every new thing, but the summer heat was quite a trial for them and so, six very tired, hot and quite dirty people arrived at the Macdonalds' house two days before Christmas. Mary and Elspeth shed some tears with their greetings, but soon after a cold wash and cooler clothes. They sat on the verandah drinking tea. They eagerly exchanged news and views of their new lives in this astounding country. Mary found it hard to believe that this fit man was her sickly brother Fergus. He was so full of life with no sign of the sickness that he had had when he left Scotland. She would be able to give her mother a glowing report.

"Fergus," she said, smiling at him, "I would never have believed that life in a town could suit you. Mother and Father will be so pleased. Elspeth dear, what have you been feeding him on?"

Elspeth laughed, "Well, I think we are all becoming bronzed Australians already. Just look at you. You must admit it is hard to get away from the sun. I don't think we are nearly as brown as you people. Mary, the food available is so good. I get such pleasure in piling the plates of my family with wonderful meat and fruit and other things we have never even seen before."

"Yes, that is the best part of this life. It is so good to see Murdoch and the children eat and eat, but the Frasers are not. Poor people! Responding to the sun as we are, burning every day. Margaret is having a constant battle with the sun and her fair-haired brood. She is not so affected, as you saw on your way here, but wait until you see poor Alec and Ian. They seem to be in a constant state of reddening and peeling."

"How is Meg coping after losing Eliza? It would be so hard to lose a wee one at any time, but for it to happen so soon after coming here. Did she want to go home after that? I think I would have wanted to."

"She is doing well now, but she found it very difficult for a time. She has been marvellous. She wanted to come to help me when John was so ill, with all her children to look after too, and she would still think of someone else. You'll see the old Margaret though. She certainly has a placid way of coping with life."

"Unlike you, dear", Elspeth put in quietly. "You don't show it much, but I know you carry things deeply. What is it Mary? Are you still worried about John? He does seem thin, but I think he is well now."

"No, I think we have Johnnie right now. He is improving quite steadily now."

"What is it, lass? Can I help?"

Mary looked towards Murdoch. He was engrossed in conversation with Fergus and the older boys. As she watched he got up and turned to her.

"Mary love, I'll take Fergus and the boys to see our wee home farm." They went down the steps and into the vegetable garden.

"Now", prompted Elspeth, "now tell me what it is."

"I don't know, I really don't know what is wrong with me. I see my men happy here. Murdoch and Malcolm just love the work, the life, the weather, the food and the potential of it all. Duncan is very happy with all that surrounds us. He is forever showing us some new bird, animal or insect - he even has me looking for them. The younger ones are happy playing at gardening and helping. We have a roof over our heads. We can see the way some day owning our own farm. Mr. and Mrs. Forrest are kindness itself, but Elspeth I hate it. I hate it and cannot seem to come to terms with it. The slightest thing gets me down. The heat, the flies... Oh! just everything. I hate it all and want to go home. Home, where it is cold, where we worked hard and gained nothing. Home where the rain was soft, the sun was gentle, the heather was purple and sweet. The mountains were misty . . . and Mother was there. I hate this place and most of all I hate myself for hating it." Her voice broke.

"Yes, and storms blew and the sea roared, the sun only peeped out occasionally and we were hungry and very cold."

"I know all that. I know I am stupid and I couldn't believe that I could be so homesick and so full of hate."

"Does Murdoch know how you feel?"

"I haven't spoken of it and I try to cover it up, for he loves this place so, but, he knows there is something. He too, thought that I was worried about John, but now he is well, Murd wonders why I am still worried. Elspeth, I don't want to spoil it for them. They all love it so. Do you think I will ever get to like it?"

"That will be up to you, lass. It's funny really, we have always looked to you as being the strong one of us. I thought I would hate a town life, but I quite like it, but, Mary, I think it is up to you. You will just have to get your priorities right and just push self down."

"I do know this, Elspeth, I do know what I should do, but somehow it seems to flood my being, this hate and loathing. I've prayed for help and just don't seem to get it."

"God helps those who help themselves, dear. You have to do your part."

"Mary, Mary, are you there?" came a voice from the house.

"It's Meg," said Mary and called out, "on the verandah, Meg."

"I'll pray, too, Mary," put in Elspeth quickly. "You will be all right, you will see," and she turned to greet Margaret.

On Christmas Eve, Alistair MacLeod, Caroline and their three children came over from Parry's farm ten miles away. Alistair seemed bigger, broader and more Scots than ever, and against him, Caroline seemed smaller, more faded than she had been. She was the only one in the whole party whose complexion had not taken the colour of the sun. She was paler, if anything, and certainly quieter. Elspeth thought she would try to seek the reason for this if an opportunity came, but it was difficult because there was so much noise, talk, catching up on each others' news. The young people left the adults and explored the Macdonald farm. The men sat on the verandah and the women worked in the kitchen preparing food for the whole family. The Christmas feast was to be eaten that evening as Alistair and his family had to be back by Christmas afternoon as Alistair had the second milking to do to let Mr. Parry's Jake have Christmas evening off with his family.

There was no time for private conversation and so Elspeth could say nothing to Caroline and felt disturbed about this. However, everyone seemed to enjoy themselves.

At the dinner table Murdoch spoke to them all, summarising their doings of the past months, before he asked a Blessing of the Lord, and reminded them of the wonderful opportunities ahead of them in this free land of theirs. He challenged them all especially speaking to the young people - to work and put their all into their efforts and God would bless them abundantly. He mentioned the sorrow of losing little Eliza and asked that He would heal the hurt in Meg and Alec's hearts.

At this, Alistair's voice boomed, "It was the Lord's will". Mary noticed many quick glances at Alistair and wondered whether she imagined some of the venom apparent in his voice. Surely not. She glanced at Elspeth and found a look of wonder there too. They exchanged looks, each determined to get to the bottom of this.

No opportunity came though as there was much hilarity that evening and the adults were happy to see the young ones taking up with the friends where they had left off months before, and didn't want to go to bed when their parents wished.

All too soon all the MacLeods left to share the Frasers' house for the night and Elspeth and Mary were at last able to share their thoughts when the last candle was snuffed in the girls' room.

"What do you think, lass?" queried Elspeth. "What is wrong with Alistair?"

"Perhaps he and Caroline were out of sorts for some reason. He was certainly a bit surly."

"Phuff," dismissed Elspeth. "I have a feeling that there is something more than that."

"Oh dear, I hope not," Mary sat down with a sigh. "Elspeth, have you ever known Alistair so aggressive before? He's always been so fun-loving, but now he's quite dour. I felt he didn't approve of the children's antics."

"Yes, but it is the children I noticed more than anything. Each time one screamed with delight, they looked towards Alistair fearfully. Oh, I must have imagined it."

"Well, something is wrong with Caro. Perhaps we can find out in the morning before they go."

Alas, on Christmas morning the MacLeods left early, calling in only to say a quick "Goodbye". There was little opportunity for more than hugs and kisses and see you at Easter time."

This last promise Murdoch had extracted from Alistair, who had given his word reluctantly, but Murdoch insisted that it should be a promise.

As they watched the family drive away: Murdoch said, "Alistair seemed to be in a funny mood. I've never known him quite so touchy."

"We noticed it too, Murd. Did Caro say anything to you?"

"There was no time lass. Here's Alec and Meg. Let's have a cup of Christmas tea. A happy Christmas to the Frasers, one and all. Who can believe that Christmas could be hot?"

"And a happy one to you too," grinned Alec. "It's hot all right. We could wish it may be a little cooler. I am not saying that I would like a cold Skye Christmas, but a little nearer halfway between would be a good thing." Saying this, he fell into a chair on the verandah, fanning his scarlet face and on seeing the teapot arrive, he said with a grin, "When an Australian is hot he pines to get hotter by drinking hot tea. What a crazy, lovely place it is."

With Alec Fraser around, it was hard to be serious at all and they just lent themselves to enjoyment on this first Christmas Day in the Antipodes. Then they fell to reminiscing, to sharing past experiences, past fun and happily sharing dreams and ambitions. To the others it seemed that all Alec wanted to do was to get rich and give his children all that he had never had. Murdoch tried to tell him that having everything wasn't important. It was lots of other things like family love, friends and having a Christian purpose that was important.

Alec sat up in his chair, his small frame to its full height, and said, "Murdoch, I have friends, I have you, Mary, Fergus and Elspeth. I have my wonderful family, Meg, my darling, and our lovely children. I don't think any of you know what you mean to me. I know you were dubious about letting me join you, but you gave me this wonderful chance and I'll not forget it. I'm not deceiving myself that the Laird wanted to sponsor me, but with your backing he did. Now I have the opportunity to give my family what I never had. Man, can you see?"

"Yes laddie, we can see. We are proud of you. We can all understand how you feel, but Alec, lad, what brought this on?"

Meg broke in, "It's Alistair, Murd. I don't know what's got into him. I thought he was a friend, but he certainly didn't act like one last night."

"Why, what happened?" they all chimed in.

Alec then told them. 'It seems that I am too Australian, too quickly for Alistair. He didn't say much but it seems he thinks that the wrath of the Lord would be upon me if I didn't mend my ways. Also that I am not a good example for our children, his and mine."

"What's got into the man? He has never been sanctimonious. Anyway, what have you done to bring on his disapproval?" asked Fergus.

"It seems that I mix with sinners at the hotel and speak with ex-convicts.

"Alec was telling Alistair and Caroline a joke that he had heard at the hotel and Alistair was horrified at him for being at the hotel. The joke was a very funny one. You know the one about the Irish fishermen, Murd. You thought it was very funny. Then when Alec told Alistair that the hotel owner was an ex-convict he was very upset indeed."

"He kept talking about the wrath of God and thumping his fist on the table. I didn't know he was that religious. If that is what being religious is, I don't think I can be."

"Alec, being religious and being a Christian are often, unfortunately, two different things. I am not one to frequent the hotel myself, as you know, but there is no call for Alistair to be so pious. Try to forget it, man, he'll probably be quite different by Easter when they come again."

"The thing is, Murdoch, he seems to blame my sins for us losing little Eliza. You know the sins of the father being visited upon the children, etc., etc. That I found very hard to take, for I love my children dearly and would do anything for them. He hasn't lost a child, he doesn't know what it is like." Alec controlled himself with a visible effort.

"He's obviously not himself, Alec. He's never given any indication of ever having thoughts like that before. I wonder if anything has happened. Now that I think of it, none of the family seemed easy. Even the children and Caroline were very quiet, weren't they."

"Yes, "said Mary, "Elspeth and I have said the same. Would it be possible, Murd, for us to go and see them sometime? I would like to talk to Caro and Easter is a long way off. When is it, by the way?"

"I can tell you that, Sis," said Fergus. "It is in March. It's early this year. Let's forget old Alistair now and we'll tell you how we live in Sydney Town. Besides, I am sure he will be all right. He's probably taking this new land a bit hard or something."

Chapter 12: *Learning so many new things*

Christmas had been hot but when the February rains came, the humidity was almost unbearable for the new settlers. No one had energy and for the first time, Mary could see that Murdoch was finding his work a trial. Not the work itself, but the effort of doing it under trying conditions. The children had no desire to run about and found that sitting in the passage way in the middle of the house was almost cool and so many hours they sat there playing. The girls had their family of peg dolls which they fed, clothed, washed. They had collected knuckle bones from the big Mutton roasts and broths, from Mary, who had taught them to play 'jacks' or 'knucklebones'. Occasionally Duncan would let John play marbles with him. He wasn't very good at the game, but was very pleased to be able to play such a skillful game. Mary would take a chair to the passage when she could and took these opportunities to teach the children the basics of spelling, writing and arithmetic. Sometimes she sewed, but best of all for the children, she would read a story to them. They had few books only, but the Bible was a great source of material for her and they all had their favourite characters.

They had the habit of getting up early in the morning at any time, but it was a greater pleasure these hot days as they kept their work to the early hours and the last cooler hours of the evening.

It was so strange to them that there was such a little difference between the days and nights. In Skye one only had a few hours of dark in the summer, with days of more than twenty hours. Then the children did not see the dark for weeks. Mary was grateful that they didn't have twenty hours of this heat, six or eight were enough. Things didn't ripen as quickly here as at home. For there the summer season was short and ripening was quick. Perhaps the longer hours of daylight were the reason, mused Mary. "Ah well," she thought, I daresay we will get used to it someday. I wonder what winter will be like."

Murdoch was fascinated by the different farming methods. The first thing he learned was that very little indeed was the same as home. One had to learn all over again. Mr. Forrest was a good mentor. He taught well, knowing his subject thoroughly. He trained his men knowing full well that as soon as their knowledge increased they would leave him and take farms for themselves. Instead of being frustrated he prided himself on his training techniques. He was extremely proud of his country and knew that good farmers would make the colony great and so he put in so many hours training his men. He looked upon it as a national investment. He told Murdoch that when the time came he would help him look for a farm. They discussed the possibilities getting of Murdoch a grant of land. Free land was quite desirable of course, but would probably be several years before such land was productive and Murdoch had no desire to ask Mary to give up the little comfort she had. So he was content to work and save until he could buy land that was already productive. This would be sometime off yet. In the meantime he was learning a great deal and he and Malcolm often talked of the farm they one day would own. They would have a dairy herd, for this was their first love, but they would also have some pigs and some sheep. It seemed treacherous that they wanted to have some of the very animals that had been instrumental in them leaving their homeland, but here the sheep caused friendly feelings and not hostile ones.

They had cause to be puzzled by this new land of theirs. They had further indication of its harshness when the hot weather turned wet. Such rains as they had never experienced fell down in heavy, soaking drops. Everything was wet and sticky and fungus and mould grew on all sorts of things. The rain didn't want to stop and soon the Hawkesbury was in flood, the clear river gone and in its place a thick, dirty mass that flooded all its nearest land. 'Forrest Park' was safe as only the river paddocks were affected and there had been time to move stock from those. The farm-houses were on high ground, but Mary could see the flood waters getting nearer the town and wondered if it would be inundated. The men were called to help neighbouring farmers who hadn't been able to move their stock quickly enough. They were all much interested in the experience, but as no known farmer was badly affected in any way they put floods down as another peculiarity of their new home.

The flood did, however, drive snakes up closer to the houses and many were killed. Mary felt she could never get used to the horrible things and once when she found herself face to face with one in the garden she just turned and fled into the house and shut the door, shrieking loudly for Duncan who dispatched it quickly, but only after Mary had forbade him to pick it up. For she had stopped at the kitchen window to watch the killing and found Duncan trying to entice the snake to bite his hat while he tried to capture it. He was quite upset with his mother when she stopped him, saying, "George does it that way, Mother, why can't I?"

Murdoch banned any further adventures of this type when he heard the story and refused to listen to any appeal from Duncan.

Autumn came and everyone enjoyed the cooler days, cold nights and an early frost. Malcolm came in from milking the cow on the first morning of frost with the bucket of warm milk steaming in the cold.

"Mother, was it as cold as this at home? It's very cold outside. I found it very hard to get out of bed this morning."

Mary laughed, "Yes, it is quite a change, my son. It is much colder at home, but somehow we are feeling it more. Perhaps it is because when it is cold on Skye it is cold all the time, day and night. Here the days are so warm that the cold nights seem to be colder.

"That may be so. All I know is that my hands feel frozen."

"It was at this time that Charles Parry sent to Mr. Forrest for help. The two men who worked on his farm with Alistair succumbed to gold fever and left Mr Parry without notice. While he and Alistair were mustering in the mountainous timber country, he'd had a fall from his horse and badly jarred his ankle. So, until he could get more labour from Sydney, Alistair had to do the work alone.

William Forrest was glad to help his friend out and came to see Murdoch and Alec one evening with the news.

"We'd be glad to go, Mr. Forrest. Mary and the boys can help here. Ian Fraser and Malcolm will do all the farm work you need to have done."

"I could send George and Mick, but I thought it would be an opportunity for you to see your sister and MacLeod."

"We'll be off in the morning, sir," said Alec.

"Good," said Mr. Forrest. "I will leave you then. I would think you would be back within a week. You can take our gig if you like, or ride for that matter."

"I think we'll ride, Mr. Forrest. If I may have 'Brownie', I am sure that Alec will want to ride his 'Star.'"

"Yes, I would like the chance of trying her out on a long run. I've only been on her locally."

"I think you got a good bargain there, Alec," approved Forrest. "You seem to have an eye for a good horse."

"I don't know why, sir. Very few have come my way."

They left early next day and as they rode up to the MacLeods' house, Caroline greeted her brother with a sob.

"What's this, lass. Glad to see your big brother?"

"Oh, Murdoch, it is good to see you." Caroline clung to him.

"We are so far from you all. Alec too, this is good. You must sit and I'll make tea for you before you go out to Alistair."

"What ails you, girl. You are looking peakie? You're not sick I hope?"

"No, Murd, I am well. Oh, here's Alistair. He must have seen you coming."

The men exchanged greetings and handshakes.

"I am glad you came, Murdoch. I badly need help at the moment. Mr. Parry felt sure that help would come from the Park. We expected that you may have brought George, though."

Murdoch looked startled at this and looked sharply at Alec who seemed not to be included in the greetings. He decided not to make anything of it, as Alec appeared to ignore it and so turned his attention to his tea.

"Caro looks a bit pinched, Alistair. Working her too hard, or has it been the heat, lass?"

"Work never hurt anyone," returned Alistair brusquely. "When you are ready we'll get on with some."

"It must wait until I have finished my tea, man. Why the hurry?"

"We have a lot to do and I daresay I won't have you for very long, so I must use you while I can."

"Come on Alec, the man wants us to work." He slapped Alec on the back and followed his brother-in-law out the door.

Alec was sent to scythe fodder and Murdoch went with Alistair to work with the sheep. There was little time for conversation all day until milking time when they all met in the dairy.

Alistair seemed to throw a word or two at Alec, but otherwise gave most orders through Murdoch. It was not until after dinner that night that Murdoch said, "Where is Donald, Caroline? I expected to see him working here. Has he found himself a job?"

"Yes, he has," replied Donald's mother. "He is working on Tregonning's farm. They have a big dairy herd and Donald enjoys it. He is fortunate, isn't he?"

"He certainly is."

"He won't be there for long though," gruffed Alistair. "He'll be working for me soon."

"What's this, Alistair? A farm?"

"We've applied for a grant on the Manning River. We will move there when we can decently leave Mr. Parry."

"But how? What will you do until it is cleared?" Alec broke in.

Alistair leaned back in his chair and gave Alec a withering look. "I believe it is quite wild country and has to be cleared of large timber, but it is the isolation I want for my family."

"What do you mean, man?" queried Murdoch. He caught a frightened look on Caroline's face.

"I mean," said Alistair loudly, "that we have brought our women and children to a sinful place and I mean to take them away from harm. The Lord said that we should not mix with sinners. 'Come ye apart and be ye separate,' said the Lord."

"Well, I've not taken that as its meaning. You're making a mistake," said Alec. "Besides, the colony seems no worse than anywhere else."

"I would expect such a remark from a sinner such as you, Fraser.

You've never been any good. Who are you to tell a God-fearing man what to do?"

"Hold hard, both of you," said Murdoch as Alec rose to his feet. "Sit down, Alec and calm down. Now Alistair, what's got into you? You never used to worry about sinners and such and I am sure we had plenty at home. I am quite sure Alec is no worse than the rest of us."

"He admitted to me at Christmas time that he consorts with sinners and convicts at the Devil's house."

"If you mean I have a drink with my friends at the hotel at Riverbend, then yes. I'm a sinner. God knows, Alistair, that I care for Him as you or Murdoch or any of you do. What's got into you? What makes you think you can judge me anyway? I think you are off your head. I only have to look at Caroline to see how unhappy she is and your two little girls creep round like mice. Mine like to sing and dance and yours...."

"Leave my family to me, Fraser. They'll do as I say. I know the Lord is full of wrath with you for He took your child away from you. I see the Lord's hand in that."

"Why, you ..."

"Calm down, Alec. Why not bunk down now and leave this to me," said the very concerned Murdoch.

With a growl and a shrug Alec left the room.

Murdoch turned to Alistair. "What's got into you, friend? You've never felt like this before. I never took you for being narrow-minded."

"Is it narrow-minded to keep your family from sin? I intend to. I will keep them isolated in the bush and keep them pure and Holy."

"You've got it all wrong, Alistair. We are not intended to run away from life, but to face it and grow strong."

"I'll not have sinners near my home and Alec is a sinner."

"If that's the way you feel, "I'll send him home for I'll not have you hurt him any further. You do him a great discredit, for he is a good and very loving husband and father."

"He can be loving and not do his duty," came the pious-sounding voice.

Murdoch gave up and bid him 'good night'. He was unable to speak to Caroline, so went into the bedroom where he found Alec on his bunk.

Alec looked up. "he's mad, Murd."

"He's something, old fellow, and I'll not have him say anything else to you, so what about leaving this to me and you going home in the morning. I can't see that there is anything that urgent to do here anyway. I wonder if it was a ruse of Mr Parry's to get us here to look into it."

"I will shove off in the morning, Murd. I don't want to make things worse for you and Caro. What will I tell Mr. Forrest?"

"You'll think of something. What a situation! I thought something was wrong with Caro."

"He's mad, I think. I wouldn't much like going to live in the bush with him in his present frame of mind."

Alec was gone before any of the household rose the next morning and Caroline asked silent query of Murdoch as he said morning."

Alistair said, "Was that Alec leaving early?" knowing full well that it was.

"Yes" said Murdoch. "As it upset you to have him here, he could hardly remain under your roof. I must see Mr. Parry this morning to offer some explanation."

"Do as you think fit," came the dour reply.

When Murdoch called in at the homestead he found Mr. Parry most anxious to discuss the situation.

"I was hoping to see you alone Macdonald, for I wish to tell you that I have a great concern for your sister and her family. You will have gathered that there is something wrong with MacLeod. Not that I blame him altogether, but I am sure that his way is not the best way to handle it."

"Why, sir, what has happened? What has happened to make such a change in Alistair? We've always been the closest of friends, but now I can't get through to him. He's never been so narrow-minded before. I cannot understand it."

Charles Parry looked very sadly at Murdoch. "Some very unpleasant things have happened and I think that Alistair thinks that he is doing the very best for his family. You see, not long before Christmas two rough fellows, ex convicts, went to the house and found Mrs. MacLeod alone. They asked for food and of course she prepared to give them some. As she did so, they crept up to her in the kitchen and handled her roughly. I am thankful to say that Alistair carne in at that time and found them. He tore into them like a mad bull and nearly killed them. I arrived at that moment just in time to stop him from killing them. Any man would have done what he did. Mrs. MacLeod was badly frightened, but I am sure she suffered no physical harm. The men literally staggered away and a few nights later their hen house was burned and some stock killed.

Well, if that wasn't enough, little Ann had a nasty experience too. Mrs. MacLeod sent Ann to my wife with a recipe or something like that. After Ann left here she met a man on the track near the bush. He grabbed her and was taking her into the scrub. Ann screamed and Donald heard her. He was hoeing and so ran with his hoe. When he saw his sister being taken away, he attacked the fellow with the hoe I would have myself, and he hurt him quite badly. Donald was horrified at what he had done. He rushed Ann to their house and then ran to his father for help, then back to where he had left the man. They found no trace of him. Alistair was roaring mad and since then hasn't trusted anyone. He is afraid to leave Mrs. MacLeod or the little girls alone at all and as a consequence is over-protective and has succeeded in frightening them with his ferocity as well as all the neighbours. It is amazing that he lets Donald work at the dairy farm."

"I am stunned. I find it hard to believe that this has happened and Alistair hasn't told me, Mr. Parry. And you say this happened before Christmas. Why, there were opportunities for Caroline or the children to share it with my Mary, but not a word was said. I thought they would have had enough feelings for us to know that we would have received it with understanding."

"I suppose it is understandable. I suppose he could think it a reflection on Mrs. MacLeod and so ban them from speaking. He's taken it very hard."

"He has taken it in such a way that I think it has unhinged him, Mr. Parry. I can understand some of it, but not all. I think he has taken the blame on himself in some twisted way. This explains why he turned on Alec the way he did." At this Murdoch explained what had happened the previous night. "I feel sure he must be blaming Alec for his little girl's death, thinking he had neglected his children for a frivolous life. At least this is how it appears."

"So it would seem."

"Thank you, sir, for sharing this with me. I must speak with Alistair and try to get him to see reason."

"Has he told you that he wants to take his family up into the bush on the Manning?"

"Yes, he has and I've tried to tell him that isolation will not do for the children and Caroline. Now that you have told me this, am sure that it is doubly wrong for them. It will only teach them to fear other people."

"Yes, I have tried to get that over, too, but he doesn't listen. "Murdoch returned to Alistair and as there was a boy helping with the work, it was lunchtime before Murdoch could broach the subject."

"Why didn't you tell me, man. Surely you were sure of me?"

"I don't want to speak of it, now or ever," rejoined Alistair.

"But Alistair, locking it up inside you won't help."

"And talking about it won't either. Donald and I are working as hard as we can and very soon we should have enough money to move, but, whatever you say, I am going away from this sinful place and taking mine with me. Now let us go back to work."

"Not until you tell me that you will come to Riverbend and discuss it with me and stay for a while before you make the break. Caroline would like to talk it over with Mary and she is my sister, you know. Besides, they have always been so close."

"She's my wife, man, and she'll do as I say. I know what is best for her and my girls. Donald will be with us and between us we will protect them. I'll not discuss it further. We'll away to work."

Murdoch had no choice but to follow Alistair back to work. He remained the week, but it was a cheerless experience. There was no gaiety in the house, no opportunity to speak much with Caroline. At one stage he tried but she silenced him by saying, "Quite now, Murdoch. I'll not hear criticism of Alistair I dislike the prospect even more than you do, but I'll do as he says. He does love us and he is anxious for our welfare, you know."

"But he'll smother you. He's acting like a tyrant. It's not right."

"I've promised that I will go and that's that. I'll not speak of it again."

"But Caro, you cannot go like this."

"Enough now Murd, no more. I'm going."

"But Caro,"

"Enough!" she said sharply and walked away. When Murdoch returned home he was able to fill in the details for Mary, Margaret and Alec. The women were horrified at the thought of Caroline and the little girls going so far away from them, and so soon. Strangely, Alec was more understanding of Alistair when he heard the story.

"I don't agree with him, mind you. I think he is making a mistake. I can see what made him decide to do it. but I think he has been pushed too far, almost over the edge, don't you think? I, on the other hand, am very pleased to have Margaret and the children so close to you. If anything should happen to me, You would be close to Meg, to help her." He turned to Murdoch and Mary. "You would, wouldn't you friends? You would look after Meg and the children?"

Murdoch slapped him on the back. "Of course, old fellow, but nothing is going to happen. You're not going to follow in Alistair's footsteps, I hope."

"No, I am not that", said Alec with such a serious look on his face. No news came from the MacLeods about their coming for Easter as was planned at Christmas and so Murdoch and Mary decided to go to the Parrys' farm to see them. Mr. Forrest lent his gig and on a misty autumn morning they set off, leaving the children under Meg's care.

Caroline was pathetically excited to see them and explained that within the next week or so they were leaving for the north. Alistair had hired a dray for all their household goods and they were to drive to Sydney where they would board a ship to take them to the Manning River. They would have to take livestock and provisions for them so they would have enough to live on until they could grow their own food.

Murdoch reminded her that it could be a long time before they were self-sufficient. Caroline assured them that Alistair had planned well and had consulted several people who had had experience of pioneering bush like that.

"But you cannot want to go, Caro" said Mary.

"No, dear, I do not say I do, but as I have come all this way from Skye, I daresay I can manage a little further. My main regret is that I will sorely miss you, my dear people." At this she rushed into Mary's arms and sobbed. "But I will do it. I will go'"

"Well, we will enjoy our short time together. We will enjoy it while we can. I have so much to tell you."

"Alistair will be so glad you have come. I know he is a stubborn, proud man, but he does love us all, you know." Caroline patted her face with her apron and began to make tea.

"We plan to stop a day or two if you will have us," said Murdoch, "will Alistair want to have us?"

"I am sure he will, Murd. He will be in soon, you will see."

So the visit passed more successfully than the Macdonalds had expected. Alistair was much more reasonable to talk to and Murdoch felt that as time passed he would get over the trauma of the two bad experiences, but he was still far from being the old friend from Skye. He could see that they sincerely thought a new start would benefit them all. They couldn't see that they were running away. He did hope it would all turn out well.

The women were tearful when it was time for farewells. When would they meet again? What would happen to the family? Mary sat silent for a great deal of the journey home and her heart was heavy for her sister-in-law. It seemed this land had cruelties beneath its surface that were past understanding. The life at home had been cold, hard and raw, but somehow predictable. Just as soon as you felt that you were coming to terms with this place, something evil would raise its ugly head and come crashing into your life and leave you bruised. Mary had a deep feeling of distrust for the whole place. It looked good, it smelled good, usually it was good, but all the time you felt that life was uncertain, unsteady, unpredictable. Where would it all end? Would they really ever find it a friendly place?

Murdoch, too, pondered, but in a different way. He felt that Alistair was going at it too hard. This was challenging, this new land, and Alistair was such a strong man that he wanted to fight it. He knew Alistair had an inner frailty that could easily snap. This new homeland was a place that needed quietly taming, like a young colt. It needed to be gentled. You had to keep a firm rein but move along in harness with it. "It has so much to teach you and we have so much to learn," mused Murdoch.

"What's that you are saying, Murdoch?" asked Mary.

"Lassie, I am just thinking how each one of we four men are handling this country. Do you know, I think Alec can teach us a lot. Although Fergus has taken to it well, too. He's entered into a new life altogether and he and Ellie have settled in like old hands. But Alec, I feel, has the makings of a good Australian. He is so happy here that you would think he was born to it, and Meg and the children too, they are all the same."

"Yes, I see what you mean dear. Aren't we fortunate to have them so near. If I am feeling down, Meg is always there to lift me up. She is a great comfort, and dear Alec, what a good friend we are finding him to be. Not the trouble we all thought he would be. Meg has always had such faith in him. She has always said that if he had a chance he would make good. You have to admit he had a bad time at home."

Murdoch looked straight at her. "You haven't really felt at home here have you Mary? Sometimes you do seem far away from me. Sometimes I want to call you back from where you go."

"I think I will just go home for a while, Murd. Don't mind me, I'll be all right. Come on, Meg and Alec will be wanting to know the news."

"Yes, they will. Come on, get up." Murdoch clic-clic'd the horse and shook it up to a brisk trot.

"I think Alec has lost his wild notions about the goldfields, thank the Lord. He seems quite content."

Chapter 13: *Alec*

"I'm off for a few days, Mary," said Murdoch, as he sat with the family over their evening meal. "I'm to go to Camden to get the sheep. Mr. Forrest had word that they are ready."

"When will you go, Father?" asked Malcolm eagerly. "Will I be able to go with you?"

"I'll be going the day after tomorrow and will be away about four days lad. I'm sorry son, I won't take you, but Duncan. Malcolm I must leave you in charge, to look after things here. Your Mother will need you and I can depend on you."

"Oh! Father." Malcolm looked truly downcast.

"Oh, Father," exclaimed the excited Duncan. "Can I truly go?"

"Yes, you can. Malcolm, you've been with me before and Duncan needs the training. Besides, Mr. Forrest is away off to Sydney and I'll need you to watch over things."

"But Uncle Alec will be here."

"I know son, but I want you here and that's all there is to it." Malcolm, recognising in his fathers voice that ordering tone that cannot be shaken, said, "Right, Father, I'll look after things."

Mary had sat watching her men proudly as they discussed further plans for the trip. They seemed to take to this new life of theirs so easily, so happily, so calmly. Who was she to shatter their lives by sharing her unhappiness with this place, this intolerance, indeed hatred, of this relentless land. The heat, the flies, the snakes, spiders, oh, just all the things.

"... and if you can start ploughing the acre paddock. You've taken to ploughing well, Malcolm. You seem to have a knack with it that I have not."

"Yes, Father, but I think it is because I love the horses so much."

"And they love you, son."

"Will I be riding, Dad?" chimed the eager Duncan.

***

"Maggie, are you there, Maggie?"

Margaret Fraser came out of the wash house wiping her sudsy arms on her voluminous apron. "Hello Alec, you're just in time for a cup of tea."

"Very well, my dear, but I've come to pack some clothes. Mr. Forrest wants me to go with him to Sydney and we'll be away for a few days."

"What! I thought he was leaving you in charge while Murdoch is away. I thought I heard him pass a while ago."

"He changed his mind and asked me to get my things and meet him as soon as I can. I'll go and get my things. You make the tea."

Alec went into their bedroom, piled as many of his clothes as he could in a pack and dropped it out the window amongst the plants in the garden, then gently dropped his gun onto this. He packed a few more of his things into a small bag and went to the kitchen carrying this.

"How long will you be away, Alec?"

"About two to three days, love. You'll be all right, won't you? Ian will help you."

Maggie seemed puzzled about this, but said nothing. Alec called all the children and gave them a fond hug, telling them to help their Mother and do her bidding.

They stood in front of their house and waved as Alec mounted his horse and rode away. Maggie stood there watching him down the road. He turned, took off his hat and waved, his red hair shining in the sun.

"Where is Dad going, do you think, Mama?"

Margaret turned to find her fourteen-year old son watching her. "Well son, he told me that Mr. Forrest wants him to go to Sydney Town with him."

"But I heard Mr. Forrest giving him the orders for what is to be done while Uncle Murdoch is away."

"Well, I am sure your Father would do nothing wrong, Ian, but it is rather odd. We'll just have to wait and see."

Alec rode down the road until he was out of sight of the house, then pulled the horse up and hitched the reins to a tree and set off back towards the house under cover of the bushes. He picked up his pack and gun and hurried back to his horse. Swinging himself into the saddle, he rode off down the road. Half a mile down the road Alec pulled up sharply and called, "Tom, you're just the person I wanted."

The old bushman stood beside the horse looking up to the rider.

"Where are you off to, Alec?" His words slurred and Alec looked enquiringly at him.

"Are you drunk, Tom?"

"Only a bit Alec. Not too drunk to say g'day to a friend."

"Well, I've got to go away for a time Tom and I would like you to give this letter to my wife. Would you do that for me?"

"Sure I will, Alec. I'll go now."

"Not now, Tom. I want you to give this to her tomorrow."

"What you up to Alec? I don't want to do nuffing wrong."

"You don't have to. Just give Margaret this letter tomorrow and here's a coin for doing it. But don't drink it all away at the hotel." Alec handed the money and the letter to the old man, turned his horse and rode smartly up the road after shouting, "Don't forget, will you old timer."

Tom stood looking after the disappearing rider and muttered, "Now I wonder what he's up to." He scratched his head, put the letter in his hat and headed straight for the public house.

Chapter 14: *Rearranging life*

Margaret Fraser had a very disturbed night. She knew Alec was off on one of his hair-brained schemes. She knew in her heart that he was not in Sydney with Mr. Forrest and had half expected him back before this, for it was like Alec to get up to some mischief and cover it up before he got into trouble. He was not bad, thought Margaret, he's such a kind-hearted person and wouldn't really do wrong. He loved the Lord too much for that, but he did get such silly ideas. He wants so much to give us everything he thinks we want. He would really like to give the goldfields a try. The goldfields! The thought shocked the worried woman. He wouldn't go to the goldfields! Oh, Alec, not the goldfields! She tried to dismiss the idea, but the thought of it kept her awake. She had slept little and was quite weary when it was time to get up and prepare breakfast for her family.

Ian dressed his brother and Effie mothered her sisters. A lovely, happy family-life they shared. All the children favoured Alec in colouring. There was no mistaking who their father was. Some had Alec's true red hair, the rest were sandy fair. They were an industrious group who loved the garden and even the six-year old, Kate, knew what was growing in her plot. The girls were very keen to be good housekeepers like their mother and already Effie could cook for the family.

As Effie served the oatmeal to the little ones, she said, "When is Father coming home, Mother? Is he coming with Mr. Forrest today?"

"I suppose so, dear. I want you to mind the little ones this morning while I walk down to speak with Aunt Mary."

It was 10 o'clock before her work was done to her satisfaction. Margaret set off for Macdonalds' house with a heavy heart. She was torn between wanting to share the worry with her cousin and not wanting to lower Alec in Mary's eyes. Murdoch was such a steady man and he couldn't see why Alec would do these 'silly things', as he called them. But Alec was so impetuous.

Mary came out onto the verandah when she heard the gate. "Meg, my dear, in time for tea. We will have it out here. I've just sent the children down to the dairy, so we will be alone."

"Oh, Mary," Margaret said. Mary looked at her quickly as she heard a muffled sob in her cousin's voice.

"Meg, is there anything wrong? Anyone sick? Can it wait while I get the tea? You just sit here while I get it. It's hot, isn't it? I thought this would be cooler, but apparently even autumn is hot here." She disappeared into the house and soon returned with a laden tray.

"Now, tell me." Mary handed Meg a cup of steaming tea. As she burst into tears, Mary said, "Goodness, Meg, what is it?" She came across and put her arms about her.

"It's Alec," she sobbed. "I know I am silly, but I don't know where he is. He left yesterday morning and I find he has taken some clothes. This morning I saw that he has taken some of our money and his gun. Mary, what will I do? Do you think he has left us?"

"Alec wouldn't leave you and your bairns, silly one. I suppose he must have gone off on some jaunt of his own."

"Mary, I think he has gone to the goldfields. You know, he is mad to have a place of our own and he dreams of getting one quickly and he wouldn't take us into the bush like Alistair has taken Caroline."

"Yes, Alec was ever impatient to get things the minute he thinks of them, but I am sure he wouldn't do anything so silly without talking it over with Murdoch."

That's just it, I think he may. He's tried to talk to Murd about it. Not for a long stay, but just to try his luck, and Murdoch wouldn't listen. I think he has gone while Murdoch is away so he cannot stop him. Mary, do you think he has?"

"If he has, Meg, he'll soon find that you don't pick up gold nuggets that easy and he will be back in a few days. I wonder where he would go. The closest would be just over the mountains, Sofala, Hill End or the like. I hope Murdoch doesn't go looking for him.

Mr. Forrest is going to be annoyed enough as it is."

"Mary, look, there's Mr. Forrest now. What will I tell him? I thought he would be home today."

"I am afraid you will have to tell him just what you told me, but I am sure he will be annoyed about it. Don't worry, he will probably not say much to you, but save it up for Alec."

Mary stood as the farmer came through the gate. She watched as he approached and thought what a pleasant man he was, one who had eased their arrival in such a wonderful way. He had hitched his mare to the gatepost and patted her lovely chestnut neck. He greeted the women as he took his hat off.

"Good morning, ladles. I saw you enjoying your morning tea and have taken the liberty of asking myself along. I know that Mrs. Mac never turns a starving man away from her door."

He chuckled as he sat down. "I also wanted to know when Murdoch expected to return. I rather urgently wanted to speak with him."

"No, Mr. Forrest, he really didn't expect to get back until tomorrow. Please excuse me while I get another cup."

"Well, Mrs. Fraser" he said as he turned to Meg, "is Alec still up at the top paddock or did he get the job finished?"

"Oh, sir, oh," stammered Margaret and then, looking somewhat sick, she stared at Mr. Forrest.

"Are you all right, Mrs. Fraser? Is there anything wrong?"

"Alec's gone and I don't know where."

Mary returned and poured the tea. She explained Margaret's plight. William Forrest was obviously greatly annoyed, but he could see Margaret's distress and so said little. They discussed the situation while he drank his tea and then he said as he rose to go, "Don't worry Mrs. Fraser, we'll do nothing for the moment. He is sure to be back soon and maybe the scallywag will have it out of his system by then. Hello it looks as though you have another visitor."

Old Tom came through the gate and ambled up the path. He took his battered hat off and said, "Good mornin' Mrs. Macdonald, Mrs. Fraser, Mr. Forrest."

"Good morning, Tom. What can I do for you?"

"Well, it's really Mrs. Fraser I wanted, madam. I had a letter that Alec gave me."

"Thank goodness," said Meg. "Now we'll know."

"Well, it's like this, you see." He shuffled his feet.

"Come on, man, out with it. Where's this letter for Mrs. Fraser?" said Mr. Forrest impatiently.

"Well, you see, Alec give me a letter yesterday and said to give it to Mrs. Fraser tomorrow, that's today and I put it in me hat."

"Where is it now?" asked Meg.

"Well, see, I dunno. I know I put it in me hat and he give me some money and now it's not in me hat today. I looked everywhere, I did, and I can't find it. I am real sorry, I am."

"I suppose you went to the hotel to spend the money. Just like Alec to give you some."

"Yes, real generous he was. It was in me hat yesterday and not today."

"But what did it say? Did you read it? asked a distracted Meg.

"I dunno what it said. I can't read, but it probably said he was going away. He looked as though he were going somewhere."

"Which way did he go?"

"Sydney way."

"Come, Tom. We'll go back to the hotel and search. Now, don't you worry, Mrs. Fraser, I'll take Tom back to the hotel and search the whole place. Someone may have seen it. I'll call back and report with the letter, I hope."

Saying this, Mr. Forrest walked down the path to the gate, unhitched his horse and stood waiting for Tom.

The old man, hat in hand, stood looking up to Margaret. "I am real sorry, Mrs. Fraser. I know I've let Alec down. He's a good bloke, Alec is, but I knew he was up to something when he give me the letter. I think I should a' come right up to you with it then. Then I wouldn't at lost it."

"Come on, Tom" called Forrest. "Mrs. Fraser knows you didn't do it deliberately. We will look everywhere we can."

The two men walked up the road towards Riverbend, the mare nuzzling Mr. Forrest as she walked behind them.

Mary took Meg into the house with the tea things, both thinking of all Tom had said.

It was nearly lunchtime before they heard the chestnut cantering back. Mr. Forrest dismounted and came quickly to the house and the waiting women.

"I'm sorry I have been so long, ladies, but I have searched everywhere. I have spoken to everyone who may have seen or spoken to Tom last night and there's not a sign of the letter anywhere. The only thing we can hope for is that it has your name on it. Old Tom assures me that there was some writing on the outside of it."

"Thank you for your trouble, Mr Forrest. What will we do now?"

"Just go home and don't worry, we'll see what develops. In the meantime, will you send young Ian to me. Do you think he would do Alec's work for me, under Murdoch's supervision?"

"I am sure he'll try to, Mr. Forrest. He is very keen to work on the farm."

"I'll be off then." Good morning Mrs. Mac., Mrs. Fraser."

"Mary, I must go. I have left Effie too long as it is. Thank you so much for everything." Margaret gave Mary a quick hug.

"Try not to worry, Meg. It will all turn out right in the end. I am sure Murdoch will come to see you as soon as he gets home."

"Oh dear, what will he say? I think he's always felt that Alec could let him down."

"You would be surprised. He was only saying the other day how much Alec has to teach us. Anyway, he will know how you feel, don't worry, he will be very kind."

"But we have let him down."

"You haven't. He won't be annoyed with you, dear."

Meg hurried off to her own home, leaving Mary thinking about the happenings of the morning and just what Murdoch would say when he came.

Murdoch and Duncan arrived next morning, dusty and dry, after driving the mob of sheep. Duncan was very tired after the days of riding, but very proud that he had been asked to do the job with his father. Mary waited patiently whilst he chatted about their doings while she plied them with tea and fresh-baked bread. Eventually he asked if he could go to find Malcolm and tell him of his adventures.

Left together, Murdoch looked at Mary and put his arms about her. "Oh, I have missed you, lass." He kissed her tenderly. "I think I love you more each day."

Mary snuggled closer in his arms and said, "This is really lovely, dear, but I've something to tell you and I want to tell you before the children come in. Come and sit down. If you hold me like this I am sure I am not going to be able to keep my mind on what I have to say."

"Come on then, lass, come into the parlor and tell me." He led her to the settee and cradled her in his encircling arm.

"Well dear, you're not going to like this. Meg thinks Alec has gone away somewhere."

"What? When?"

Mary told him the story as she knew it, Murdoch listening intently, sitting up straight and looking straight at her.

"I am afraid I agree with Margaret. The silly man has the idea that there are nuggets lying around waiting to be picked up. He'll soon be back when he sees how many people never see a speck of gold."

"You don't sound as surprised as I thought you would be, Murdoch."

"I suppose I half expected it. He talked about it a fair bit some months ago when we first came here, but lately he hasn't said much at all and I thought he'd got it out of his system."

"There's another thing though that puzzles me. Old Tom said he was heading Sydney way. If he was going to Sofala or Hill End he would have gone the other way. What do you think?"

"Yes, that's a teaser. Maybe it was just a ruse."

"You won't go after him then, Murd?"

"No, lass, what's the use. I have no idea where he has gone, if indeed he has gone to the diggings. Besides he would never stay away from his family long. You know how much he loves Meg and the family."

"I thought that would override any thoughts of goldfields."

"Yes, but when Alec gets an idea he just doesn't listen to reason. He's heard men's stories about the hardships, but he doesn't choose to listen to that. He only thinks of finding gold to buy a farm for his family. Dear, silly old Alec, he does learn the hard way. I think this business of Alistair pushed him into doing it. He may think he can show Alistair that he can get a farm for his family too. I wonder if he has thought whether the boss will thank him for this escapade."

"What will Margaret do in the meantime? Mr. Forrest did ask her if Ian would do his father's job for him until he returns. Do you think he can?"

"Ian is a good lad and is going on for fifteen now and Malcolm and I can help. I think we can fill in, between us."

***

The dusty horseman could see lights twinkling in the dark. He thought they were still a fair way off, but found them much closer than he thought.

"At last," breathed Alec, "Ballarat at last."

He was so intent on the town ahead that he didn't see the two. They sprang out at him, one grabbing the reins and the other pulling him off the horse. Alec fell to the ground, knocking his head on the rock beside the road.

One of the attackers peered at him in the gloom. "Gawd, mate, we've done him in. Lets get outta here."

They went through his pockets, taking everything they could find and mounting the horse, they galloped off, leaving the unconscious man under a bush.

Chapter 15: *Snakes!*

No word was heard from Alec. Daily they expected to hear and William Forrest made discreet enquiries, but no reports of his whereabouts were forthcoming. They were at a standstill. One week went by, another, and still no word. Then came very heavy rain and again the Hawkesbury was in flood. This time the water rose to be so high that several neighbouring houses were inundated. Many animals were lost and a number of travellers to the goldfields over the mountains were held up and had to have temporary accommodation until the water went down. Murdoch sought the acquaintance of some of the prospectors and felt able to share Alec's story with them. He asked them to plead with him to return if they met up with him. He told them to assure Alec his job was secure if he came back immediately, but if he delayed very long Mr. Forrest would not be able to keep it."

The waters remained high for nearly a week and on returning to the river, they left a deep sludge all over the pastures. Dead animals, tree trunks and all kinds of debris littered the once tidy pastures. Even some household furniture was found. One large cedar table was found standing right way up, caught against some rocks, looking as though it was ready to be used for a meal, the rocks beside it for a seat.

Again the snakes invaded the high ground and with them came tragedy.

On the first fine day Duncan decided to explore the mud-covered paddocks, looking at all the odd things brought down by the river. Small John trotted behind him, both becoming extremely muddy and wet in the process. Duncan flicked the piles of small twigs with a gum stick that he carried, laughing at the rubbish as he sent it into the air. Johnnie gleefully ran, trying to catch the flying sticks, when he suddenly shrieked and screamed.

Duncan turned and, to his horror, he saw a snake attached to the little boy's leg. As he ran forward the sleek, brown, slithery animal released its hold and made away.

"It bit me, Duncan, it bit me."

Duncan grabbed the little chap and ran with him towards the house on the hill above. John was quite a burden for the twelve-year old lad. He gasped for breath as he ran, but was able to yell at intervals. In the paddock above the homestead, Murdoch and Malcolm heard the faint sound, saw Duncan struggling with his load and ran.

Mary, too, heard him and ran towards them. She took Johnnie in her arms and ran crying into the house, Murdoch and Malcolm not far behind.

"A snake. He's bitten, quick, make a tie for his leg," cried Mary.

Murdoch quickly tied his handkerchief round the tiny lad's thigh, yelling at Malcolm, "Quick, run for Dr. Kenny."

They tried to remember all that Mr. Forrest had told them to do and felt so helpless as they watched the little chap sink before their eyes. By the time they heard the welcome sound of the doctor's arrival, they knew in their hearts that it was too late. It was! Another cruel blow to take. Where would it all end?

Mary clutched the little boy's body to her, her eyes searching his, willing him to live. Murdoch took him away from her and she burst into bitter sobbing. She looked accusingly at Murdoch,

"Why, oh Murdoch, why? He's so little." The question that every mother asks at such a time.

They laid him in the churchyard near Eliza Fraser. Two little people that this hard land had taken.

Murdoch worried about Mary a great deal as she seemed to withdraw into herself even more. She found it so hard to resume normal life and even her daughters felt that she was far away from them.

Murdoch could see that she often had tears on her face and so felt that she would soon recover from this, their bitterest blow. Two weeks after the funeral, Murdoch came to Mary and said, "Mary love, I have more bad news. I've heard that they have found a man's body way down the river. He had red hair. It could be Alec. We will have to go and tell Meg. Will you come with me?"

Mary looked up with bitterness and hate shining out of her eyes. "I should have expected it. This place will kill us all. Why did you bring us here?"

"Mary, pull yourself together! I am not enjoying this anymore than you are. Don't blame this land for everything that happens. These things happen everywhere. Oh, darling lass, don't let this break you. You're strong, you must beat it."

Mary dragged herself out of the chair. "What can I do then, Murd? How can I help Meg? What can I say to give her any comfort?" she said in a defeated voice.

"We can be with her when she wants us. We can comfort her. That's what we can do. Come on, lass."

Meg received them cheerfully, giving Mary a hug. "Oh Meg," cried Mary, "more trouble. More tears."

"Why, what's happened. Are the children sick?"

Murdoch quietly gave Meg the news. She was stunned for a while, her face, pale and drawn. She sat silent for some time, then she looked at them both and said, "Thank you both for your help and concern, but I am sure it isn't Alec. I am sure I would know if he were dead. No Murd, it isn't Alec., I know it isn't."

Her eyes flowed with tears and she looked quite pathetic sitting there. Mary suddenly knelt beside her and burst into tears too. Arms entwined, they sobbed, then gradually calming, sat back to face the problem.

They could not move Meg from the conviction that Alec was still alive somewhere, but it did bring matters to a head. Mr. Forrest came to see her, allowing her to stay in the cottage until she could find somewhere to live, but he would need the cottage for a new farm hand who would be commencing work shortly. Ian could have a job with him at the Park, so they wouldn't be destitute. He also suggested asking Mrs. Milne at the store whether she would rent her cottage to Meg, as she lived at the shop now that Mr. Milne had died.

Meg followed this up and found that the storekeeper was sympathetic. She agreed to let her cottage to Meg, but warned her that it would be a tight squeeze for six. When Meg returned to make final arrangements about her move to the cottage, Mrs. Milne said, "Mrs. Fraser, I have been wondering if you would care to help me in my store? Since my husband died I have had Lizzie Downs to help me, but she is marrying and going with her husband to work on Shorts' dairy farm. If you do this, you could take over the quarters at the rear of the store. You would find them more commodious than the cottage."

"Oh, Mrs. Milne! Oh, thank you, but I have no experience in such a position. I would be quite useless, I am sure."

"Would you care to try it? I feel moved to offer you this because I know you are a woman of trust. I am sure you would soon learn. It would help me, too, for as I am getting old, I do not want to be at the store the whole time and if you are there, with perhaps some of your children to help you, I would find it a help."

"I am overwhelmed! May I please consider it and speak with my cousin, Murdoch Macdonald, about it, please?"

Meg waited until that evening to see Mary and Murdoch, leaving Ian in charge of the children. She told her news and finished by saying "I really do not feel confident that I could do it."

"Well, lass, it would certainly be a challenge, but not beyond you," said Murdoch. are very capable, Meg, and I think you should accept it, don't you, Mary?"

"Yes, I do. I know just how hesitant I would be, Meg, in your position, but think, dear, of the opportunity. If you take this job you will fare quite well and still have the children close by you."

"But what will Alec say when he comes home? He wouldn't like me to be doing this. I know that none of you think he will come back, but I know Alec. He wouldn't leave us for long unless things have gone wrong for him and at the same time, I know he is alive."

"We understand how you feel, Meg, but dear lass, he wouldn't want you to starve."

"No, he wouldn't. Oh Murdoch, why doesn't he come? Where do you think he is?"

"See here, lass, Mrs. Milne knows your story and she knows that you'll not want to work when Alec comes back, so if she's prepared to have you under those conditions, I'd say 'yes'. You know that we do feel that he won't come," Murdoch put in softly. "I think perhaps you are not facing reality."

"I know you think that, but even though it seems a lifetime to me, he's only been gone a few weeks. He will come, You see."

Murdoch gave her a quick hug. "Alec has a wonderful wife."

Chapter 16: *The Store*

Meg settled into store life better than she had imagined. Mrs. Milne moved to her cottage on the edge of town and the arrangement suited both women admirably. The house at the rear of the store was larger than the farm-house at the Park, the garden not as well-developed, but the yard was large enough to be a satisfactory play area for the smaller Frasers. As it was well-fenced, Meg had no worries about the children while she was in the shop. She soon learned her work and her natural manner was excellent with the customers. As time went on, "Mrs Milne was able to leave more to her, especially as twelve-year old Janet was proving a valuable assistant. She enjoyed weighing sugar and flour, rice, etc., packing them neatly into bags and pricing them ready for sale. Ian made sure that all the heavy bags were brought in from the storeroom to the shop each night, ready for the next day's sales. It was soon a family effort, with even Janet at 12, Effie, ten and Jamie, eight, doing jobs around their new home.

On occasions Fergus MacKenzie came through the town on business, buying stock and selling to the country storekeepers from Mr. Trent warehouse. He usually stayed with the Macdonalds, but he always spent as much time as he could with Meg. Meg found him a fund of knowledge about the latest stock to arrive in Sydney. He arranged with Mrs. Milne to send to her all the newest things and so she often had articles as quickly as they appeared in Sydney stores. Fortunately the store was a large one and they were able to display their wares, especially their clothing, in a way, on advice from Fergus, that kept a continuous flow of women through the door looking at the latest fashions. Even the poorest women were constantly coming, just to look at the clothes. When they came to look, they often bought some little thing that they could afford.

No word came from Alec. The Macdonalds felt certain he was dead. They knew Alec would never leave his family completely and so felt sure that even if it was not his body found after the Hawkesbury flood, then something equally as devastating had happened. Meg was still certain he was alive and was worried that something had prevented his return and so several times through the following winter Murdoch had asked for time off to go to the goldfields over the mountains to search for him. He found no trace of him at all which went to reinforce his idea that Alec was dead.

All this time Murdoch and Mary were planning and saving for their own farm. Mr. Forrest told Murdoch that as time went on and he felt Murdoch would be able to run his own farm, he would help him look around for a suitable one. Murdoch assured Mary that he had no intention of taking her into the bush as Alistair had done with Caroline. He didn't think they would have a big farm when the day came, but he wanted it to be their own farm in a place where they could expand and so settle Malcolm and Duncan nearby when the time came for them to branch out. So they all worked very hard preparing themselves for that grand day when they could move to "Duntulm", the name they all agreed to grace the gate of their dream. Mary and the boys worked on their little farmyard and learned in miniature how to run pigs and fowls and ducks and all the other things that would help them in their future independent life.

A year passed and then some months and still no Alec. Thankfully, Meg was quite the storekeeper now and Murdoch felt that it was time to start looking for somewhere of their own. Mr. Forrest asked about properties each time he went to a sheep sale or met any farmers in the town. In the meantime they worked and saved.

There was a dairy nearby that fascinated the Macdonalds. The Pollards came from Cornwall. Mrs. Pollard had worked as a dairy maid and he a dairy hand. They had toiled long and hard and now owned their own dairy farm. Mary loved to visit the dairy and some day dreamed of having such a one. Emma-Jane Pollard became one of Mary's close friends and never seemed to tire of teaching Mary what she knew. The Macdonalds, of course, had only one house cow, but all this information Mary stowed away for the day when they would have a dairy of their own.

Pollard's dairy was built low into the ground for coolness. It was a large stone building with several netted windows. The room was whitewashed and soot-less. You would never see a cleaner one or a lighter one and it was always cool. All round the dairy was a shelf that held all the necessary utensils, each one clean and sparkling. Big bowls were to be seen, full of rich, creamy milk for setting the cream, scrubbed wooden buckets with polished brass bands and several butter churns standing in a corner. There were slabs of polished stone where Mrs. Pollard made her delicious butter, golden yellow and artistically 'patted' into patterns and moulded shapes with a design on the top of each pat, that told the name of the dairy. In the room adjoining there were cheeses on racks and some hanging to ripen, vats of curdled milk-cheese in the making and sides of bacon covered with cheese cloth. At the far end of this room were baskets of eggs.

Further away again was the milking shed and here too, cleanliness was the rule. The stone floor was bare of any evidence that a large herd of cows came to it twice a day. The sloping floor allowed it to be washed down with ease. The cows coming into the bales at milking time to happily lip the feed in the boxes and each cow coming into the shed in turn and entering its favourite bay, waiting patiently to be tethered. There was a shelf that held several well-scrubbed wooden stools for the milking hands.

Sometimes Mary came down at milking time just to watch all the ordered busy-ness of this delightful place. She was encouraged by Mr and Mrs. Pollard to ask questions and to help when she wanted.

"I know how you feel, Mrs. Mac.," William Pollard told her.

"When we came to the colony we didn't know we would ever have a chance to have a place like this. I reckon I have a dairy as good as the one we worked in at home. I am really proud of it. So if we can help you and your man, we are only too happy to show you."

"We really appreciate it, Mr. Pollard. We wouldn't expect to have a place like yours. You see, there are no dairies like this where we come from and so we surely couldn't do what you do. I think I could manage some of the things and I want to do them well."

"You are welcome, Mrs., with anything we can help you with."

All information she obtained was shared with the family over their meals. All had the same ambition, to work for a place of their own, something unachievable in Corbost, Skye. She shared it all too, when she wrote to her people back home, trying to put the feel of the place on paper so that those at home would know a little of what they were experiencing in this land of strangeness.

Chapter 17: *Felling Timber*

The timber was huge. Great trees grew profusely in this beautiful forest, this forest of hardwood eucalypt that was superb for building. Alistair hated cutting the massive giants, but they grew in such soil that the farmer in him won each battle as he pondered the demise of these monarchs.

They had cleared quite a lot of the land which simply cried out to grow all the things Alistair asked of it. The season had been very good and his stock and family looked very fit.

Donald and his father worked well together, the perfect team. They worked so hard that they had little time to think of life away from this lonely place. Everywhere there was beauty and who could want more? Yes, they had settled in better than they could have dreamed."

Caroline missed the family, but she and the girls were kept occupied with all the things that needed to be done in their snug, one-roomed log farmhouse. She had hated the thought of being so isolated from the family but, now they were there on their farm, she was content.

They had seen almost no one since their arrival many months before. Their only access by land was a very rough track along the river. In fact, only one visitor had found his way to the farm. That was the parson from the town down the river. He had heard some settlers had come to this lonely stretch of the river and called to meet then. Caroline was amazed when his lean figure appeared at the house one day and was very pleased when Alistair greeted him with friendliness, though he gave him no encouragement to return or send anyone else to visit them, in fact, he made it plain that they wanted no visitors. The parson doubted whether anyone else would venture this far.

So each day was filled with work, either on farming or clearing and very quickly they forgot to expect anything else.

"I think we'll take the big one next, Donald. I can't think why I kept leaving it, but we've cleared all round it and now I think it time."

The nearly sixteen-year old lad was now almost as broad as his father. Hard work and the good plain food Caroline provided had strengthened him and his muscles rippled as he and Alistair cut deeply into the wood, axe chop and axe chop alternately. The giant was many feet in circumference and it was late in the morning before they heard the first crack of the timber.

"Its coming, Father."

"Just a little more, son."

"Father, watch out! Run."

The big tree seemed to twist as it fell towards the running men, then Alistair tripped. As Donald paused to look at his father, they were engulfed by leaves, twigs and branches. Donald screamed as a branch tore at his leg, but no sound came from Alistair.

"Did you see that, Liz? Come on."

"Jake, you fool, leave them alone. You can't go down there."

"But, Liz, they hurt. You can't leave that kid down there."

"And get yourself hung. Go if you like, but I ain't."

"Look, Liz, we know there's no one on this farm but them two and the wife and kids up at the house. If we help them, they might help us."

"Help us get caught, more like. Just look at us. Who would believe we are anything but what we are? We even look worse than when we arrived in the colony and that's saying something. Have sense."

"Look, Liz, I don't reckon we could stick it much longer on Abo tucker. If we help them now, I don't reckon we'd be worse off than we are. We could always go bush again. Come on."

Jake went down the hill to the clearing where the huge tree lay, fallen into the nearby crop. The branches lay thick and he could see no sign of Alistair or Donald, but he could hear a moaning and struggled through the tree towards the sound. He found Alistair lying still under a large bough and he called to Donald deeper in.

He found the boy under a mass of greenery pinned by the leg under a branch. He easily lifted it off and tried to clear some room to see how badly the boy was hurt. His arm and left leg were twisted unnaturally. By this time Donald was conscious and wondering about the strange figure who had appeared from nowhere.

"We'll soon get you out of this," said Jake cheerfully.

"Father. Where?"

"He's over there. He's alive, so don't worry. We'll get you out first." He then called, "Liz, come here and help me."

Donald gazed at the two dirty, ragged people and was only too pleased to let them help. He hurt too much to wonder much about them.

Jake cleared a way through and soon he was able to drag Donald by the shoulders and pull him free. Liz tried to make him comfortable in the ploughed field.

Jake didn't like the look of Alistair, in fact, was surprised to find him still alive. But he was, with both legs pinned under a huge bough.

"Come in here, Liz, and try to help me lift this."

She struggled through and found that they could only move it slightly.

"Look, if I use this as a lever and push it up, do you think you could hold it up while I drag him out?"

"I'll try Jake, but I don't reckon I could."

With much heaving and resting and heaving again, Jake eventually pulled the big man out.

"Is he alive Jake?"

"Yes, he is. His legs are smashed and he's got a cut on his head, but he's all right, I think. All we have to do now is get them on the dray. That's gunna be a job."

They managed it by using the backboard of the dray and manoeuvring each patient onto the vehicle. A slow procession moved up the rise and into the clearing where the house stood. Ann saw the dray come up to the yard and ran to her mother.

"What is it, child?"

"Some people with our dray, Mama."

"Quickly, take your sister and hide under the bed, like I told you to do."

Caroline saw the children safely under the bed, grabbed the gun beside the door and stepped out, leveling the gun at Jake as the dray pulled up. She gazed in horror at the two ruffians, thinking that they could mean nothing but trouble.

"Put your gun down, Missus. We won't harm you. Liz and me, we've come to help you. Look here in the dray. The boss and the boy have had an accident. Look."

With a look of horror on her face, Caroline drew near the cart and peered over the side. "Alistair, Donald. Oh, dear Lord, please help me."

"Well, Missus, I don't know if He will, but we will. We'd better get them inside."

Donald was stirring. "Mama, is Father all right?"

"What happened, Donald?"

"The tree fell. I think these people will help."

"We will, Missus. We'll try to get your man into the house while he can't feel it, because his legs are hurt bad."

"What will I do?" Caroline cried in anguish.

"Now, Missus, we'll manage."

With a struggle the three adults carried first Donald, then Alistair to their beds. Jake cut Alistair's trousers off and inspected his legs and considered how to set the breaks. There were no bones sticking through, so he felt he could try to straighten the limbs out and tie them to pieces of wood. Whether they would be any good … he sighed. "Well, it's all we can do."

"They need a doctor," said Caroline faintly. "Would you go and try to get one?"

"No, Missus, I wouldn't and I won't waste me breath telling you why now. I must get to work on this bloke."

Alistair was breathing evenly but still hadn't stirred, so using some pieces of timber, Jake splinted both legs. It was a difficult job and needed all his strength, but when he was done he thought they looked straight and even felt pleased with his work.

"I think he's all right, Missus. I am not much good at this, but I seen it done before. It's the best I can do. I got to do the young fellow now. It will hurt him, so why don't you busy yourself washing the boss and try to keep away from your boy and let me get at it."

Caroline had hardly taken in that these two strange unkempt creatures had taken over her house. She felt so helpless and Jake seemed to know what to do. She wondered what Alistair would think but at that moment it didn't seem to matter. She heard a yell from Donald and then silence.

"He's fainted, Missus. That's a good thing. He'll be all right. This is much easier. I'll get his leg fixed fine."

They tore up some of Caroline's precious sheets to bind the broken limbs and soon had them as comfortable as they could. Donald woke feeling very sick and sore, but looked better.

"I can't thank you enough, but I think I can manage now,"

Caroline said uneasily, not knowing quite what to do with Jake and Liz.

"Could we have some tea, Missus, and something to eat? We ain't had nothing but black's tucker for ages."

"Blacks!" said the startled Caroline, as though she hadn't enough to think about. "Are there blacks here? We've never seen them."

"Yes, Missus, there are blacks here. Me and Liz have been living with them."

"Where are you from?"

"I don't need to tell you, Missus, but we would like some eats."

"Yes, of course, would you like some broth?" She ladled the rich mutton soup into big bowls and broke pieces from a fresh loaf of bread and put them on the table. The two starved people literally shoved it into their mouths while Caroline watched in amazement.

The two little girls had crept out from under the bed while Alistair and Donald were being tended and sat staring at the wild looking couple in complete silence.

Jake finished his soup and pushed the plate away. "That was lovely, Missus."

"There is more if you want it."

"Yes, I would," Jake said "Liz would too, wouldn't you, Liz?"

Liz had said very little and looked about her continually, rather like a caged animal and now she just sat and looked up at Caroline who was amazed to see tears running down the filthy face. "Oh, Missus, if you only knew what we been through."

"Now, Liz, hold on to yourself." Jake looked at Caroline. "Now, Missus, I been thinking. Liz and me, we've had a rough spin and it wasn't our fault, but it seems though you can't manage by yourself with the boss and the boy laid up. What about giving Liz and me a go at helping you."

Caroline looked helplessly at first one, and then the other. "But you're so ..." She couldn't finish.

"I know. We're dirty. You'd be dirty and in rags if you done what we done. Give us a chance, Missus, we'll clean up and if you could spare some clothes, well, we'd look all right then. Missus, we won't hurt you, we'll help you. All we want is tucker and clothes. Please, Missus, give us a go?" he pleaded.

"My husband doesn't encourage strangers" was all Caroline could think to say.

"He ain't in any state to say anything, Missus, if you don't mind me saying. And how are you going to manage if we don't help?"

"I don't know, I don't know! I must have help from somewhere. If only Murdoch were here. I can't manage Alistair and Donald can't help."

"You got us, Missus. We'll clean up if you will give us some soap and water and you'll see, we'll look better soon. I must say I've seen Liz look better than she does now."

Caroline was too concerned about her own folk to really give much deep thought about her guests. She handed soap and some clothes of hers and Alistair's to them and told them to go to the shed for their toilet. She had no idea who they were but had a feeling that they would be escaped convicts. The thought horrified her, but she shrugged it off as something she would face later, as her concern was for Alistair.

Donald was awake and fairly comfortable. He was very distressed at his father's state. Every now and then he raised his head to look across at the large bed where Alistair lay.

"Mama, he will be all right, won't he?"

"We hope so son, but let us have a word of prayer about him."

They bowed their heads.

"I have been praying, Mother. Mother, what are we going to do? And who do you think these people are?"

"I have no idea, Donald, but they probably saved your lives. If only they were cleaner. Well, we'll see when they return. Perhaps Father will let them stay when he wakes."

"I don't think Father will be fit to say anything." He glanced towards his father. "Is he hurt badly?"

"Both his legs are broken, son. I think the man has done well with those and I do think he is waking, because he moves his head and his hands now and wasn't doing that before."

When Jake and Liz returned they were much improved. Liz's dress was not a bad fit, but Alistair's clothes hung on Jake.

"The boss is bigger than me, Missus, but Liz will make them tighter, if we can keep the clothes. She's good with a needle and if we had a comb we could make our hair better. I'll shave my beard off if I could borrow the boss's razor, please, Missus."

They certainly looked less wild when all this was done and Liz even gave Caroline a shy smile. "Thank you, Missus. Oh, Missus, I do feel clean now. You are good."

Caroline could see that she was still inclined to be misty eyed and decided she couldn't be as hard as she had at first seemed.

Jake looked over to Alistair. "I think he's rousing. He's moving more. Thank goodness we got him fixed up before he woke. My Misses, you must have wondered about us bringing your menfolk in like that."

"I still wonder - er ..."

"Jake's me name. At least it will do for mine."

Caroline hardly knew what to do with them and her eyes kept wandering to Alistair as he appeared to be more restless.

Jake took over "Listen, Missus - er ... "

"MacLeod" put in Caroline.

"Mrs. MacLeod, listen, Missus, you just look after the men and tell us what to do. You can trust us, we won't steal anything. Liz's a good housekeeper and she'll do anything you want. Won't you, Liz."

"Yes, Mrs. MacLeod, I want to help you, truly I do."

Caroline was only too anxious to give her mind to her men and so Jake took over the outside work and Liz worked under her directions around the house.

Alistair opened his eyes as they ate their evening meal. He looked at Caroline and said, "Donald?"

She was able to quieten him by saying, "Donald's all right, Alistair. He is here in his bed."

"Good," said Alistair and went to sleep again. She sat by them all night, tending them as they needed. She had worried about housing Jake and Liz, but Jake announced that they would be quite comfortable in the hay shed. He instructed her to bolt the door inside so she would feel safe, but not to hesitate calling him if she needed him.

"A strange pair," she thought as she slipped the bolt.

The next day Alistair was conscious for longer intervals and occasionally watched them with a doubtful look on his face. It was some days before he could take in the fact that Jake and Liz had come to the rescue when they did. He took the news quietly, being too ill to really do anything else.

By the time he was able to sit up and hold a conversation, Caroline knew the gist of her two helpers story. Jake told her as they sat by the fire, one evening.

"Yes, Missus, we were convicts. I guess you know that. We ain't done nothing real bad, but I guess you have only got our word for that. You see, I got a sentence for stealing a feed. We lived in Middlesex, near London, me, Mum and the kids. We didn't have no Pa, 'cause he died years ago. Well, some boys and me we saw a man pushing a cart, of meat going to the butcher. We hustled him and stole some of the meat. Well, they caught us and they give us seven years. But we've both finished our time. I was in the hulks for three years before I come out to Sydney Town and I got here when I was twenty.

"Poor boy" said Caroline.

"It wasn't all bad," said Jake. "The hulks were bad, but I like the life out here. Better'n living in ol' England I reckon. It's warmer, anyway. Well, I was working for Mr. Mitchell out near Camden and he and Mrs. Mitchell were good people, but Mrs. Mitchell died and the boss seemed to go off a bit and then he started drinking. When he drank he got fighting mad, but he was all right when he was sober. Well, he had a housekeeper after Mrs. Mitchell died and one night he got so mad drunk that he punched her down and killed her. Nothin' happened to him and then he got Liz in her place. He kept off the bottle for a while, but then he started again. In the meantime, I fell for Liz and we wanted to get married. Mr. Mitchell, he arranged it and twelve months ago we got married." He looked down at Liz and smiled.

"Six months ago, Mr. Mitchell, he got drunk again and he hit Liz and I saw red. I didn't mean to hit him, but I did and I hurt him real bad, mebbe I killed him. I knew no one would listen to me, an ex-convict and I was a goner, so Liz and me, we just lit out. We went to Sydney and a sailor got us a ship and hid us. We didn't know where we were going and didn't care really. We set sail and then one night he came for us and told us to hop overboard and swim across a river. We did and found some blacks who let us live with them and we've been there ever since, but it's lonely out there and we used to come down close to your farm and watch the men work and you and the little girls, just to see some white folk. I don't reckon anyone would be looking for us and I reckon we could stay here forever and no one would find us."

The prospect of hiding fugitives from the law did not appeal to Caroline, even though her sympathy was with them. What Alistair would say she could only imagine.

"Liz, what did they send you to the colony for? I couldn't think it was too bad."

"Missus, I think Liz will tell you some day if she wants, but not yet. Just believe me, she's all right."

Liz looked at Jake with scared eyes. Then to Caroline. "I think I will tell you, Mrs. MacLeod, some day, but not yet, not now."

Alistair's recovery was slow at first, being too sick to ask many questions and only too pleased to think that Caroline was not alone.

When Caroline suggested again that Jake might find a doctor for Alistair, he refused, saying, "No, Missus, I would do a lot for you, but I don't go to town for you yet awhile."

She had the same reply when she suggested taking a letter for Murdoch. However, time passed and her patients improved. Jake made a sort of walking splint for Donald and a pair of crutches so he could hobble out of bed and sit in a chair. Alistair was quite unable to leave his bed. As time went on he sat up watching all about him. He learned Liz and Jake's story and to Caroline's surprise said nothing, but seemed a little tight-lipped. He looked up at Jake and said, "Well, I thought about what Caroline would have done if you hadn't turned up when you did and so I just accept that you were instruments of the Lord. I cannot thank you enough for what you've done and shall be ever in your debt."

"Boss, I've been called a lot of things in me time, but I ain't never been told I was a instrument of the Lord."

So a strange friendship developed between the large farmer and the ex-convict.

Caroline was amazed at the continued care Jake gave Alistair and the patience with which Alistair accepted his ministrations.

In two months Donald was quite active and tentatively putting his foot to the ground. Alistair was a more difficult proposition, for even after that time, Jake could see that there had been little or no healing of the bones.

"It's no use, is it Jake? Be honest with me, man. Surely I should be getting better by now."

"Now, Boss, you be patient a little longer."

"Jake," thundered Alistair, "tell me, I am not a child."

"All right, Boss, I will. I don't know much about broken legs, but I can see that your right leg moves where it shouldn't when I move you. I just dunno what to do."

"Murdoch, that's who we want. We need Murdoch here, but how to get him?" He talked it over with Caroline and decided that when the parson came, (he said he would come again), they would send a letter to Murdoch asking him to come and take the family back to Riverbend until Alistair was better or perhaps a doctor in

Sydney Town would be able to do something. They would leave the farm in Jake and Liz's care.

When they told the pair what they had decided, Jake and Liz were overcome that the MacLeods felt so confident about them, but as Alistair said, "Jake, if I can't trust you after all you've done, well, I cannot trust anyone."

"But, Boss, look at what you've done for us. We think we could make a real go of it here and soon we'll be so fat that no one will recognise us. Anyway, without my beard, I look different. One day I'll be game enough to go to town, just to try it out."

"Jake, I'm wondering if you would take our name and call yourselves our cousins. It would give you some standing and a reason for taking the farm over. Maybe, man, I'll not be able to come back, so you could keep it going until Donald can come back, if he wants to."

"Boss, Boss, thank you. Jake MacLeod, eh? Liz, how does that sound? Jake and Liz MacLeod. Aw. Boss."

So the letter was written and when the parson came two weeks later he assured them he would send it on, at the same time passing very few remarks about the 'cousins' on the farm. As he only saw them from a distance he had no need to know anything about them. He was more taken up with the story of the tree fall and Alistair and Donald's injuries than inquiring about the stray 'cousins'.

Chapter 18: *Murdoch helps again*

Mary found it hard to wait for Murdoch to come home the day the letter arrived, but her excitement turned to sorrow as Murdoch read it to her. He looked at her as he finished ...

"... and so, Murdoch, you see the predicament we are in. We are sure Alistair's legs are not healing and we must move him somewhere where we can get help. We appeal to you, brother, and you Mary, to help us and we need monetary help as well as physical help as our resources are low. We pray that Alistair will soon mend and we can repay you in time, but in the meanwhile we need you, dear Murdoch. Please, please come. Dear ones, you will find Alistair a changed man, a humble and loving one. He is now so patient. With my love, Caroline."

"Well, poor Caroline, poor Alistair. What a terrible time they have been through."

"And poor Donald, too. Mary, love, I'll have to go and see Mr. Forrest now, I think. He will know how to arrange things."

"Yes, Murdoch, you must go. Why did they have to go so far away? How long will you be away? I daresay Mr. Forrest will be put out with your going."

"He is not one to kick about an accident. I don't know how long I will be away, but perhaps Mr. Forrest will have some idea. How fortunate that those friends are there to help Caroline. How would she have managed otherwise? It will use some of our money up, lass."

"We mustn't worry about that now Murd. We have no choice."

Mr. Forrest saw that there was no alternative but for Murdoch to go. He offered money to help, but Murdoch refused.

"It is enough sir, that you are letting me go. I am sure Malcolm and Ian will do as many of my jobs as they can and I will not be longer than I can help"

Murdoch made his way to Sydney and thence by coaster to the Manning River. In the town nearest the MacLeod farm he hired a horse from the hotel and made his way up river to the farm. Caroline had her arms in the wash tub when she saw him come up the track.

"Murdoch, Oh, Murdoch, I knew you'd come."

"Caro, dear lass, it is good to see you" he said as he dismounted, hugging her to him. "You couldn't have found a place more isolated, sister. I didn't think I would ever get here."

"Come inside quickly, Murdoch. Hitch the horse there and we'll attend to it later. Come and see Alistair."

The door opened and Donald stood there smiling. "Uncle Murdoch, it is good to see you. We do need you."

"It is nice to be needed, lad. How is that leg of yours? Your arm too?"

"My arm is not so bad and my leg is too, but slower than my arm, thank you Uncle Murdoch."

They walked in to where Alistair was propped up in bed. "Alistair, my friend," was all Murdoch could say as he saw the pale pain-lined face of the man.

For a while Alistair said nothing, just clasped Murdoch's hand in his, then he said, "Man, it is good to see you. We had to call on you to get us out of our mess. You didn't waste time getting here either."

They sat and talked while Caroline prepared tea. Murdoch heard the story that Alistair had to tell and he told it with a humility that Murdoch had never heard in him before.

"I had to come here, Murd, to lose myself. Praise the Lord have found myself. I can honestly say that even though I cannot yet walk, I am content. I am surprised at myself, I am happy."

"It is a good thing to see you so, my friend. I feel sure you will be right in no time. Tell me, were your legs set straight?"

"As well as Jake could do them. They even seem straight now, but Jake thinks they haven't healed, especially the right leg. We haven't dared get me out of bed as we are sure they won't hold me up."

"Here come Liz and Jake now, Alistair. I'll make fresh tea."

Murdoch greeted the pair with friendliness and with thanks for their care of his sister. "They could all have died," he said, "and we are grateful."

"We think we have a lot to thank them for. They have been that kind to us, Mr. Macdonald. If you only knew."

"He does know, Jake. I have told him the full story. That is only right."

"Yes

"It is Boss. If you are going to leave us in charge, it's only fair."

"Is that right, Alistair? Will you leave Jake in charge?"

"Yes, I will, Murd. There's no knowing how long I'll be and Jake and Liz will stay, either until we all get back or at least until Donald comes, and there will always be a place for them here."

"I am sure they would look after the place very well."

"Do you object being part of the scheme, Murd? I must admit don't like being party to any wrongdoing, but I feel that if Jake did kill Reginald Mitchell, it was in defense of his wife and it could not be called murder. It is only his past that would cause him trouble, I would think."

"Did you say Reginald Mitchell? Of 'Longacre Park', near Camden?" Murdoch asked with a chuckle.

"Yes, that's it. We worked at Longacre."

"How long ago did you hit him?"

"Nearly nine months ago, now."

"Well, I collected some sheep from him personally only three months ago for my boss, William Forrest of 'Forrest Park'. He wasn't dead then, in fact he looked remarkably fit and Mrs. Mitchell did too, so I think you are hiding for nothing."

"Well, well. Liz, did you hear that? I didn't kill him. I like Mr. Mitchell and I 'm glad I didn't kill him."

"Mr. Macdonald," said Liz, "did you say Mrs. Mitchell? But she's dead, his wife."

"I believe she's a new wife, Liz. In fact, I did hear that he had married his housekeeper."

"So, maybe he has stopped beating up housekeepers."

"Well, all I can say is, she is a massive woman and I think could keep him under control."

"Oh, Jake, we can make a new life for ourselves now. No more hiding and dodging and being ashamed. Oh." Liz fled from the room sobbing.

"'Scuse me," said Jake, as he followed his weeping wife.

"Well, Murdoch, you are a bearer of good tidings. What a relief to poor Jake. A relief to me, too, for I am not a lawbreaker by habit, but I wouldn't let him down," sighed Alistair. "I must say I am very happy about it. Jake's a very good fellow. I don't really think he is cut out to be a murderer."

"If you could have seen them, Alistair, that day they brought you home, you would have believed anything. They frightened me silly." said Caroline.

"Me too, Mother. Each time I woke and saw Jake, I thought I was having a nightmare" laughed Donald. "What a good fellow he is."

Caroline had been so certain that Murdoch would come that she had a great deal of the packing done and he was surprised and pleased to hear that they could move off as soon as he thought they could get berths on a ship. So, in a few days, they loaded Alistair, the children and Caroline on the wagon and set off for the town, with Jake driving and Murdoch riding his hired horse. Liz came too and they all treated it as a picnic until the time came for farewells. It was a happy day for them all to remember.

At the hotel, Liz clung to Caroline, "Oh, Missus, you're that good to us. Thank you, we'll take care of everything, never you fear. When you get back you will find everything ship-shape."

"Yes, Boss, you'll see we will do everything you want done and you send Master Donald back any time you like. We'll look after him. And you and Missus come back soon."

"Take care, Jake. Get along home now, man. Goodbye and thank you."

Caroline and Murdoch left Alistair in their room at the hotel and went down to the street to see them off.

"If you go now you will be home before dark, Jake. I will know you are safe then" said Caroline, giving Liz a last hug.

"Yes, Missus. I'm going to take Liz along to the store. Just to look, mind, because she hasn't seen a store for that long. That is, I think she deserves it.

"Aw, Jake."

"Now just a look, mind, no hankering after anything."

"No, Jake. Goodbye, Mr. Macdonald ."

"Here, Liz, buy something with this. I would like to make it more," Murdoch said as he handed sixpence to her. Liz, too overcome, just beamed at Murdoch as Jake drove them off.

"Good people, Caroline. The kind to build Australia into a big country. You go back to Alistair, lass, and I'll see about a ship. I do hope one comes soon."

Alistair travelled on a stretcher that Jake made for him and everyone saw that he was involved with everything going on. They had waited a week, wondering whether their slim resources would last the journey back to Riverbend, when a ship came in travelling south.

It was only a short voyage to Sydney and as soon as they arrived they hired a wagon to take them to Elspeth and Fergus's house with almost the last of their money.

Caroline wept a little as Elspeth greeted her. "Come in, love, we have everything prepared. We have a room made ready and we'll keep you here until Alistair is if it and well." And so they stayed.

They decided that the two little MacLeod girls, Ann and Jane, would go to Riverbend with Murdoch, leaving Donald with his parents so that a good doctor could look at him too. Murdoch took his nieces to Parramatta by ferry the next day where they caught the coach west to Riverbend. Fergus had provided the money for the tickets.

"I want to do it Alistair" he said "for I have an excellent position and am making good money. I seem to have fallen on my feet and want to share it with my family. So, Murdoch, you go home and leave these three with us and we'll see they get the best of attention.

Ann and Jane were excited to see the bustle of the city then the ferry ride to Parramatta and a coach ride too, were almost too much for them and they were very tired little people who finally arrived at Aunt Mary's house. Mary greeted them with relief.

In spite of the best treatment, Alistair's leg refused to mend. He suffered a great deal of pain, but was always patient. Elspeth refused to let Caroline work in the house, saying that she looked really pallid and that she needed a rest more than she did. Donald had healed well and very soon was allowed to join his sisters at Riverbend.

Finally the doctor told Alistair that he would have to lose his leg as it hadn't healed at all. Caroline took the news harder than he did, saying that a big, strong, healthy man should heal a big strong, healthy bone, but apparently the bone had been crushed when the tree fell and so refused to knit. His left leg did heal eventually, but remained weak for some time.

"Jake will be upset, Caroline" Alistair said, "but the doctor assured me that it was no reflection on his first-aid."

"Alistair, how will you manage? What will you do?"

"We'll just have that leg off for now, love. Don't worry, I'll manage. It will be better than lying in bed all the time, looking at four walls. I will be able to get about on crutches. Hush now, lass, I will be all right."

He was. He went into the Sydney Hospital and had the leg amputated above the knee. He was soon better than he had been for months. His left leg was now able to take his weight and he learned to manage crutches with an ability that amazed his family.

Fergus wondered what Alistair would do with his life. He had a feeling that farming would be too difficult for sometime yet. He was right. Alistair announced one day that he thought he would go to Riverbend to live and start a little school for the farming children there.

"It is something I want to do and I know I can do it." said Alistair

Fergus went with them to Riverbend when the time came for them to leave Sydney. Mary and Murdoch rented a house in Riverbend for them and were able to furnish it sparsely. The house had a big, wide verandah along one side. Murdoch, Donald and Malcolm had turned it into a very good schoolroom by filling in the open side and putting two windows and a door in the wall, so that the schoolroom had a separate entrance. They also made long tables and forms for the pupils when they came. Alistair began with the children of the family, his own daughters, Ann now twelve, Jane ten and Alec's children, Janet, fourteen, Effie, twelve, Jamie, ten and six year old Kate. Murdoch and Mary's daughters, Catherine and Mary Ann, aged twelve and nearly eight, brought the number to eight. Jamie Fraser was put out when he discovered that he was the only boy, but when the nearby town and farm folk heard about the little school, he soon had male companionship and was content.

William Forrest came to see Alistair one afternoon after school. He had watched with interest the planning and establishing of the project. He admired the Scots folk who had come to live among the people of Riverbend and was ever keen to see how they coped with the difficulties they encountered. He had great admiration for them. He hadn't been very attracted to Alistair on the ship, as he didn't appeal to a man with a great sense of humour, but he was the first to admit, how wrong he had been when he saw the new Alistair.

The man had taken his tragedy with a fortitude that was truly admirable. His experience had had an enlightening effect on his character and instead of the taciturn man he had been, he was now a quietly patient man with a jolly manner with the children.

"MacLeod," he said on this afternoon, wonder if you want some more pupils? Our governess, Miss Phelps, is to be married soon and is leaving us. We would be pleased if you would take our children into your school."

"Thank you, Mr. Forrest. I've no presence though of being a good teacher. I love the children and aim to teach them to be useful people."

"What made you turn to this? What made you feel you are fitted for it? McWilliam tells me you are teaching his children Latin. Man, where did you learn Latin? It doesn't sound like what I know of the highlands."

Alistair chuckled. "Well, sir, I've always had a mind for book-learning and have read all the books I could get hold of. My father was educated with the old Laird when they were youngsters and the Laird's father sent them off to Edinburgh for more education.

So benefited by my father teaching us. He became factor to the Laird, so his education was always useful to him. My father passed it on to all his children and insisted that it would be someday of use to us. It seems that it was worthwhile. I suppose you are surprised, Mr. Forrest?" He smiled.

"Nothing really surprises me about people I meet in this colony. I've grown up with convicts who range from lawyers and doctors, down to the worst criminal, so nothing surprises me now. I take it you are happy to have my children then?"

"Willingly," Alistair laughed up at William Forrest. "If I have any more I will have to enlarge my schoolroom. Come and see it."

He painfully got up from his chair and hobbled out to the schoolroom. There he eagerly showed all the work that Murdoch and the boys had done making the place Alistair's pride.

"MacLeod, I'll be paying you, of course, for my children's education. You cannot do without payment."

"You are right, sir, I could not afford to take children without payment. I must charge for my teaching."

"I'll pay you what we were paying Miss Phelps. Willie will have to go to school in Sydney soon, but you will have Catriona and Grant for some time."

"You're not sending them to school in England then?"

"Indeed not, I want them to be Australians. They would lose touch with the colony if they were sent away. Besides, I couldn't do without them."

"Aye, it is good to have your children about you."

"I'll bid you 'good day' then, MacLeod. Mind that you are strict with them."

Chapter 19: *Ballarat, Victoria*

The valley had been beautiful before the inhabitants took over. It had grassy slopes down to the bubbling creek the eucalypts standing serene and graceful, lords surveying all around.

Now all was mud, mud when it was wet and dust when it was dry. No grass, just mud and dust and all through this desecration was a city of tents. Tents everywhere and of every description some so small that they barely covered the needs of one miner and some quite large that housed a family.

This was Ballarat, one of the many such valleys in the diggings, where hundreds of people came for the gold that would give them all they wanted so they thought.

Bill Turner had been working his claim for a year now. Backbreaking work at the best of times, but worse since his mate Larry McGuire had died a few weeks ago. Now Bill had to work the claim alone. He dug the spoil and when his buckets were filled he had to go to the surface and wind the windlass to bring the buckets up for washing day.

He thought he'd had enough for the day, so he packed his tools away and headed for the pub. As he walked up the hill he saw a group of louts throwing stones at something huddled under a bush. Hearing a whimper he went to investigate and saw that it was a man crouching there.

"Get away, you rotten louts. What are you doing there?"

The boys ran away and Bill got in under the bush and pulled out a cowering, bloody mess of a man.

Bill knew the little white-haired man who just lay in a heap, a shivering mass.

"Ah Scotty, what on earth have they done to you? Come on up, can you stand? I'll help you to my tent."

No one knew where Scotty had come from. He'd been around the valley for longer than Bill had. No one knew anything about him. It was said that he staggered into someone's camp one night, bloodied as he was now, and not knowing who he was or from where he had come. Most people were kind to him. He lived on the edge of starvation because the residents of the valley were too poor to take on another mouth to feed. So, many helped to keep the man in food and clothing. They named him Scotty because of his brogue. Anyway, he knew no other.

He was a sorry mess when Bill looked at him in the light of the lamp. He cleaned him up as best he could and bedded him down in Larry's bed roll.

The little man said nothing but sat up and gladly ate the stew that Bill offered him.

Scotty was up and about in a ten days and tried to repay Bill's kindness by working around the camp. He filled the gap that Larry's death had made and Bill was glad enough to have him. Scotty had very little to say, but was quite a cheerful mate to have. He was very easy-going and agreed to do anything to help that he could. They soon became firm friends once the work of the claim was shared. For many months Bill watched over little Scotty who was still very wary. When any young men were around in groups, Bill tried to act as buffer. One day while Bill was working down the shaft, a group of young fellows came tearing through the camps in high spirits, not meaning any harm.

Scotty was in the process of bringing some buckets of spoil up on the windlass. When he saw the young ruffians heading towards him he panicked, dropped the handle of the windlass which flew round, hitting him hard in the midriff and he turned in mid air as he shot headfirst down the shaft. Luckily the buckets caught half way down on the ladder and so he only fell about ten feet, but he was badly hurt.

Bill was in a terrible predicament as he was below the buckets down the shaft and couldn't get to the injured Scotty. The boys who were the cause of it all had seen what had happened and formed themselves into a rescue team.

Poor Scotty was broken once more in many places. He was a sad sight when they got him onto a stretcher.

Bill eventually struggled out of the shaft, covered with dirt dislodged from the sides and out of the buckets. He tried to make his friend as comfortable as he could but didn't think much of his chances of recovery this time. "Poor Scotty, he's a goner this time, I think," muttered Bill as he washed him.

Scotty was making no sound, no movement.

Dr. Landsdowne came into the tent and knelt beside the injured man. He found a broken leg and he thought a broken spine and perhaps a fractured skull as well.

"Just keep him warm, Bill, there's nothing else you can do. I'll set his leg while he cannot feel it, but I don't think he can move his legs anyway. His arms look all right and he's moving those."

Scotty was still unconscious the next day and the doctor shook his head over him.

"He'll be a lucky man to survive this Bill, and even if he does he may not want to. I'm sure his back is broken and he will never move again. What's to become of him? Do you know anything about him?"

"No, I don't, Doc, nor does he. I daresay you know as much about him as I do. Anyway, he's me mate and I'll look after him while I can."

"You're a good man, but I don't think you know what you're taking on."

When Bill awoke the next morning he looked over to his mate and saw his eyes on his own.

"Hello, old mate, how do you feel?"

"Not very well, I must say, and I don't seem to be able to move my legs. What happened to me?"

"You fell down the shaft, Scotty. Don't you remember?"

"No, I don't, I'm sorry, and I don't remember you. Should I? You seem to be my friend. How did I get here? I think I can remember two men coming at me out of the dark. Where's my horse, my clothes?"

"Well, Scotty, you just lie still and don't fuss yourself. It looks as though I've got some talking to do, but that can wait." Bill stood thinking, looking down at Scotty. "Do you remember your name, mate?"

129

"Yes of course I do, it's Alec, Alexander Fraser. How long have I been here?"

"Well, I'm Bill Turner and mate, but as I say, we've got a lot of talking to do, but now isn't the time. Do you feel like a pot of tea and some breakfast? You stay still while I get you some.

"Thank you, Bill. I seem to have no choice, and anyway, tea sounds great."

After feeding his patient, Bill waited for Dr. Landsdowne impatiently. He refused to be drawn into explanations with Alec, anyway, he was not well enough to be too curious. He slept, Bill thought, or at least he lay with his eyes closed.

It was late morning when Dr. Landsdown's horse trotted up the slope. Bill hurried to meet the doctor and kept him out of earshot.

"He's awake, Doc, and has his memory back, at least he remembers who he really is and doesn't seem to know about the last year or so. Seems he was attacked by a couple of men. He remembers that. His name is Alexander Fraser."

"Did you question him, Bill?"

"No, Doc, I tried to head off too much talk. I didn't think I should let him talk. He'll be too ill to worry anyway. Let's go and look at him."

The doctor bent down as he came into the tent. His patient looked up.

"I'm Dr. Landsdowne. I hear you are Fraser. You've been knocking yourself around, man."

"Yes, I'm not feeling too sprightly. Tell me what happened, Doctor, I'm all at sea."

"Let me look at you first before we have anymore talk. Lift your leg. Hm. Lift this arm, now the other. Does your broken leg hurt?"

"I can't seem to feel my legs at all, Doctor. What's wrong?"

After the examination the doctor said, "I imagine they call you Alec or Sandy. Yes?"

Alec Confirmed he was known as "Alec"

"Well, Alec, you've certainly had a bad fall, but it will be a while before we know how bad, so you just lie still and let Bill look after you. I don't want you getting yourself upset, but when you feel up to it you and Bill can talk and get things sorted out."

Bill and the doctor left the tent and went out of range.

"I just don't know what to say, Bill. I'm afraid he's a cripple for life. Try to find out if he has any family and whether we can get him to them. There is little I can do, but he will need constant care and you cannot do it."

"How much can I tell him, Doc?"

"I really don't think it matters, man, he's little use to himself like that. I know that sounds hard, but what can anyone do? People like Alec often contract pneumonia and die unless they have good nursing."

"You tell me what I'm to do and I'll do what I can."

Dr. Landsdowne gave Bill a quick run-down on the required nursing care and left him standing thoughtfully overlooking the valley. He turned and went back into the tent to find that his new/old friend had fallen into a deep sleep.

Over the next few days Bill tried to ward off too many probing questions, but the day came when Bill thought it time to tell his story and hear Alec's, if he would tell it. Bill had asked few questions during this time, so was quite curious to piece the stories together. They had grown close during this time, Alec quickly realising that without Bill he could do nothing. As it happened Alec began his story without any prompting. He told Bill of Margaret and their children, his job on Forrest's farm, he even told him about his leaving, and the letter, and for the first time felt shame in the telling of it. "You see, Bill, I just didn't think. In fact, I didn't think much about anything at all. I can see that I've just had ideas and acted on them. I haven't been much good to Margaret. She'll be wondering where I am now. Tell me, Bill, how long have I been here?"

Bill heaved a big sigh and said, "Well, Alec, here it comes, two years."

"Two years! Oh, no Bill not two years. How, how can that be?"

Bill was filled with compassion as he watched the tears stream down Alec's face. It was a situation that Bill felt unable to cope with. After some uncomfortable, interminable minutes, Alec turned to Bill.

"Tell me," he said, "tell me all about it."

So Bill told him all he knew as gently and kindly as he could. Alec's eyes did not leave Bill's during the telling and all he said as the story ended was "Thank you, Bill" and extended his hand to take Bill's in his.

Alec lay there, a jumble of thoughts shooting through him. "Margaret - Margaret with no money. What would she have done all this time? Murdoch would help, but what a burden for him. Oh, why did I always act first and think after? Why - why - why? What can I do?" His thoughts were agonising to him.

"Bill, what will I do? What can I do?" came sobbing from him.

"Don't worry old man, we'll come up with something."

Bill left Alec alone, thinking it the best thing. He knew that only time would heal. He wasn't really sure in his own mind how to sort it all out anyway. He picked up his tools and climbed down the ladder to the mine and began digging, his mind working on all aspects of the situation.

A few days later Bill came into the tent. "Ready for tucker, Scotty?"

"Bill, I wish I could get it like I used to," and laughed at his mate's blank look. "Yes, I'm beginning to have bits of memory back. It's so hard to sort it out. Just like dreaming of being two people."

Bill looked down at the pale man in the bunk, his once red hair a sandy white, his small, wizened body hardly seen below the blankets.

"It's good to know that it's coming back anyway. Just don't try and one day it will all be there."

"One day, yes, one day," came the sour voice. "Will I have a 'one' day? What's to become of me? I can't stay here. I won't be a burden to you, what about my family? I still can't write to them. What would I say? It tears me apart wondering about them. What must they have thought of me? I only intended to be away for a few months."

"Now, it's no use going on about that. You won't help yourself get any better if you do."

"I'll never be better Bill, and you know it. What use can I be to anyone?"

"You shut up. You're me mate, aren't you? You leave the worrying to me and just get better. By the way, you'll be all right if I go up to the assay office this afternoon?"

"Yes, Bill, I'll still be here when you get back," he said bitterly, then with an effort more brightly, "You got some good specs?"

"Well, I have some, but will tell you all about it when I get back."

Bill returned just before dusk and headed straight for the tent.

"Alec," he said eagerly, "we're on our way home."

"What! What do you mean?"

"I told you, you were me mate, Scotty, and you are. When you fell down the shaft and knocked the buckets, there was quite a fall from the side of the shaft and I found some nuggets there. I took them up to the assayer and I sold them. Not only that, one of the big companies has bought the claim, so you and I are going home, mate. With money from the gold and money for the claim, we're rich, boy."

"But the claim's yours, Bill, it's not mine."

"Well, I went right down below the seam, Alec, and you found it for me. I always meant you to have Larry's share anyway so we split it even, mate."

"Bill!" came the exclamation.

"And I've bought a spring cart and we pack up and leave for home as soon as we can. Think you can make it? I'll make you a bunk on the wagon and you'll be quite snug under the cover and will ride back to the Hawkesbury like a king. I'll drop you off with your Maggie and kids and then it's home to old Sydney Town for me."

"Do you mean it? I don't have to go empty-handed back to my girl?"

"No, old timer, you'll go back better off than that there prodigal son."

Bill was as good as his word. Within twenty four hours they were packed into the wagon and with two good horses were on the way.

Alec was never very forthcoming about his trip south, but spoke a lot about Scotland. Bill too, talked incessantly, mostly about his life as a youngster in Sydney. His grandfather had come out in the third fleet in 1792. He had been convicted for stealing a shirt from a hedge around a parson's house. He and his friends each got seven years transportation. Apparently, James Turner as a go-ahead young man, for he soon made good and with in a surprisingly short space of time became an inn and toll keeper in

Parramatta. He married a convict lass and they had eight children. Their son, Thomas, was Bill's father. He became a farmer and did well. Bill had never been interested in farming, for it seemed such hard work and for little had always gain, he reasoned. Now that he had capital, his mind turned constantly to farming and he was glad to talk it over with Alec.

Alec was one of those people who was very knowledgeable about his way of life, but never seemed to be able to pull off any of the ideas for himself.

"I just didn't go about anything the right way, Bill. Murdoch really valued my opinions, but I always seemed to make a mess of things for my family. Bill, what do you think they'll do when they see me?" This question recurred most often in his conversation.

"We'll just have to wait and see," was all he would get from his friend.

Long weeks later the dusty wagon pulled up at Macdonald's door. Bill climbed off the wagon seat and hitched the horses. On the verandah he called out, "Are you there, missus?"

Mary came to the door and eyed the stranger warily. "Yes, what can I do for you?"

"Are you Mrs, Macdonald?" enquired Bill.

"I am," said Mary. "Is it my husband you're wanting?"

"Well, yes. I would like him to come, Mrs. Macdonald. Would you send one of the children to fetch him if he's not far from home, and then could I have a word with you?"

Mary turned and called Malcolm and Duncan who were eating their midday meal in the kitchen.

"Duncan, run and get Father. This -er -"

"Turner's the name, Mrs. Macdonald, Bill Turner."

Mary was very curious about this secretive stranger and asked him inside, telling Malcolm to pour tea for him. Within five minutes they could hear Murdoch and Duncan come through the yard and soon introductions were made.

"You look as though you've travelled far, Mr, Turner."

"I have that, Mrs. Macdonald. I've come from Ballarat, from the diggings."

"I hope you did well," said Murdoch.

"Quite well," said Bill, sizing these people up and liking them.

"But I have something for you and need your help."

"What is it, man?"

"I've got Alec Fraser in the wagon."

All four Macdonalds said, "Alec Fraser!"

"Yes, and a broken, sick man he is, too." Bill quickly outlined the story.

"Dear Lord, we never thought of a thing like that. We didn't know where he got to. We couldn't make out where he was."

"I must go to him Murdoch," and Mary almost ran to the wagon.

"Alec, Alec, dear silly Alec," said Mary, as she knelt beside him.

"Where's Margaret, Mary? We went to the house and she's not there. Oh, I'm so glad to see you, oh, Mary, I am so sorry and look at the mess I'm in. What's to do?"

"Hush now, Alec, we'll get things sorted out. Margaret is living at the store now, she's quite a business woman."

"Will she forgive me, Mary?"

"Of course she will. You know Meg is the easiest person we know."

Murdoch joined them in the wagon and looking at the small, sick man, he found it hard to control his voice. "Alec," was all he could say and he took the sick man's hand in his. He felt the heat surging through Alec and he could see that the colour in his cheeks was not a healthy one.

"I'll ride to the store, man, and tell Meg. Bill will bring you up slowly and Mary and Malcolm will go with you to show you the way."

Turning to Duncan he said, "Son, you are in charge here and we don't know how long we will be."

Duncan said "Yes Father, and I'll saddle Brownie and bring her round."

"I'll ride bare back, son, so hurry along."

As soon as the mare was brought round he jumped on her back and sped up the road towards Riverbend. Bill looked after him. He took his hat off and scratched his head. "He can ride all right. You wouldn't know she was not saddled."

135

Duncan said proudly, "He can that, sir, and he had never ridden a horse until he came here. He took to horses and I love them too. 'Bye, Mother, we'll be all right. You stay at Aunt Margaret's until you fix everything up."

Murdoch entered the store and was relieved to see no customers. He said, "Effie, dear, look after the store, will you, while I speak to your Mother."

"Yes, Uncle Murd, is there anything wrong?"

"I'll tell you later when I've spoken to your Mother. Is she in the house?"

"Yes, just call out. She's not long gone in."

"Are you there, Meg?" called Murdoch as he reached the neat, clean kitchen.

"Yes, Murdoch, come in. You're just in time for tea. Sit down." Murdoch came round the spotless, well scrubbed, white pine table, took the teapot out of Meg's hands and said, "Sit down, dear, I've something to tell You."

"Oh, Murd, is it Alec? You've heard something of Alec?"

"Yes, dear, he's on his way here. He's sick, Meg, in fact, I think he's very sick, so sit down and I will tell you all I know."

He quickly told her the story that Bill Turner had told him. Effie came in as the story began and when Murdoch finished she came to her mother and held her hands tight. By this time they were both sobbing.

Margaret said, "Oh, Murd, I didn't think he would want to leave us to fend for ourselves. I thought he must have been dead to be away so long and yet all this time I knew he wasn't. I couldn't understand it. Please bring him to me and we will look after him, won't we, Effie?"

They all went through the shop when they heard the wagon. Murdoch called, "Malcolm, run and ask Mrs. Milne to come and look after the store, if she will. Explain what has happened. She will know that Margaret won't want the store this afternoon."

Margaret had scrambled into the wagon. She fell on her knees beside Alec and no one heard what they had to say to each other, but they remained entwined for some time.

Chapter 20: *Homecoming*

Murdoch came to the rear of the wagon and said, "Meg, dear, can you get a bed ready for Alec? I'll carry him in if you go and turn it down."

He helped Meg down and she ran into the house and quickly prepared a bed for Alec then Murdoch carried him in.

"I've sent for Mrs. Milne, Meg. We'll take Bill with us for the night. Alec will only want you and the children tonight we'll come to see you in the morning."

"Thank you, Mr. Turner. I am so bewildered that my manners are wanting. You will come to see us in the morning, won't you? Murdoch and Mary will look after you. I can't take it all in yet, but I will be more organized when you see me then."

Murdoch rode back beside the others in the wagon, leading his horse. The boys helped Bill unhitch the horses and feed them. Bill was then free to tell them all he knew of Alec but didn't mention the gold or money. He felt that that was Alec's privilege to tell. In the meantime Mrs. Milne had taken over-the store for the day and with Effie's help they left Meg and Alec to catch up on all that had happened during the lost two years. As she washed him and tended him carefully, she found it hard to keep back the tears. His battered emaciated body was a pitiful sight. He read something of her thoughts and said, "I'll not trouble you dearest. We must face it you know. I had to get back to you. I couldn't go without explaining what I did and why I did it. My darling, I wanted so much for you and the children. I didn't intend to go for so long, you know. Mary tells me that you never got the letter. What must you have thought of me. Oh, love, how could I have done it to you?"

"Hush, love, I knew you intended nothing but good for us. I thought you must have died, but yet couldn't really feel that you had.

I just knew that something had stopped you from coming back. It was so hard to keep on believing though."

"It must have been a bleak two years, lass. I nearly went out of my mind thinking of it when I came to my senses. Oh, love."

"Let's not worry about that now, Alec. We will make up for lost time." Then she asked, "Alec, can you move at all?"

"Only my arms and head, love. I am like a baby. And we will have to face the fact that I cannot live for long. We must not fool ourselves. I heard the doctor talking to Bill and he doubted whether I would live long. He said that people like me usually go off with pneumonia and I haven't liked to tell Bill that I have felt bad these last few days. I get sweats and I don't think that's good." He smiled, "Meg dear, I have something to show you."

"Can it wait, dear? I would like Dr. Kenny to see you as soon as he can come.

"No, love, I want to show you this. Please take the leather bag out of my pack. Bill put it in there."

Margaret took all of his few possessions out of the pack and at the bottom she found a heavy wash leather bag. She brought it to him and he took the gold nuggets out and put them in his hand.

"There, lass, that's what I went to Ballarat for, but, of course, I had no idea that I would get them this way." He then told her the story of how Bill found the nuggets. "Bill insisted in giving me a half share of the money he got for the claim too. It is deposited in the bank for you. Did you ever think of having so much money in the bank, Meg?

Well, you have now, and with the money these nuggets will bring, I can leave you secure, lass."

On saying this he seemed to shrink back into the pillows. Meg was alarmed at his pallor now and quickly put the nuggets into the bag and back into the pack. She went to the shop and said, "Effie run for Dr. Kenny and ask him to come when he can."

"Alec," She sat beside Alec and caught up his hand. "I am not going to give you up without a fight and fight I will. Dr. Kenny will tell me how to look after you and if these nuggets are going to be of any use, they will buy help to make you as well as we can get you."

Her optimism was short-lived as Dr. Kenny could only endorse what Alec had heard the Ballarat doctor tell Bill, but he thought that with careful nursing they could get him over the fever that was affecting him now.

The children were burning with curiosity to see their father and it was difficult for Meg to keep them away. She could see that Alec would settle down better if they all came in to sit quietly while he looked them over. They found the white-haired invalid hard to recognise as their fiery-haired, boisterous father. Alec wanted only to feast his eyes on each loved one and wonder at their growth in two years. Just on dusk Ian came racing in from the farm and falling on his knees, he held his father close and repeatedly cried, "Father, oh Father," and with tears running down his freckled face, he said, "Father, we are so glad to have you home again, we missed you so."

Alec was astounded that this big seventeen year old was his Ian. A man, a man, so like himself. He felt a surge inside. He must stay with them all until he could teach them that his past ways were not the best. He must stay to steer them along the right path. He glanced at Margaret and saw that she had caught his thoughts. They smiled above their son's head and Meg felt a confidence flow through her. He would do.

"Well, old man, you look fine," was Bill's remark when he saw Alec the next morning. Wouldn't have believed it. I can see that Mrs. Fraser is the miracle-worker you said she'd be. He never stopped telling me that I had to get him home to you and he would be fine."

Murdoch and Mary followed him into the room as Meg brought the tea tray in.

"I am afraid Alec didn't get much sleep last night. We had so much to catch up on that sleep seemed unnecessary. It was enough just to be together."

"I daresay, Meg," said Mary with a chuckle. "Whatever you have done to him, he certainly looks a lot better. That is no reflection on your attention, Bill."

"The children are spoiling us. Effie brought us breakfast in bed, a thing I have never had, and we had a real sleep in. Mrs. Milne is looking after the shop and we are enjoying ourselves. It is so wonderful to have my man home again."

Alec just beamed and held her hand and Mary said, "I don't think any of us had any idea what you went through, Meg, you always put on such a brave front. I don't think you felt very brave at times though, did you?" She poured the tea as she could see that Margaret had forgotten it.

Meg jumped up and laughed, "Well, I am not going to think about that any more. I feel nineteen again, quite light-headed in fact. But Mr. Turner -"

"Call me Bill. Mrs. Fraser. I'm not used to the mister bit"

"Well, Bill, we have so much to be thankful to you for. Alec has told me so much about your kindness and devotion. We shall always be grateful and will always have a special place in our home for you. In fact, our home is yours, Bill." As she said this, she went to the pack and brought out the leather bag and tipped the nuggets out onto Murdoch's hand. He looked at the golden rocks and was speechless. While he stared at them he handed them to Mary who was equally as stunned.

"Do you mean you struck gold after all, Alec?" as Murdoch said this he looked at Bill.

Bill explained the nuggets and continued, "You see, me and me mate Larry, never made a go of it and then Larry up and died. Right after this, Scotty here almost falls in me lap and he takes over as me mate. I missed the seam when I put the shaft down, but when he took his tumble, Alec unearthed the nuggets and put me onto a seam. I sold the biggest nuggets and then was offered a good price for the claim. We split the money and I gave the other nuggets to Alec so he could give them to Mrs. Fraser. You see, he's me mate, so we split."

"I now have a fat bank balance, Murdoch, and just had to get here to give these to Meg. But man, what a mate Bill is, I don't deserve it at all, do I, Murd?"

Murdoch found it all rather much to take in and was so pleased for the Frasers', who, he thought, did deserve this good fortune.

"Murdoch, you know I am not experienced with money and

you know how I get carried away. I think I have learned my lesson, but could you help me sort it all out? Will you advise me? I am so grateful to you, all four of you. You've done more for me than any other people I have had anything to do with."

"We will help all we can. I cannot say I am used to selling nuggets, but we can but try. There is so much you can do with this money, you must plan it so that you can live on it. You must put those nuggets into the bank before they disappear. They must be worth a fortune."

"Oh, I will do that. Meg can take them there today. But I did want to show her what nuggets look like. I daresay we won't have others. Perhaps you would like to go with Meg now, then I think we will all feel safe about it."

"The nuggets can wait Alec. I won't leave you yet."

"No, Meg, I think you should go. Murdoch and Mary will go with you. Bill can wait here with me. Won't you, Bill?"

"Yes, I will, Alec. Then I must head off for Sydney Town, as I've plans of me own. I wouldn't mind being in on this consulting business, Murdoch, if I can, because I want to buy a farm and I think you could help me with that."

"I certainly will help all I can, Bill, but I am a newcomer. too."

Chapter 21: *Alec's new life*

Alec recovered from the fever he came with, but remained a very frail man. It became the habit for all to meet in his room frequently and share their doings. Alistair was one of Alec's first visitors, making a painful effort to see the man he had been so resentful of. They greeted each other with a love and understanding that neither would have dreamt possible when they had last met. Painful experiences taught a lot. These two who thought they had so little in common now found much to talk about. Alistair shared openly his reasons for their journey north and spoke of lessons learned with pain.

Alec found he was better able to speak of death and Meg's future with Alistair than with Murdoch, for he found it difficult with Murdoch. Murdoch always appeared to be so sure of where he was going and what he was doing that to someone like Alec he sometimes seemed a little remote. Not remote really, but just not able to understand someone like Alec who at times appeared to blunder through life. As Alistair had admitted his mistakes, it encouraged Alec to see him in a new way. Because of his talks with Alistair he was able to speak to his children in a manner he had not been able to before. He had always been fun and ready for a romp with them, but now he was able to understand them and share their problems as he never had before. So the wild Alec became the kind, understanding and considerate Alec. He hadn't lost his sense of humour and was ever joking with visitors as though he hadn't a trouble in the world. Even though he was much better than when he came home, he didn't really improve in health. Meg fed him the best food she could get for him and tried to build his small frame up, but he remained very frail.

The families loved Alec even more than they had done. They had always enjoyed his love of fun and no one had ever taken him very seriously, but now he was quite a new man. He was someone to whom they could confide, someone with whom they could share little worries.

Ian carried his father out onto the verandah of the shop when it was fine and warm. There he would hold court, people stopping to speak to him whenever they came to the shop or drove by. He was always encircled by his friends. Meg watched him carefully noted when he showed signs of tiredness and never hesitated to enlist the help of a brawny farmer to carry him to his to bed.

What a Christmas they all had together! What a lot they had to celebrate! Fergus and Elspeth came down from Sydney, taking extra time off from the warehouse and announcing that he would not go back until after New Year and Hogmonay. So, on the Festive Day they gathered on Macdonald's side verandah that had been cleared of beds and belongings and they set trestles up and loaded them with all the good food that this new land had provided for them. Food that they had never seen in Scotland. They were now used to the wonderful fruit and meat that Australia excels in, but Mary thought they would never really take for granted the beautiful peaches-apricots-plums and berry fruit that grew so prolifically in the area. Her table had fowl, mutton, beef and turkey, all grown on the Park. Mr. Forrest saw that his workers all had a great feast for Christmas time.

Apart from the food, the family celebrated the wonder of being together again. Mary refused on this day to think of her baby Johnnie and little Eliza Fraser lying in the churchyard of the Riverbend church. As she walked to church that morning she had glanced in the direction of the little headstones marking the graves and smiled when she thought of her little son, once again feeling his arms about her neck. She had shrugged the feeling off, knowing that one must not live in the past, but try to come to terms with the living.

She had noticed Meg look in the same direction as she too entered the church. Even in her new-found happiness Meg could not forget a missed little one. A mother couldn't. Dear Meg, she was so happy now that she had her Alec back again, even such a frail Alec as she now had. Meg was determined that she would make Alec well and keep him with her as long as it was possible.

Already she had made Alec feel how important he was to the family and how necessary it was for him to stay alive to be there with them all, to be counsellor and mate.

And Caroline, what a change in Caroline! She had always been overshadowed by Alistair, but Alistair in his new role as schoolteacher seemed now to be able to bring Caroline right out of her shell and blossom. She encouraged her husband in his new life and together, they were making such a success of all they attempted.

"Then there's me," said Mary to herself. "Somehow, all the others have made such a success of all they attempt and I just go along, working with a heavy heart, not coming to terms with this land at all. What is wrong with me? Am I just downright selfish or something? I can never seem to like the place."

"Come on, Mary, you're standing there in a daze. Are you back at home again?" Elspeth slipped up beside her and put her arm around her waist. "Come on, lass, we have a hungry family to feed."

After their huge meal the older girls decided to give their parents a rest and offered to clean up afterwards. They shoo-ed them out onto the verandah at the front of the house and brought them tea. The men settled themselves around Alec, who lay on the wheeled stretcher that Murdoch had made for him with Duncan's help. The women sat and chatted about all the things that had happened to them throughout the year.

"They will be getting our news at home soon," said Mary. "Meg, what a happy time for them to get your news of Alec. Happy I mean, that he is here with us, not that he is sick."

"Yes," said Meg eagerly, "not that Alec is sick. I think he is quite well now, don't you Mary? I think he is looking much better."

"You cannot deny that, dear. You are looking after him very well. I must admit that I thought you wouldn't have him for long when he first came home, but these weeks in your care have made a difference."

"He is going to be even better, too. I am determined that he will be quite better. I don't think he is worrying so much about being a burden either. He was thinking that he should die quickly to get out of our way but I am sure we convinced him he is necessary to us."

"If anyone can make a success of Alec's health, it will be you, Meg," said Caroline. "You really are wonderful, the way you can run the shop and tend Alec."

"But he is no trouble at all. He needs little attention. The children love him so that they are fighting to do things for him. I thought it would wear off, but they never seem to think of him as an invalid. He is their precious father who needs their attention."

"Dear Alec!"

"What are you women talking about down there?" called Fergus.

"We have a great idea. Come and listen to it."

"You have, you mean," said Alec.

"But you all agree, don't you?" laughed Fergus.

Elspeth joined in, "You have to watch this husband of mine he is always getting us involved in his great ideas. What is it now, oh honourable task master?"

"We are going to celebrate Hogmonay. We want to celebrate in fine style and have a celebration New Year. What about it lassies? Will we have a dance and song night in the old style?"

"What a grand idea," Elspeth clasped her hands. "We can make all our Scottish dishes and invite our friends and neighbours and show them what we do at home. What do you think, Mary?"

"Yes, I think it a very good idea. Oh Murdoch, it will be like home again."

"Not quite, lass. It will be very hot for dancing a reel, but I daresay we need not wear our hot clothes. Yes, I do think it a good idea. I am sure we could have it in Mr. Forrest's barn. There isn't much there at the moment and I am sure the boss will be only too happy for us to use it. Mrs. Forrest will want to be in it as well. Yes, let's do it. There is a lot we have to be happy about, isn't there? A few old traditions would be a good thing in this new land. We could show the neighbours what we Scots can do."

The young people threw themselves into preparing the barn for the dance. In fact, the whole town was quite excited about it. Mrs. Forrest took over the supervising of all arrangements and soon had the women baking for hours to feed the hungry dancers. As many Scottish recipes were used as possible and Cornish, Devonshire,

Yorkshire and Irish women found themselves cooking dishes they had never heard of. The Scottish women were given the task of making those that needed that special traditional touch. And so the supper table was loaded with delicacies that were absolutely mouth-watering. Mrs. King, the cook at the Park, had surpassed herself in making dishes that even the Scottish people had not seen. "We have never had these ingredients," said Mary. "We have heard of them, of course, but they didn't come our way."

They felt that there had never been such a New Year's Eve. Mary, and Elspeth looked their families over as they gathered in their finery to go up to the dance.

"You will do us credit, won't they, Mary? My! Girls, you do look pretty and so grown-up, we will have to keep the boys away," laughed Elspeth.

Mary glowed with pride. Murdoch looked so tall, slim and brown after his years now in the sun. Malcolm, Duncan and Donald were not far behind him in height, nor were Fergus and Hamish. "Fergus, I do wish Mother could see you. What a different person you are. Not the skinny, sick, pale man who left Scotland. I am proud of my family."

"It is a grand country to get well in, Sister. Could anyone not get better in such a place?" retorted Fergus.

Murdoch looked at Mary and smiled, giving her a quick hug. "No one could be unhappy in such a place, eh lass?"

Mary only smiled back and said, "Let's be off. The dancing will start before we get there."

They all walked up the neatly tended road to the barn, such a different road to the one they trod over two years ago when the weeds had grown apace while Mr. Forrest had been overseas. There were now well-trimmed hedges along the farm roads and the place had a much loved air about it.

Murdoch paused and looked over the paddocks, the pastures running down to the river, the Blue Mountains towering above them. "I thank God we came to the wonderful farm and found such a boss as Mr. Forrest. I thank God we had sense enough to not go poking for gold that we most probably never would have found.

I thank God we came to this land in the first place. I thank God." It was almost a festal shout. He was so obviously moved that they all stood in silence, watching him and feeling what he felt. Murdoch repeated his cry of his first 'Forrest Park' morning, "Isn't it grand to be alive? Come on everybody, why are you standing there mooning at the scenery? Let's go dancing." He took Mary's hand and ran up the roadway. "Come, we are going to have fun." he cried.

"You big boy," laughed Mary, trying to keep up with him. The children ran too, leaving Fergus and Elspeth to saunter along watching them.

"They seem so happy, don't they, Ellie?"

"I think they are, truly are, I mean. But I still think that Mary hasn't woken up to that fact yet. It will hit her one day. I do wish she wouldn't live in the past."

"Wise old Elspeth, you always know what everyone is thinking, don't you?"

"Old yourself," she laughed. "Come on, I want the first dance with you."

"I would like to see anyone take that away from me. You're mine my girl."

"Come on, you two. What kept you? Mother, I want the first dance."

"No, you don't, young Hamish. I have spoken for your Mother for the first dance. You go and find nice young lassie of your own," said Fergus.

The barn looked beautiful. The young people had spent all the day decorating the rafters with ferns and greenery of all kinds. Sandy McNabb was tuning his violin and looked as though he was ready for the first reel. He drew his bow across his instrument and bent his back as he started into a rousing Scottish tune. Soon, there was a floor full of people giving themselves to the music, laughing, dancing and calling that infectious whooping sound that the folks felt necessary to their fun. The music tempo was exciting and people who had never heard the Scottish rhythm were compelled to take part and learn the steps of those very beautiful dances. The old musician alternated the reels with other more recognisable tunes for the English ears and so each was able to learn the others methods of social exercise. The young people soon picked up the steps and very enthusiastically shared the fun with their parents.

Alec bemoaned the fact that his dancing days were over and Alistair sat by his side as they watched with interest their offspring stepping out with gusto. Both men urged their wives to participate in the dancing, assuring them that they did not wish them to miss out on the fun. Alistair had never been much of a dancing man, but Alec had, as you could expect such a man to be. At first it almost hurt to see the others swing almost through the steps, but he hastily took himself in hand and told himself that he was very pleased to be there at all. He did appreciate all the family had done for him. This wheeled stretcher thing that Murdoch had made allowed the family to push him to church and to other functions that otherwise he would miss. He always had been a gregarious man and he especially liked to know what was going on around him. He wasn't a gossip, but rather, a mine of information about the affairs of the district. Alistair had never been a popular man with his fellow adults, but the new Alistair had a great rapport with children, so it was not so surprising to find him surrounded by some of his pupils. As Alec's cronies were continually coming to speak with him, Alistair moved away from the stretcher, his little circle of friends moving with him to let Alec entertain his friends in comfort.

In between the dancing there were songs and poetry. The Scots folk felt that an evening like this would not be complete if there was not a verse or two recited and all of their friends were skilled in these arts. Fergus sang some Scottish songs and was received by the people with a great deal of appreciation. His voice was a pleasing baritone and the songs he sang were the beautiful island melodies that were tinged with a sadness. Quiet Caroline proved to have a very robust and rich contralto and many were surprised to hear her. She sang with a skill that would not disgrace a professional performer. Murdoch and Mary sang a sweet duet and later, Murdoch said some wonderful poems right from the Highlands. He began with a Scots poem on the 'Massacre of Glencoe'. "He always begins with that," said Alec, "but he gets better after he says it. It seems to relieve his feelings or something."

THE HEATHER TO THE HAWKESBURY

After the 'Massacre', Murdoch did go on to more delightful works and he was able to show his Scottish brogue in full when he recited some of Robbie Burns and then Sir Walter Scott to finish up.

"Dear friends, I have shared with you some of the poetry of our land. They tell something of the feeling we have for our homeland and I am sure that you feel that your poetry shows yours. But we have a new homeland now. This land of Australia. I am sure that as time goes on, many poems and stories will be written about this great south land. I have tried to find something that was written about it recently[5] and have learned to know a great man who comes from this very Hawkesbury area, Charles Harpur. This is his poem on:

A Midsummer noon in an Australian Forest

Not a sound disturbs the air,
There is quiet everywhere
Over plain and over woods,
What a mighty stillness broods.

All the birds and insects keep
Where the coolest shadows sleep,
Even busy ants are found
Resting in their pebbled mound.
Even the locust clingeth now
Silent to the barky bough,
Over hills and over plains
Quiet, vast and slumbrous, reigns.

Only there's a drowsy humming
From yon warm lagoon slow coming,
'Tis the dragon hornet—see!
All bedaubed resplendently,
Yellow on a tawny ground,
Each rich spot nor square nor round,

[5] Charles Harpur was born at Windsor, NSW 23 January, 1813.
This poem was first published in *The Empire*, 27 May 1851.

Rudely heart-shaped, as it were
The blurred and hasty imprint there
Of a vermeil-crusted seal
Dusted o'er with golden meal.
Only there's a droning where
Yon bright beetle shines in air,

Tracks it in its gleaming flight
With a slanting beam of light,
Rising in the sunshine higher
Till its shards flame out like fire.

Every other thing is still
Save the ever-wakeful rill,
Whose cool murmur only throws
Cooler comfort round repose;

Or some ripple in the sea
Of leafy boughs, where lazily
Tired summer, in her bower
Turning with the noontide hour,
Heaves a slumbrous breath ere she
Once more slumbers peacefully.

Oh 'tis easeful here to lie
Hidden from noon's scorching eye,
In this grassy cool recess
Musing thus of quietness.

There were many who were not appreciative of much poetry, but this moved everyone there. That this Scotsman could feel the wonder of this new land made them, too, think of the atmosphere of the place. Most had come to Australia in recent years and even those who hadn't, could remember the strangeness that took a deal of getting used to. Murdoch's efforts were much appreciated.

Mr. Forrest stood and invited Alistair to say grace before they moved to the supper tables, and while waiting for Alistair to come forward he said, "Friends, I want to say something which is in my heart, and which I feel must be said. I count it a blessing to me that these four families of Scots folk came my way. I liked them on sight and I hope I do not embarrass them by saying this, but say it I must. I have watched with interest the fortunes of these fine people. We thought we had lost Alec, and to our relief, we found we had only mislaid him."

"Thank God you found me again," put in Alec.

"Yes, we do thank Him. I am sure he watched over you lad. We thought we had lost Alistair to the bush up north and are very pleased to have him back in our midst, even though he came back missing a leg. It hasn't stopped him much. We are very pleased indeed to see the family once more re-united. I felt I had to speak because to me, these four families represent the future of Australia. I am only mentioning them because it is their celebration tonight, but there are many more of you good folk who come into these categories. First I see Murdoch as a typical farmer who has little in his thoughts but his farm and his family and all that revolves around these. I am sure he will get himself a farm in the near future and perhaps begin an Australian dynasty. Then we have Fergus who thought he was coming to Australia to die and what happened? He became a business man who typifies the new strain of merchantmen who will spread out over this vast continent and service the people in all walks of life. We need a Fergus in our lives that we may live in some comfort. Then we have Alistair who represents to me the academic Australian."

"Oh, no sir, not me," put in Alistair hastily.

"Yes, Alistair, I count you as representing the intelligentsia of our land. We have no renowned seats of learning as yet in our country, but look to people such as Alistair who can share their knowledge with us and teach our children. I happen to know that he has a certain talent for preaching that I hope we can take advantage of in the near future."

"We all appreciate the fact that we have a fine school in

Riverbend and can send our children to Alistair to learn the necessities of life. Lastly, I come to Alec! Alec, I think, shows us what the Australian man is to be best known for. Alec will always give us mate-ship and friendship. Alec will give us humour and wit and a knowledge of life that we will all, at some time, appreciate. We will always need an Alec in our lives to share our happiness with and to share our worries. Our little mate! I cannot miss saying a few words about the Scottish ladies. I won't speak about them personally, for I feel they are alike in the main thing that is necessary for the perfect wife. She must always be a good backstop for her husband. I have first-hand information about this, for the good Lord blessed me with the gift of a grand wife, and she too, from Scotland, as you know. A wife must face the things that are not to her liking with a fortitude that is never flagging. She must follow her mate to the ends of the earth. She must be guide, comforter and friend, wife, a mother and good organiser. My friends, I suggest to you that we have such women, with us tonight in Mrs. Macdonald, Mrs. MacKenzie, Mrs. Fraser and Mrs. MacLeod. Ladies and gentlemen, I give you a toast to our friends."

Supper followed and some had found it hard to wait for the speech to finish before starting their meal, for meal it was. As well as the Scottish food that is present at such functions, such as every kind of oatcake that could be made, shortbread and haggis, there was a grand array of food that the Australians thought necessary. Fine hams, beef sliced thick and several legs of mutton, as well as poultry and huge turkeys. There were crisp bread and cheeses, yeast buns and cakes and every kind of fruit in season, raw and preserved. Bowls of thickened cream and healthy yellow butter were dotted around the feast.

"Thank you for all the amazing things you said about us, Mr Forrest," said Murdoch when his boss came to talk to the four men who were gathered together talking about the speech that he had made.

"You make us hang our heads, that you think so of us. We do not deserve it."

"I beg to differ, Murdoch," came the rejoinder. "Allow me to know the country I grew up in and allow me to know which are the men who are successful in this country. I have seen men from all walks of life make a go of this place and I have seen men from all walks of life make a mess of it. It isn't a matter of who you are, but what you have in you. I know that England is a land full of classes and to a certain degree I think that this has been brought to Australia, but I am sure that in the long run classes will not matter. What will matter will be what a man puts into his life. His willingness to work and willingness to adjust to the conditions he finds himself in. This is what I feel is so admirable in you four. You adjust and you do not complain about a bit of adversity, take it in your stride."

Forrest smiled at the men, patted Murdoch on the back and bid them 'goodnight'. Murdoch's eyes followed him across the room, then turned to his friends and said, "We fell on our feet when we met up with that gentleman, didn't we? I wonder where we would have been if we hadn't?"

Chapter 22: *The New Generation*

"Uncle Alistair, are you there?"

"Yes, in the schoolroom. Oh, it is you, Duncan. Come in, my boy."

"Hello, Uncle. I've come to see you."

"Well, come in lad, don't stand on the doorstep. What have you there?"

Duncan came into the schoolroom to find his uncle sitting at his desk, marking lessons on a pile of slates. The boy seemed rather ill at-east and red in the face.

"Uncle," said Duncan. "You know that I like making things and have made quite a lot of things for my insect collection. Well, I got to thinking that you are finding it hard to get around easily and I thought this might help."

He brought a contraption from behind his back and proffered it to Alistair. The man could see that it was a wooden leg, a peg leg, the sailors called them. He took it from the boy and looked at it. "Why Duncan, I don't know what to say, but thank you."

"Uncle you don't have to wear it if you don't want to. I won't be hurt, truly I won't, and no one knows that I have made it. It's just that I have noticed how tired your good leg gets, doing all the work and I thought if you could have something to hold you up, you may not get so tired. You see, it goes on like this and it has a harness on it to help you keep it in place. If this one doesn't fit, then I can make one that does. I saw a sailor with one on the ship and it was amazing what he could do."

"My boy, how thoughtful of you. I have often thought that I perhaps could get something like this one day. It would be grand if it worked. Let's try it."

"I made the peg part of it longer than I thought, so we could trim it to the right size. I brought the saw to cut it. I hope it fits.

I padded it inside to make it comfortable."

Alistair stood up and tried the thing gingerly. "I think I will have to wear it under my trousers, son, but we will try it over them first to get the length."

"You mean you will try to wear it, Uncle? You really don't have to if you don't want to. I didn't tell any one in case you didn't want to wear it."

Alistair laughed at the worried look on the boy's face. "I want to wear it if we can get it to fit, Duncan. I think I am a very lucky man to have a nephew who wants to be so helpful. You have made it very well. Look, I think with a bit of trimming, I could manage it well."

"Stand up and I will see what length you should have it and I will cut it down."

At this stage the door into the house opened and Caroline came in. "Hello, what are you two up to? It is a leg! Where did you get that, Alistair? Duncan, did you make it? What a good laddie you are. Does it fit Alistair?"

"Caroline, isn't this fellow a marvel? Fancy him thinking this up. Do you know, I think it will work. Can you mark where you should cut it, Duncan? What about me standing on the edge of the step and you could measure it then?"

"I don't think I should cut too much off it at first, Uncle. I would rather have it too big at first."

Very soon, with adjustments, the leg was ready and Alistair took a few steps.

"I think I will keep the crutches at first until I get the feel of it, but sonnie, I think it will work."

Duncan beamed at his uncle taking his first few steps. "You take it easy, Uncle, don't fall. You will be careful, won't you?"

Duncan left Alistair and Caroline to try the leg alone. He was a happy lad to see his plan had worked. His father had made a good workshop in the shed at home and was only too pleased to encourage his son to make woodwork a hobby. Murdoch had always been quite capable of making furniture and the necessary things one needed around a farmhouse, but Duncan showed a skill in making really fine articles. He was nearly fifteen now and still interested in all the natural things around him. His collection of insects was quite remarkable and his woodworking skills came in handy for this hobby, for his specimens were housed in cabinets that any collector would be proud to have. He had made chests with tight-fitting drawers that kept unwanted parasites out. Duncan's present of a leg for Alistair gave their relationship a new dimension. Alistair soon took more interest in him and found what a keen brain he had. Duncan was most appreciative of this new friendship and was able to talk to Alistair about the Latin used for the names of some of the insects he had caught. Mr. Forrest had lent the boy a book he had that illustrated some insects which seemed similar to the ones he had caught. Duncan dearly wanted to know the meaning of the names. This was a hard time for Alistair, for the Latin he had seemed to bear little resemblance to the language of the books, but they worked together on it and the friendship grew.

Malcolm Macdonald, Ian Fraser and Donald MacLeod were all, by this time, working on 'Forrest Park'. They were around seventeen now and almost men. Hard work was a way of life to them and they were all keen to learn well and someday have farms of their own.

One evening after dinner, William Forrest walked down to Macdonald's house, finding them on the verandah. He joined them and said, "Murdoch, I have a proposition to put to you. I have a friend who lives near Yass. He has a big run and many cattle. With this gold fever that most seem to be suffering from, he cannot get men enough to get his stock to market. We can buy good beasts at five pounds a head and I know that we can get ten pounds here. I thought you might care to take the three boys, Malcolm, Ian and Donald and go down for some. I would like to stock my new hill paddocks and I would like some for sale. If you would care to, you could buy some yourself and bring them with my lot. What about it?"

"That sounds a great idea, Boss. The only thing is that I wouldn't like to leave my wife for that length of time."

"Oh, Murd, don't worry about me. Duncan will look after me. How long would you be away?"

"I think you would get there in a week, Murdoch," said Mr. Forrest, "and after that it would depend on how much food there was on the way back. Several weeks perhaps. We would keep an eye out for Mrs. Mac, Murdoch. We wouldn't let you get lonely. What about the other lads. Do you think they would like to go?"

"I am sure of it. I feel a bit concerned about Ian leaving Mrs. Fraser, but now that she has young Benson working for her, she should be all right. He could help her with Alec, too. Janet and Effie are big girls now. I think that would be all right. Alistair, too, would be happy to see Donald have the experience."

"Talk it over anyway. Don't make up your minds right now. Think it out and let me know in the morning. If you think you would like to do it, I will go over to see the MacLeods and the Frasers tomorrow."

"How soon would you like us to go, sir?"

"In the next week or two, I should say. I will write to Guthrie Carmichael and tell him the plan. We'll have to get horses ready too, and equipment. So about two weeks, let's say."

The boys were very anxious to go and thought the journey an exciting one to look forward to. Malcolm asked his father, "Would I be able to buy a bullock with my five pounds? Then I could get ten pounds for it at the sale. It sounds like easy money. Father."

"I don't think money comes easily son, but you certainly may if you would like to risk your money. You have to get your animal back and you have to choose one that will bring in top price. I imagine the others will wish to do the same."

Ian Fraser said much the same to Alec, but with a difference. Alec was rather inclined to indulge Ian and allowed him to have twenty pounds to buy four cattle if Murdoch was agreeable.

Alistair had little enough to give Donald, but gave the lad ten pounds, hoping to double their money. Donald had five pounds of his own and so hoped to get three good beasts. "Father, I was thinking about this could you give thought to this proposal? If I do what is planned and the scheme works out, I would like to do this as often as I can and work hard at it. I may not even have to go as far as Yass each time. I would like to earn money quickly, working for two years, and then I would like to be a preacher.

By this time I should have enough to see me through for a while. I will study hard and perhaps you could help me with this. I daresay I could preach while I work, so to speak. I mean that I could preach in towns that have no ministry and when I find a good lot of cattle, buy them and head home and sell them. What do you think of that?"

"Well, let me think about it, son. Let us see how this works out first. I find that these get-rich-quick schemes sound all right, but don't always work out. As for the rest of your idea, I go along with that. I am proud to think you want to give your life to doing this. I did think you might want to return to the Manning River. You are a very good farmer, son."

"You are a good farmer too, Father, but you seem very happy to be teaching the children here. You could go back to farming, you know."

"Yes, I do know, but now have no inclination to do so. Jake is doing as well, if not better, than we were and I appreciate the money he sends me. I am as happy here as I have ever been in my life Donald and do not wish to disturb that. Your mother is very content here with her family and I want that to continue."

"You will think about my project then?"

"I certainly will. There may be some sort of training you can do, or some sort of study. I will try to find out. In the meantime, don't expect to make money that easily."

On the day before they planned to go, Bill Turner, Alec's old prospecting mate, came up from Sydney to visit Alec and look around for a farm. He came to the house to see Murdoch and was interested in their preparations and sat talking to Murdoch while he worked. "Makes me get itchy feet, seeing you get ready for a trip like that."

"Why don't you come, Bill? I am sure we could use your experience. We are not very used to big mobs of cattle, you know."

"Well, I dunno. Would you mind if I did? Me time's me own. Yes, I think I would like to go. Get me hand in for when I want to buy for me farm."

"We will be glad to have you."

"I'll go and break the news to Alec. I came to see him and I'm running out on him straight away."

"Alec won't mind. In fact, he will be glad that we have an experienced hand to guide us."

So next morning an excited Macdonald family rose to say 'goodbye' to their father and brother. They walked up to the yard at the Park where they were all to meet and found Donald waiting ready. Ian and Bill came soon after and with 'God speed' from Mary and the family, they set off, Mr. Forrest giving them last minute instructions. They each carried a heavy pack containing tucker[6] and clothing and soon were out of sight.

They were able to cover about thirty five to forty miles a day and found the going quite easy. At night they camped out as the stars shone brightly in clear skies. The days were warm, just right for travelling and they were pleased to see that there was ample feed for animals for the trip home. None of the Scots folk had been south of Camden and so after that town were most anxious to see the country. They were surprised to see such lovely mountain country and the farms that lay along their route. They called in at several of these places and were always offered hospitality in the form of food and shelter should they want it. The boys liked to camp out and so they usually refused. Near Goulburn they stopped at a beautiful dairy farm owned by Dick Hassel and his son, where they were hosted in the usual way and directed to Carmichael's farm where they were to collect the cattle. They still had many miles to go, but Mr. Hassel knew Guthrie Carmichael, as everyone seemed to know everyone in the back country, and was able to give good instructions as to how to make a more direct route than going through Yass. As they travelled they arranged for yarding for their mob on their return journey and were surprised to find that this was very easy to do. Bill suggested that as the farmers were in great trouble getting their beasts to market, they were only too pleased to be helpful to anyone who may take theirs sometime. Certainly, Donald and Ian showed interest in doing this, Donald seeing that he would be able to put his plan into action if all went

[6] Tucker = Australian word for Food

well, and Ian because he liked the adventure of it and wanted to make money.

Over their camp fire at night, they had the opportunity to get to know one another better. There was little opportunity for chatter in their lives at home. In Murdoch's spare time he usually spent it with Alec and did not see so much of Ian. He often had thought how alike he and Alec were and wondered whether Ian had that same, well you couldn't call it unsteadiness, that Alec had, but it was a certain something that made Alec what he was. A good fellow for all that, mused Murdoch, but he had a real knack for getting himself into trouble.

"What are you young'uns going to do with yourselves when you settle down?" asked Bill on their last night before collecting the cattle.

Malcolm said, "I have no thought but to help Father buy a farm. I am wondering whether this type of trip will help our goal come nearer, Bill. I hope so."

"Yes, it will be interesting to see how it goes. It seems too easy to me, but I reckon it should work. Mind you, it's no fun in a drought, but the seasons here have been good by the look of it, and barring accidents, we should do well with it. I brought some money to buy some if they are good and I checked with the meat bloke in Penrith to see whether the price is steady there and he assured me it was."

"I have brought money to buy three," said Donald. "I do hope the scheme works, Bill, because I have a plan if it does."

"What is it, Donald?" asked Murdoch. "Something serious, I imagine."

"Oh, I'm not all that serious, Uncle Murdoch. I like a bit of fun. But yes, this is serious, because I want to go into the church and I thought that if I could make enough money in two years bringing cattle up from the back country then I would be able to train or something. Father is going to try to find out for me, but I couldn't do it alone. I would have to have help and it might cost more than I would like to spend."

"Is that what you would like to do, Donald? I wondered at your not returning to the Manning."

"Father said I could do that, but for one thing I would be too far away from the family and as they are not wanting to go back there, I wish to slay as near as I can."

Bill said, "I think you could make it work out, son, and I don't think you would find it hard to get companions. I've heard of several decent blokes who want offsiders to do just this. I could tell them about you. I am sure they would take you along. You can always buy beasts to sell and add it to the mob, like you are doing this time. I heard about a big mob of fifteen hundred go up from the real outback and into Bathurst to the goldfields. I think if you are keen you will find a lot of this work to do."

"What do you want to do, Ian?" asked Murdoch.

"Well, I too, want to help my father get into a farm. Mother and I think he is well enough for another move. We would like to think that at least he could call himself a farmer, even if he does have to direct us from his bed. After all, look what he did so we could have a farm. So I want to farm for Father."

"And I want to be near them, too," put in Bill. "I reckon I want to be near me little mate, so if we can get a farm close by, I'll be there to lend a hand when they want it."

"What sort of farming are you going in for, Bill?"

"Well, it won't be dairying, like you want, Murdoch. I reckon I don't want to be tied down to cows twice a day. A man's got to have some time for himself, so I reckon I'll grow a bit of crop and have some cattle run. I saw a decent-looking farm the other day that had a bit of hill country at the back of it, that should be right for cattle."

"Where is it, Bill?"

"Not that far from Riverbend on the Jingalong Road. It backs onto some good Crown land too, that looks interesting. I could get a lease on that too. There's a decent farm near it too, that I want Alec to look at that backs onto the same Crown land. I think it would be good for Alec's horses."

"So your Dad's going in for horses, Ian? He's a dark horse himself. He didn't tell me that."

"I think he thought you may not like it. He said you might think that horses are too chancy."

"As a matter of fact, I don't. Horses are bringing in a good price at the moment. I daresay he isn't thinking of race horses, is he?"

"We would like to have thoroughbreds, Uncle, but we do think they are a bit chancy. No, we are wanting Clydesdales. We would like to try to build a good stud of Clydesdales. We would have others, too, but they would be our specialty. What do you think about it Uncle?"

"Well, I think you and your father would do very well, Ian. You still have a lot to learn about them, as they are really very new for you, but you and your father both have a real love and talent with them, so you should do very well."

"When we get back we want you to have a look at the farm, Murd, and get Mr. Forrest, too, if he will come, to advise us. Will you?"

"For what it is worth, I certainly will, Bill, but I am no great authority on farms, you know. I will be hoping that Mr. Forrest will advise me when I can go looking for a farm myself. I am sure he will help, both you and me. He had always said he will. I wondered when Alec would start thinking farms. I am sure he feels that Meg has had long enough in the store. I know she likes it, but she really doesn't have to now and I am sure Alec would like to see her settled in her own home."

"Before he dies, do you mean, Uncle Murd? Do you know, I don't think he will for a while. I think he'll stay for a bit," said Ian seriously.

"I think you are right, lad."

"Me little mate's got a lot o' courage," put in Bill.

Chapter 23: *A New style of farming*

The party found Carmichael's cattle station quite easily. Murdoch liked the look of this country west of Yass. So different to the closed in Hawkesbury River farms. Guthrie Carmichael was an Englishman who was making a real job of being an Australian squatter. His cattle and land were in excellent condition and Murdoch could understand his concern, when he saw the quality of his stock, at his not being able to get them to sale yards. Murdoch, Bill and the boys had their choice of beasts at five pounds a head and it seemed as though they would have quite a deal if the price was what they expected it would be in Emu Plains near home. They took a herd of two hundred and Murdoch silently wished he had more capital to spend on buying more. He hoped he would be able to return during this winter and get more for himself.

They had quite a pleasant stay at The Downs, Mr. Carmichael proving to be a very generous host. They saw quite a lot of the property and were very impressed with the working of such a large run. The place seemed immense to the men of the river farms, but none were really tempted to want a big place like this. Just as well, for it would take more capital than they had together to set up a place like this.

They left on their way home after a three day stay, with a promise of more animals if they would care to return later in the season. Donald and Ian made a promise that they would do this.

They had quite an uneventful journey home. They took it slowly and were happy to see that the cattle lost no condition, but with such good grass all the way, they considered themselves fortunate in their first venture. They were relieved when the stockyards at Emu Plains came into view and they could yard the beasts for sale. Murdoch then took the rest to put in a paddock at the Park, ready to move the following day or so to the wooded hill paddocks that Mr. Forrest had recently acquired for such stock. They got the price they had wanted and they felt very pleased that the deal had gone so well. Mr. Forrest showed his gratitude by giving each of them an extra beast to sell. They all felt rather pleased at that, even Bill, who looked upon himself as quite a capitalist these days.

A few days after their return, Murdoch shared the ambitions of the group with Mr. Forrest and asked if he would look at the farms Bill and Alec were thinking of buying. With the boss's assent he arranged for everyone to go and look at them one fine autumn day. They loaded Alec onto his stretcher and put it into the wagon and, with wives and children and picnic baskets, the party set off. Mr. and Mrs. Forrest came with their three children in their gig and the day took on quite a festive air. Ian and Malcolm rode alongside.

The farms were about a mile apart, both backing as Bill had said, onto a strip of fairly rough wooded ground that should be ideal for stock. The farms were cleared and the ground sloped gently down to a creek that promised a good supply of water all year round, a necessity in this dry land. There was no house on Bill's proposed farm, but on the one that Alec would buy there was a small farmhouse that would need a great deal of improvement before being able to house the Fraser family in the style that Alec wanted for his brood.

They pulled up in the shade of a tree on Alec's farm and made a picnic camp. The men lifted Alec out and put the wheels on his stretcher, then set off to inspect the farm, walking slowly over the ground and every now and then stooping to pick up a sample of soil to look at it, smell it, feel it and then discard it.

A chuckle bubbled out of Mrs. Forrest as she watched procedure. "I love to see them do that. I wonder if it is really necessary to go through that little rite. I am sure I would only look down as I do now and say what a lovely place to live. Oh, Mrs. Fraser I do hope your husband buys this. I am sure it would be a lovely place to live."

"I hardly know how to breathe, I am so excited, Mrs. Forrest. I cannot believe that it is happening. I know Alec has been talking about this ever since he came home, but it never seemed true that we would have enough money to buy a farm, just like that," said Margaret, clasping her hands together.

"Enough to buy some good stock too, Meg" smiled Mary. "Isn't it wonderful that Alec is able to do this for you."

"Before he dies, do you mean, Mary? Do you know, I don't think he will. Not for a while anyway. He is so excited about this. He can hardly contain himself. I cannot imagine how he has been able to wait so long. I felt sure he would rush out and buy the first farm he saw. I think he must be learning patience."

"Yes, Meggie dear, I think he has learned the very hardest way. I agree with you that I think he will defy the doctors this time. You are looking after him so well that I am sure he won't die yet," said Mary.

"Let us walk over and have a look at the cottage."

The three women walked over to the poor little house, leaving the children to follow or stay and play as they liked. The grass was green and good and so the girls were soon busy in their usual games.

Mrs. Forrest wrinkled up her pretty nose. "I cannot see you in this place, Mrs. Fraser, knowing how well you look after your house and shop."

"No indeed, I think it is not much good. You couldn't do anything much with this. Bill suggested that we build another one completely, if Alec buys it."

"It is just the right place for a house though, isn't it, Meg? You would build right here, wouldn't you? There has been quite a nice garden here at one time too, but I do not think the last people cared much for that. Look at the lovely creeper on that trellis. Oh, and Meg, look at the roses."

"They are really beautiful, aren't they?"

"What about cleaning this verandah up a bit and having our picnic here?" said Mrs. Forrest. "I think if we settled here for our meal, Mr. Fraser would be on flatter ground for his stretcher."

"That's a good idea, Mrs. Forrest. I will go over and get the lunch. The children can help me bring it."

"We will tidy the old table and chairs up and have it ready when you get back."

When the men returned the women had the lunch spread out

on a pleasant cloth on the old table and soon they were sitting along the edge of the verandah, eating their lunch and discussing the merits and demerits of the place.

"I do not think you know what you are eating, you men. You are so wrapped in the discussion that you are just eating anything I put in yours hands," laughed Mary.

"No, love," said Murdoch, "I am eating a bannock and a good one it is. I would know your bannocks anywhere." He broke off wondering at the laughter from the women.

"Well, you are wrong. Meg made those bannocks and Mrs. Forrest made these. So I did not bring any today."

"Well, they are good anyway. I like bannocks." He turned to Mr. Forrest. "Well, Mr. Forrest, what do you think of it? What is your opinion?"

"Yes, I think they are fine bannocks, too."

The group roared with laughter, knowing that Murdoch had really meant the farm when asking for Forrest's opinion. Murdoch was quite taken aback at the turn of the question. He joined in the laughter.

"Yes, sir, very fine bannocks, but what of the farm?"

"Yes," said Alec and Bill together, "What do you think, Mr. Forrest?"

"I think it is a fine place. There is a good depth of soil on it and the pasture looks right. It has the makings of a good farm. I don't need to go into the hill country because I have just taken some of it for my own cattle and had quite a good look at all the country round here. I think if you could get it at the price you mention you will do well."

Alec looked pleased. "Yes, I am very pleased with it. It is even better than Bill said. What do you think, Murdoch?"

"All I can say, old man, is that if I was the envious type I would be envious right now. It is a bit above my touch and I would like to see you and yours in it."

"When you have finished your eating, let's go and look at mine. What will you do about the house Alec. Do you want to look inside it? We could carry you in if you want to," said Bill eagerly.

"No, "said Alec firmly, "I have seen enough of it from out here.

I am going to have a new house for Meg and it will have just everything she wants in it."

Meg beamed. "You'll spoil me and I won't want to work anymore, just sit and look at the scenery."

"That I must see, Meg," said Murdoch. "We'll all sit here to see you sit with nothing to do. You just wouldn't know how to, woman."

They packed the picnic things up and once more piled into the wagon. Bill's farm was not too far down the dusty road. They turned through a good gate and could see that the fencing was quite superior to that on Alec's farm.

"We will need good fencing on our place first off, Father," said Ian, riding near the wagon so he could speak with his father, "and we will need lots of yards and housing for the horses," his face eager in the bright sunlight.

"We will, son, we will indeed. We will need a lot of new things. The first though will be a new house, I'm thinking."

Bills' farm was almost a replica of the first one and the fences were good all round the farm, as well as first rate sheds and yards.

"I, too, will build a house, but I'll bet you it won't be a fine one like the one you'll build for your missus, Alec. But, I dunno, mebbe I will settle down with a missus of me own. In that case I would need a big one. You'll have to advise me on that, Alec."

This remark was greeted with roars of laughter, with Bill joining in. Of course he'd meant a big house not a big Missus!

So, Alec and Bill bought their farms. Very quickly they had builders in to talk of plans for houses. They decided in the end to have two similar houses. It seemed that everything that Alec wanted was all right for Bill. In his eyes Alec could do no wrong.

On one of his trips out west, Fergus called in to see the Frasers and asked Meg about the store. He had a feeling that Mr. Trent would be interested in buying this from Mrs. Milne, as he aimed to have a string of stores along the route west and thought that as this store had proved such a winner, his boss would be interested in acquiring it. Meg suggested that he ask Mrs. Milne about this. She said that this lady was very upset to think that Meg would leave the store when her new house was finished on the farm.

So, after having afternoon tea with Alec, he made his way to Mrs. Milne's house to discuss the plans with her so he could speak to Mr. Trent at a later stage, and later to the Macdonalds where he stayed the night. Over an after dinner cup of tea they discussed all the exciting plans that the Frasers and Bill were making.

"Trust Alec to want to build a mansion," said Fergus. "It will probably end up most unsuitable to Australia's climate."

"Nay, Fergus, you are being unfair there," said Murdoch. "Alec is being remarkably sensible. You see, he plans to start a real dynasty of Frasers and so, is doing things properly. I imagined he would build a castle or some such, at least to have a magnificent set of stairs or something, but he isn't. Mind you, I think Meg put her foot down about that. She wants a place that Alec can move around in and so they are to have a long, low house in the very modern style that seems to be developing here in Australia now, and of course, it will have a wide verandah round it."

"Yes," said Mary, "I think it will be a lovely house. It will sit snugly against that hill and look right over the valley."

"Just like the house that you will build, eh Sister?" queried Fergus.

"No, not at all like the house of my dreams, Fergus. Mind you, the real thing will probably end up being quite different to the one in my dreams."

"When will you be thinking of looking for a farm, Murdoch" I imagine you will have quite a bit saved up now. Do you keep looking for the ideal spot?"

"Well, I would like to think so, but I do not seem to be saving as quickly as I hoped. But we are getting there. We did make a good start with stock recently. We all went south and brought up a mob of cattle that proved to be a winner. I think it could be a risk though and I do not want to lose my money on such a venture."

"Why," asked Fergus, "tell me more."

Murdoch told the story of their trip to Yass and young Donald's plan for making money.

"Well, I see quite a lot of the country' as you know, and I do know that any who will move stock for the squatters are very popular people. I think you could make quite a lot of money that way, but I imagine you would have to leave your job at 'Forrest Park' if you wanted to take it on permanently. You would buy a farm quickly that way."

Murdoch laughed as he caught Mary's quick glance at him. "No need to worry, lass. I do not intend to do that. No Fergus, if I can get an occasional trip in I will be quite pleased, but I am not risking my job. I am a patient man."

"I know that, Murdoch. Never a more patient man than you."

"When the time comes we will get our farm and we will work to keep it."

During that winter Donald made repeated trips into the country and brought stock to market. He was pleased to see his bank balance grow and felt that if he went along at that rate he would be soon able to really look into the way he could enter the church. It was not easy for anyone in his position, as there was no training for men like him. Most Presbyterian ministers had come already trained from Scotland and the young men who wanted to go into the church often went back to Scotland to train. His father had approached the Rev. Hugh McFadden and had discussed it all with him. Mr. McFadden wanted to see Donald next time he was in the district and try to work something out. Donald never seemed to be at home when the Reverend gentleman came to Riverbend and Donald thought that if he did not see him soon, he would track the man down. Mr. McFadden was forever on the move and did not seem to travel in any set way. He just went to where he felt anyone needed him. Donald so wanted to follow in his steps.

Donald had few adventures on the road. He had employed a local lad to join him in his venture. Young Bert Jenkins was a willing boy who understood stock well for his fifteen years. His father was quite a bad farmer and his family not much to be recommended, but Bert didn't seem to have the slacking tendencies that his father had. He admired Donald and was willing to do anything he asked. They stayed on the southern route most times, for Donald knew the country well now and was able to use yarding where he wanted. The squatters trusted him to get their stock into market safely and so he bought a great number to the sale-yards over the next months.

The Frasers were moving into their farm in the spring and Bill was to stay with them until his house was built. Mr. Trent had bought the store and Meg still ran it and was able to stay until she wanted to leave and go to her new house.

Chapter 24: *Changing Views*

"**D**o I pay you to lean on your shovel and gaze into space, Macdonald?"

At this, Murdoch spun round and looked at his boss leaning on the gate, shaking with silent laughter.

Murdoch chuckled as he dug the tool into the earth and joined Mr. Forrest at the gate. "I really have been working, Mr. Forrest," he said.

"I know you were, Mac, but you were so deep in thought just then, I thought I would give you a jolt. Not worried about anything, are you?" the farmer queried.

"No, not really worried, but I really am concerned about when I should make that move. The others are settled now, and somehow I cannot bring myself to uproot Mary and take her somewhere that will mean very hard work and very little return for quite a while. I am wondering constantly just how to make a move. I would appreciate your thoughts on the matter and I know you do have thoughts about it, sir."

"Don't tell me there is an envious streak in you after all?" queried Forrest, with a smile. "Don't tell me you wish to keep up with the Frasers and Bill Turner?" He leaned against the gate and put his pipe between his teeth and proceeded to roll some tobacco in his hands. As he filled his pipe he watched the Scotsman, this man whom he admired very much indeed.

"You know, I don't do any of those things, Boss. No, I just cannot see how I can buy a property and stock and have enough money to build a home and then live until we start paying our way. All this without putting too much strain on the family. I want to look for a place and while building up the stock, keep my job here, if you would be agreeable. Or, I wonder whether it would be better to leave the whole idea for another year or two. I just do not know. We are very happy, sir, and I think we will find it as hard to leave the Park as it was to leave Scotland. I am a man who likes to stay in one place."

"We certainly do not want you to leave, but I would like to see you settled in a place of your own. How long is it now, four years?"

"Yes, it is four years this next spring. So three and a half now."

"How's Alec managing?"

"Very well," said Murdoch eagerly. "The place is shaping well. It's hard to believe that they bought it twelve months ago and it must be six months since they moved into their house. They are truly happy. Their first foals will be coming soon. We are very pleased to see them so well settled."

"Yes, I know you felt they were quite a responsibility when you first came, but I think you can rest easy now."

"Alistair is doing well too, Mr. Forrest. His school is growing and he will soon need a second assistant. This will mean that he will need more room, too. He certainly found his niche. A big surprise, that."

"In fact, you have all been surprising people. Murdoch, do you think Mrs. Mac. would welcome us if we asked her for a cup of morning tea?"

"I am sure she would. Are you encouraging me to loaf, Boss?"

"It will be the day when I see you loaf, Murdoch. Come, let's go, and explore that Tea Pot."

Murdoch collected his shovel and threw it over his shoulder and joined Forrest on the track.

"How is young Donald MacLeod getting on with his plans for going into the church, Mac? What a good lad he is."

"Yes, he is that, one of the best. He has worked very hard with the stock and by now must have quite a bank balance. He shares everything he earns with his people, but even so, must have quite a lot set by. He is to begin training with Mr. McFadden, you know. His lack of formal education was to be a stumbling block, but after he was examined by the Board, they were well satisfied that his knowledge of the required subjects was good. His father had taught him well and they were impressed with his grasp of Latin and other subjects. I think he will enter a training like and apprenticeship with Mr McFadden."

"I am sure he will be a very good shepherd to any flock he has. I will be interested to watch that lad. I think the experience he has gained working on the stock has been very fruitful for him. Look, there's Mrs. Mac. wondering why we are not working on this lovely Saturday morning. Good morning, Madam." Forrest doffed his hat to her. "We two thirsty souls wonder if there would be a spare cup of tea in the offing?"

"Good morning, Mr. Forrest. I assure you, you are always welcome. Is something wrong, Murd?"

"No, nothing, lass. Mr. Forrest found me leaning on my shovel, gazing into space and he decided that I might work better if we had some tea. Or perhaps he is going to give me the sack, don't know. Anyway here we are."

"Well, do sit down and I'll bring the tea. I've just made some griddle cakes, so we'll have a party."

The men sat quietly on the sunny verandah. Mr Forrest smoking and Murdoch waiting expectantly. He had a feeling that his boss was brooding on some idea and he wondered.

It was only a matter of minutes before Mary returned with the laden tray. "The kettle was boiling," she said and gave a quizzical look towards Murdoch. He gently shrugged his shoulders as an answer and smiled.

"Excellent tea, as usual, dear lady. What a delightful place you have made, Mrs. Mac. You have the touch of the homemaker."

The front garden of the cottage was always neat and tidy and even in the late autumn there were still flowers.

"Well, I do like flowers and chrysanthemums can look so petty. I am fortunate that the soil is so good."

It was not until they had finished their cakes and tea that Mr. Forrest pushed his chair round to face the Macdonalds and said, "I saw Archie Scattersgood in Sydney Town when I was up through the week. In fact, I brought him back to the Park with me."

"I heard that Mr. Scattersgood had gone to the northern rivers, or at least, I thought I heard that," said Murdoch "why he would want to leave 'Scattersdene' I wouldn't know. It's a fine place."

"Yes, Mac, I thought we would have a good neighbour in Archie.

You know they both loved the property. What a name to call it though … Scattersdene! They planned their house and then decided to live in Sydney until it was built. So Mrs. Scattersgood and the children moved into a lovely home in Rose Bay until this house was finished. Archie never liked town life, so he decided to go and look at the north while his family was safely in town. He fell in love with the northern rivers and bought a place up there, on the Clarence River somewhere. He then decided to move there instead of settling here. So he sent for his wife and little ones and stopped the building of this house. He always did have itchy feet. I don'r think he will settle anywhere. Anyway, Mrs. Scattersgood set sail with the children and unfortunately it was in the "Fair Maid". As you know, she went down in a gale and many were lost. Mrs. Scattersgood and the three children were all drowned. Archie is devastated, as you can imagine."

"Poor man, he would be," said Mary. "Poor Mrs. Scattersgood and those dear little children."

"What a terrible tragedy," said Murdoch.

"I found him at the hotel, putting all his Australian business in order prior to going home to England. He was trying to sell all his property, and he has a lot of that, except this property here. Apparently his wife really loved 'Scattersdene' and so he feels very sentimental about it."

"Perhaps he will come back again soon, when the pain wears off a little," said Mary.

"No. Apart from losing his family, he has had word from England that his father is now frail and so he is going back to run the family estates which are quite considerable and he is heir. No, he wants to be free of all his property here, but he doesn't want to see this property go on the open market, but wants to choose the new owner himself. He wants to find a good solid family man who will love the place and I have suggested you Murdoch." William Forrest finished quickly and looked intently at the two surprised people before him.

"Oh, no" cried Mary.

"Oh, no," echoed Murdoch. "It's too big. We haven't that kind of money."

"Well, there's more to the story, As I said, Archie is very sentimental about this and if he can find the right man, someone who will build the farm up to what he dreamed of, and somebody who will build the house he began, he will let it go very cheaply. He wants the place his wife loved so much to become a reality. What do you say?"

"Well, sir, what does he call cheap? I couldn't ever imagine having a place like that. Why, it would be like having a 'Forrest Park.'"

"Well, what's wrong with that? Any complaints? I've told Archie a great deal about you and he would like to meet you both to talk it over. The only thing is that you will have to come to see him now and decide quickly, for he wants to put the sale through before he leaves, and that is very soon."

"You mean right now? Today? How can I make a decision like that in five minutes?"

"I would suggest that I leave now and you talk it over quickly and then come up to the house. Say, in half an hour."

"Why, Mr. Forrest, Mary hasn't even seen the place and I'll not buy it if she doesn't like it."

"I've thought that out. As soon as you've talked it over with Archie, gather up the family and take them over in my carriage. Mick can drive you and you can do it in comfort."

Mary had sat stunned all through this and all she could say was, "I have to change my dress."

"I daresay you will, Mrs. Mac. I'll leave you to it. But hurry."

Mary laughed. "You designing man, sitting there quietly all this time with this going round in your mind."

Mr. Forrest held out both his hands and took theirs. "My friends, I am so glad this has happened. I can see you both in this fine place and we won't lose you, you will be close by." With that he hurried down the steps with a wave of his arm.

"Well, we'd better hurry. Where are the children, Mary?"

"The girls are at Meg's, Murd, but Duncan is working on his insects. I'll call him."

"Yes, he must go for the girls and then call Malcolm to be ready to go to the farm. Mary, can you believe it? Can it be true?"

"Mr. Forrest seems to think so, but it is all so sudden."

"Yes, lass, we'll probably have to make up our minds quickly. This afternoon most likely."

They quickly changed after dispatching Duncan for the others and were soon making their way up to the big house. Alison Forrest met them at the door and impulsively hugged Mary and said, "I do hope it all comes true. Come in, come in."

Archie Scattersgood was a man much changed since they last saw him when he used to drive his family through Riverbend. He looked grey and withered after his ordeal. They found him easy to deal with and soon found that he seemed more eager for them to have the property than they were. The questions Murdoch asked him pleased him and he was much interested in the ideas they had had for the farm of their dreams. He questioned Mary about their children, their ages and their interests. On learning that they had lost their son, John, he was almost overwhelmed and shared with them that his only son had been John too and had been the same age. After this it seemed as though he wanted to give them the "Dene" as he called it. When Murdoch asked the price he astounded them by saying half the amount they had expected. He even said, "That is the first figure we will discuss and will speak further on, after Mrs. Macdonald and the family see it this afternoon. William tells me that you can all go this afternoon? I am sorry it has to be rushed, but you see I sail for England at the end of next week, so things must be settled by then."

Mary clutched Murdoch's arm as they walked home in silence and it wasn't until Duncan came racing up to them that they spoke.

"Are the girls here, Duncan?" Have they changed? Did you get Malcolm?"

"Yes, Mother, to all those questions. Malcolm has gone in to change. What's it all about, Mother? Father?"

"Go and change your clothes, Duncan and we will tell you together. Put on your grey trousers. Do go on. We will tell you soon."

"Right, Mother, I'll go. This must be something exciting."

Mary, still clutching Murdoch's arm, said, "Murd, we cannot possibly do this, can we? It just doesn't seem right somehow."

"Right, love! It would be quite right for me to put you in such a grand place, for that is where you should be. But possible, yes. Possible because Archie Scattersgood wants to make it possible.

I've been thinking. You know, William Forrest is a wily man. Tell me, how would you have described Mrs. Scattersgood?"

"Tall, dark, slim, with an olive complexion."

"Yes, and how would you describe yourself?"

"Tall, dark - oh, I see what you mean, dear. That and our losing Johnnie. Yes, Mr. Forrest would have thought of all those things. But I feel all right about that, Murdoch. I mean, because I resemble Mrs. Scattersgood and us losing Johnnie, is not playing on Mr. Scattersgood's emotions. It seems as though we just seem to fit into what he was looking for. We aren't taking advantage of him. He seems very happy about it all."

"I agree, love. I wondered why he was so happy about it and now I see why, that's all. I am sure we couldn't take advantage of him. He appears to want to practically give us the place. Makes me think of Alec and his gold nuggets. Perhaps we have found one, too."

"Let's go and tell the children. I buttered some griddle cakes and put them into a basket with some lemonade, so we can have lunch on the way."

Before they had discussed it at length, Mick drew up in the carriage and they drove off great excitement. The "Dene" was only two miles from the Park, so soon they were walking across the green pastures of the sloping paddocks. Mick joined Murdoch and the boys in the examination of soil and grass and agreed that they couldn't be better. The fencing was excellent, so too, the sheds, barns and yards. There was a cottage on the property and Sam Whittle lived in it and tended what stock there was. Murdoch called in at the cottage and explained what they were doing and Sam seemed pleased to see them. He asked quietly if there was a chance of staying there, but Murdoch said that it was too early to make such a decision. He would certainly consider him, though, if he could.

They joined Mary and the girls and walked to where they could see excavations and piles of bricks. A huge shelf had been dug snuggly down a gentle slope and they could see that foundations had been started. The plan was that of a large house and there were cellars and store rooms already built. Part of the walls of the lower floor were laid with the lovely warm-coloured brick and thousands of the same bricks stood in piles waiting to be laid in place.

"I am glad it has only reached this stage, Mary, for you can still change the plan to what you want. It has to be what you want."

"You'll have it then, Murd?" she asked.

"What do you think, love?"

"Well, I know nothing of the farm, Murd, but who could do anything but love it." She turned away from him and looked down the slope across the green pastures to the river below and the Blue Mountains in the background. "Murdoch, it is breathtaking. I could look at that view for hours."

"And so you shall, lass, if we buy it. You shall have a big, clear window with just this view and a special chair that is yours." He gave her a quick hug. "Apart from the view, what do you think?" he asked.

"From the little I have seen, I would say that it is more than we have ever dreamed of. It is, isn't it, love? Is it possible that we could own all this, free of debt?"

"It is hard to absorb. What do you think, lads?"

Malcolm and Duncan came up as he said this.

"Father, everything is here already. Sheds, yards and even a milking shed. Not a big one, of course, but it's there. Father, could this really ever be ours?" asked Malcolm.

"Father, do say it will be," put in Duncan.

Mick came up behind the boys and said, "I reckon you'd do well here, Mac. You have the boys to help you and I would say it is a chance in a lifetime."

"Yes, I find it a bit overwhelming, Mick. I never thought to start like this. It is big enough for a dairy, crops and grazing. I still can't believe it and I half expect Mr. Scattersgood to have changed his mind by the time we return."

He hadn't. Archie Scattersgood had liked the Macdonalds a great deal and felt very happy that he was able to leave the place his wife had loved in such loving and capable hands.

When Murdoch went back to the Park to close the deal, he tried to show his appreciation to the man, but was rebuffed and told, "I feel content that Louise's house will be lived in and loved as she would have. I feel grateful to William for bringing me to see you and to seal this contract. I am returning to Sydney on the morrow and would be grateful if you could come to my solicitor in Sydney next week when we can have the papers ready for you to sign."

"I will certainly do that, Mr. Scattersgood. What day would you like me to come?"

"Wednesday should suit. I will look forward to that. Let us shake hands on it, man."

"I think this calls for a Scotch whiskey all round. What do you say? Archie? Murdoch?"

"By all means," said Scattersgood.

"I'm no'a drinking man, as you know, Mr. Forrest, but I think this is one time I will break my rule."

"Good man," Forrest laughed and poured the drinks.

Chapter 25: *The New Farm*

Things moved fast and very soon Murdoch had the title to the new farm. It was many months before they contemplated a move though. Murdoch was quite happy to remain where he was until the new house was completed. When this was done he and the boys would go south for stock before the final move. Malcolm, in the meantime, left his job at the Park and was fully able to do all that Murdoch wanted at the new farm with Duncan's help. They changed the plans of the house a little. There were many minor decisions to be made and so the finished building felt very much their own. Murdoch saw to it that the living room had a large, low picture window that took in the view that Mary loved so much. The furniture they had was quite inadequate for so large a house, but they wouldn't worry about fully furnishing as yet. They would hasten slowly and so buy choice pieces that fitted in when they could. He would even try to get some Lenehan furniture for his lass, it was supposed to be the best in the country.

"Your 'Duntulm' will soon be ready to receive us, lass," Murdoch said as he came in one day. "Painters have nearly finished and I think we may set a date for a move."

"Do you think 'Duntulm' is a suitable name, Murdoch? When you made that promise to me before we left Skye, I really didn't picture anything like this new house of ours. Old 'Duntulm' is such a bleak ruin of a place that it really doesn't compare."

"But it is the dream castle I always promised you, love, so Duntulm it is."

"Oh, Murdoch, I find it still hard to believe. The house is so huge after this cottage. Do you know, I will be sad to leave here."

"Then you are happy here, Mary? I think you still have your heart at home. Sometimes I feel that only part of you came here with us."

"Don't worry about me, Murd. It is only that I find the big house a bit intimidating. So big and empty."

"Aye", lass, I know how you feel. But when we get our own things and all those lovely curtains that you and Meg have made are hung in the windows, you'll see, it will soon be a home not a house. When do you think we should move?"

"When did you tell Mr. Forrest that you will go for stock?"

"We should leave next Monday, I think, and you and the girls will stay here until we return. So really, I finish my job here this week. Well, we've had a good beginning, thanks to Mr. Forrest."

"Are you sure he is happy for us to stay until you return?"

"Yes, love, and I promised him that I would ride over each day after we move, to work here until the new man arrives."

Donald MacLeod had arranged with one of his dairy farmer friends to have stock ready for Murdoch. So he and the boys set off the following week to collect their herd of heifers and cows in calf. By the time they had dropped their calves, all would be in readiness for the dairy to go into full swing. Murdoch was certainly not disappointed in Donald's eye for stock when he saw his new herd, a good mixed lot that would produce quality milk. The return journey was to be slow so they could get them to their new paddocks in top condition.

Mary and the girls had come over in the gig to hang curtains and were delighted to see Murdoch and the boys turn in through the gate with the herd. She stood at her window and watched the cows saunter down the slope into the creek paddock, a roan beast with high, sharp horns leading the rest to the water. Mary started counting them, but as she looked at each one searchingly she lost count.

"How many do you think, Mother?"

Mary looked at Catherine standing beside her and Mary Ann jumping with excitement. Mary laughed, "I don't know, dear. I started counting but forgot when my eyes rested on each one. But there seem to be quite a lot. We will think it is a lot when we have to milk them."

"Can we go down now, Mother? They are nearly all through the gate.

"Yes, run down and tell the men that I have the kettle on."

Mary had the fire going for their own lunch, she had not been expecting the men, and she now quickly put some kindling onto the glowing coals and by the time the men came in she had the kettle simmering. She heard a quick step and was soon in her husband's strong arms. As he kissed her hair and lips, Murdoch said, "A wonderful home-coming, dearest love. If I had a chair to sit on I would have you on my knee. It is grand to see you, Mary love. I am never happy away from you."

"It's good to have you home again, my dear. I like you being home, too. Did you have a good trip, Murd? The cows look good to me."

"Yes, Donald did a fine job for us. There are a few old cows, but mostly young cows and heifers. They are a very docile lot too, only one with any wild ideas."

"The roan with the long horns that led them in, I'll be bound."

"Yes," chuckled Murdoch, "but Thompson said that she is a grand milker and has good calves. We brought some steers up for Thompson and dropped them off at the sale yards. I saw Bill Turner there and he said that I could have that young bull that I had my eye on. I am pleased about that."

"You seem to have a big herd, Murd. How many are there?"

"Yes, I got more than I planned. I have forty. But they were so cheap that I thought I may as well while I have the chance. We'll build the herd up to more than that though when we get going."

"Are the boys coming, Murd?"

"Yes, dear. Where can I wash?"

"The water is on in the bathroom, Murdoch. Just fancy having a bathroom with running water. We are so spoiled. There are towels there, too."

Mary listened to him as he splashed in the basin and smiled to herself. It was good to have him home. She laughed as she heard the children come. Catherine was bossing the boys and telling them to wash their hands in the wash-house and wipe their feet carefully.

They sat round on packing cases and whatever they could find and ate their meal while exchanging news of their doings during the last few weeks.

Moving day came and from early morning to afternoon the two drays from the Park plied between the cottage and the new farm with possessions and furniture. With the last of the loads, Mary shoo-ed everyone away with instructions for Murdoch to come back for her later, after she had finally cleaned the house well enough for the new farmer and his family.

She was surprised how quickly she was done and concluded that houses were much easier to clean without furniture. As there was nothing to sit on she wandered around for a while, then decided to walk through the paddocks to the top of the rise above the Park.

It was a glorious spring day, a soft warm, blue and gold day. Mary sat on a rock looking over the Park's land. The river glistened in the sunlight and the mountains, that unreal blue. "What a place it is," she thought, "if I didn't hate the place, I daresay I could love it. What a cruel place it is. It looks so green and soft and friendly and pleasant, and it isn't. I suppose if one had been born here and didn't know any other, one could love it. After knowing Skye, with the bright greenness of the fields, the misty days and the soft blue ones, and the purple heather and the wonderful mountains, the white thatched cottages and the white and black faced sheep, and Mother, oh, it is all so far away and I want it all so much. Dear Mother, will I ever see you again? This horrible cruel land that took Johnnie and Lizzie Fraser. I can see the churchyard down there with all its tombstones. Those two dear little ones. Oh, Mother, I don't know how I got through those days after I lost my baby. And look what it's done to poor Alec and Alistair. What a cruel land it is. Harsh and tough, it just looks nice and hides a nasty heart." A kookaburra landed in the tree above Mary. "Yes, you can laugh at me, laugh all you can. Even your laughter is harsh. What a land." She sat there looking around her, her eyes misty, but not really shedding tears.

"Murdoch loves it so and so does Fergus. What a strong, healthy man Fergus is now. You'd never think he was a frail, sick man as he was when we left home. I suppose I must be thankful for that. I mustn't wallow in self pity. Try, you silly woman, to make the best of it. Go on, try."

She took a deep breath and looked around her and then towards their new farm. Well, there's certainly a lot to be thankful for there. Murdoch and the children although Malcolm and Duncan children no longer, they all love their new place. Alec, too. Who would have thought that Alec would be the first to own a farm. Such a farm too, and their lovely new home. Well, everything has turned out well there.

Alistair and Caroline and their family, too. Lots to be happy about there. Donald, a son to be proud of, and the little girls were promising to be beautiful girls in manner and face.

Fergus and Elspeth and theirs were right the moment they stepped ashore in Sydney Town. They now live in a new house at Rushcutters Bay. Fergus has the look of a prosperous businessman now and Hamish is only too happy to follow in his steps. Elspeth, too, takes to city life as though she was born to it."

"Now, our family. Yes, there is so much to be thankful for. Who could have expected to be practically given a farm as Mr. Scattersgood did? That wonderful farm with all its prospects for the whole family. There is enough on the farm to keep the family together, always, so I need never fear that I will lose my children like Mother did. No, I do have a great deal to be thankful for. Why do I hate it so? This land of heat, flies and drought, this land of warmth, sun and plenty. Why do I hate it? Do I? Think, woman, do you know? I don't think I do. I think I have just made a habit of hating it without thinking it through. I can see its potential. I can see its warmth embracing my loved ones. I can see our roots going down into this strange land. I can come to terms with it. I can love it! I do!"

She stood up, saying these last words, over and over, "I do. I do.

A twig cracked and she saw Murdoch coming up the rise. She waved gaily. "Murdoch, come quickly and see what I see." She ran to him. "Murdoch, look all round you at the beauty. I can see what you have seen all along. I can see us being part of this land. I can see us really belonging here. I can see it and I love it."

He clasped her to him and his voice broke as he said, "Oh, love, how I have prayed to hear you say it. It was all that I needed to make life perfect. Love, we can really begin to live. Let me take you home to Duntulm."

"No, Murdoch, that's all wrong. It can't be 'Duntulm'. That's living in the past. We have a future and we must call our new home something that fits into this world. Let us thank God and then go home.

So they stood on the hill and praised God for their lives and then, like two children, they held hands and ran down the hill to begin their new life in this new land, a life that was filling the hearts of each one of the new settlers.

To some, the old land called as it had to Mary. To some, it meant a new beginning and forgetting everything about the old. To all, it is a land of opportunity. Every man, and woman had a chance to make something out of it. It really tested you, but by and large you got out of this land rewards, if you were prepared to work.

So Mary enjoyed those summer evenings when she could sit at her window and look out upon the piece of land that was their own. Her chair was placed so that when she could take a moment she would sit and watch her family at their work and when time permitted, their play.

She called it her picture.

"Murd, I've just had an idea" called Mary softly. "Do you think our mothers could make the trip out here from Scotland now that both our dar's are gone. We have so much room and I think they'd really love it?"

And so Mary was content.

Chapter 26: *Epilogue 1*

The old man in the old leather chair sat looking at the picture, "Granda, are you awake?"

Duncan turned and smiled at his granddaughter. "Janey, dear, come in. Yes, I am awake. I am just looking at Mother's picture.

"I shall always remember you sitting in your chair, looking through the window."

"It was my mother's favourite place. In fact my father had this window put in just for her, and bought her this chair in her old age."

"I must admit, Granda, I have often had a sneaky try of it myself. Only when you are busy outside. Granny would never let us sit in it if she could hear you about, though. She says that it is your own special place."

"Your grandmother spoils me, my dear. I really shouldn't claim it as mine, you know, but I must admit I have pleasant dreams in this chair. I always dream of our childhood here and the happy times we had. We were a happy family, Jane, and I have always been thankful for it."

"Well, we were always happy too, Granda, until we lost Mummy and daddy."

"I hope you are happy here with us, dear. Although it can't be much fun for a young lass here with only old people like us to live with, but I know what you mean, dear. I was so pleased to see how happy you all were. Life is not quite the same without them, is it?"

"No, Granda, but I do love being here with you and Granny. Colin, too, is very content, but then, as long as he has his fingers in the soil he would be happy, even though he does miss Daddy so much."

"Yes, it was bad enough having your father go away to war, but to come home safely and then for him to get that dreadful 'flu, and your dear mother, too. I still cannot quite take it in."

"Try not to worry about it all, Granda, we just want you to get better. We don't want you to do anything foolish."

"Well, it seems ridiculous to think that an old fellow like me could live through the epidemic and yet lose our dear ones. Oh, Janey, life was so good."

"Granda, please don't think of it. Try to forget it now. Granny will scold me for letting you get upset."

"I know, dear, but I try to put on a happy face for her. Thankfully she didn't get the horrible illness. She would have hated not being able to look after me. She seems to love fussing around me and I'm afraid I like her doing it too. Do you know, Janey, I do love your Granny."

"I know you do, Granda. You are such a pair of old love birds. I think it must run in the family. Daddy and Mummy were too. And I suppose I will be too, when I fall in love."

"Anyone in mind, dear?"

"Not really, Granda. I think I am having too much fun with our set to pick out anyone special."

"Yes, there is a great deal to be thankful for having a large family in one area. We seem to have more cousins and nephews and nieces in this place than I can keep count of."

"Yes, it is a lot of fun. There's always something doing. In fact, there is a party at Frasers this weekend, but I am not going."

"Why, my dear? I think it would do you good to get out and you have not been out much lately."

"No, Granda, I really don't want to. It is a bit soon yet."

Losing Andy and his wife, Betty, had been a terrible shock to them all. Duncan closed his eyes and thought about it all. "We were so happy. I did look forward to passing the farm to Andy and his family. Now it would only be his family. What a tragedy it was, this 'flu. So many of their old friends had gone with the wretched disease. When he opened his eyes again he found that Jane had gone. What a sweet child she was. Such a comfort to Cattie and him. They were quite a compensation to them after losing their precious son and his wife. Colin was shaping up well, though. He is so like me in many ways, even to liking my bugs, smiled Duncan. He lay back in the leather chair looking out the window at the farm below. Then he closed his eyes, thinking of all that had gone by during all his years in this wonderful place. He remembered the day his mother first called this property 'Alawah', which she had heard was an aboriginal word for 'make your home here' or 'remain here'. She had been very excited about this and thought that it was just the right name for it, but it just didn't fit and after the first trees in the orchard were planted she changed it to 'Nerrigundah', which actually means 'place with many berries', it was just right! It seemed right to us, too, and so our lovely farm became 'Nerrigundah' and not 'Duntulm' as she'd wanted when she'd left Scotland! Mother was so at peace and so loved this place. So were both our grandmothers, when they eventually came from the homeland."

Mother seemed to be the motivating force in the family. Father adored her so much he was content to stand back and just do what she wanted. He was always there, the strong tower of strength. What wonderful parents we had. We were so fortunate. On looking back I can see that she seemed happier here than she had been in our time at 'Forrest Park'. Perhaps she just needed to be in a place of her own. She seemed to be full of life when she brought us all here. Funny, I always think of mother running things, but I am sure Father was the real head of the family. It was as though he let Mother have her head and content to let her to let her run along, but be the wise backstop, always there when we wanted him. I have never really compared him to the uncles. I suppose because we took all the family for granted, everyone seemed to fit into their own niches.

"Gosh, I'll never forget taking Uncle Alistair that wooden leg I made for him." Duncan chuckled and didn't realise that he had said this aloud.

"What are you chuckling about, you silly old man?"

Duncan opened his eyes and smiled at his wife. She was quite a small, rotund woman, several years younger than her husband. She had a bright, fresh complexion and seemed to glow with health.

"Hello, love, I didn't hear you come in. Where's Jane?"

"Oh, she's coming. She is just waiting for the kettle to boil. I think I hear her now. Yes, here she is. Can you manage the door, Janey?"

"Yes, Granny. I see Granda is awake."

"I don't think I was asleep. Was I?"

"Well, dear, I called to see if you were and you didn't answer. So I just waited until Jane came. Then you started laughing to yourself. I must admit Duncan, it is good to hear you laugh again. Are you feeling better, dear?"

"Yes, Cattie, don't worry, I'm fine now. I am so stupidly weak, that's all. I'll soon be out and about with Colin again."

"Well, dear, I am sure that you will find that Colin is managing very well with out you."

"Don't worry, Cattie, I am not going to interfere with the boy, but you know I just like to potter about and see what is going on."

"You can see from here. That will have to satisfy you for a while."

"Very well, dear, let's have that tea now. I know when I am defeated."

"Granda, tell me about Uncle Alistair's leg. What was amusing you so?"

The two old people smiled and Duncan said, "Well, lassie, you will have to know something of Uncle Alistair before you can really appreciate it. Remember, he was the schoolmaster. Soon after we came to 'Nerrigundah', Father gave him four acres on the road and he built the school.

"Yes, I know that much. I always felt it was our school and truly loved that place."

"Well, in a way, I suppose it was 'our' school. He was a very good teacher, was Uncle Alistair, but before he was a school master he was a farmer and rather a daunting character. He was very strict with the children and in comparison to us I don't think his children had much fun. I suppose he was a rather pious man and seemed to be scared that if anyone laughed they would tempt the devil, or something."

"But he was very kind, dear. I loved being in his school."

"Oh yes, Cattie, but that was after his accident."

"What happened, Granda?"

"They'd moved up to a farm on the Manning River. At least, it wasn't a farm when they went there. They just carved it out of the bush. A tree fell on him and crushed his leg and he had to have it off because it wouldn't mend. It worried me to see such a big man hobbling around on one leg and a crutch and so I made him a leg. I was quite proud to think I could make one and it turned out to be quite a reasonable one at that. But you've no idea what I went through on the way to the house on the day I took it to him. I had no idea I was so scared of him until I knocked at that door. Anyway it fitted and the dear old soul wore it for some time until he got a better one."

"Yes, I can remember him stomping around on that. I knew you made it and was so proud of you. I think I was in love with you even in those days, old man."

"You seemed to be forever trailing around after me, m'dear can't say I minded."

"Were your two families close then Granda?"

"Yes, my father and Mr. Forrest were the best of friends and for that matter, our mothers were too, weren't they, Cattie?"

"Yes, they were very fond of one another and so we were ever in and out of one another's homes, especially when you moved here, Duncan."

"Yes, I am sure our parents wanted us to stay in the right places and not intrude. Anyway, you were a bit small then."

"Daddy loved Mr. Mac. like a brother and your father felt the same about Daddy. It was a grand life, Duncan, wasn't it?"

"Do you remember coming to Australia, Granda? How old were you?"

"Yes, I remember. I was twelve. I remember Skye very well and I remember that filthy ship, too. Sometimes I can still smell it, particularly when I am in the pig yard," he said with a chuckle.

"Surely not that bad?"

"Well, perhaps not quite so bad, but after the clean smell of Skye we thought it was very bad. That is probably where my little brother, Johnnie, first got sick."

"I didn't know you had another brother, Granda."

"Yes, Johnnie. He died soon after we came here. He died of snake bite. He was with me when it happened. It was a terrible day. I always felt responsible, I was supposed to be looking after him."

"Oh, I'm so sorry. Tell me about Uncle Malcolm, Granda."

"We all worked together on 'Nerrigundah' for some years. It was a dairy farm then, you know. We made it a very big dairy and did quite well, too. Malcolm married Charles and Isabelle Parry's girl, Laura, and they, had a tribe of children. Seven, I think, eh, Cattie."

"That's right. Mr. Parry was a friend of my father. In fact, Charles Parry and John Trent, whom your Uncle Fergus worked for, and Daddy were on the ship that Duncan came out on. That's where they all met. My Dad saved Mr Trents son Hugh from going overboard."

"Oh, I see."

"My Uncle Alistair went to work for Mr. Parry when we first came to Cattie's father at 'Forrest Park'. That's how it all started. As my brother, Malcolm, had married Laura Parry and when her father died the place was left to her and so they moved out there. It was a grazing place and that suited Malcolm down to the ground and he was very happy to leave 'Aroona' to Father and me. We carried on with the dairy for some years and by that time our Grandmas, Catriona Macdonald and Margaret MacKenzie had to come all the way from Scotland only Mother, Father and the girls lived here in this house. When we married we lived in the cottage at first. It is not here now, Jane, but you can still see some of the trees your grandmother planted in our garden. She always was a great gardener. Her mother brought it out from the homeland when she came. It was a wonderful gift."

"You mean where the Rowan tree is, Granda?"

"Yes, lass, that is where we started our married life. We loved it, didn't we, old girl?"

"Yes, we did. That's where your father was born, Jane."

"We had to wait a long while for him, too. We didn't think we were going to be blessed with children and then we had Andy. Life was good. We stayed there until my sisters married and we moved up here. We lived in the ground floor and Father and Mother lived up here. By this time we had closed the dairy. It was getting too hard for Father and Mother, especially for her, and Father could see it was telling on her so we went into grazing too. And then I began the orchard. I had planted an acre of citrus some years before, just to try it out and as it was successful, I planted more and look at it now! The paddock I chose for the stone fruit was good and fertile but a really big flood came and took most of them, and it was followed closely by a big frost. We lost many of the remaining apricot trees."

"It's beautiful."

They looked out onto the beautiful big trees, line upon line of oranges in one block, lines of Valencias here, Navels, Sevilles and then grapefruit, mandarins, limes and stone fruit of every kind. "It is hard work though, Duncan. You have worked hard on all this to make it so." Catriona gave his hand a squeeze.

"Yes, we have worked hard, but that's what made life good, working hard and seeing something for it. It hasn't all been good. We lost many trees with frost, flood and disease, but has all been worth it. Now Colin is taking over and it is good to see. Your father trained him well, Janey. I was blessed to have a son and grandson carry on in the work I love so much. More than my Father could say. I really wasn't cut out to be a dairyman and he knew it. He never did imagine that I would have gone in for trees in such a big way though, but I think he would be pleased. I wonder what Mother would think of her picture now?"

"Ever since I can remember, I have seen you sit there after meals and look out at the farm Granda. Remember how I used to creep upstairs when Mummy thought I was in bed and get into your lap and curl up and go to sleep. I must have been an awful nuisance. Mummy always knew where to find me."

"We are very fortunate that Andy brought his family here to share our lives. I do think families should live together. We have always been a 'together' family."

"Tell me more of the family, Granda. What about the Frasers?"

"You've heard about Uncle Alec striking it rich in Ballarat and so I won't go through that again. I think even the smallest ones in the family know that one. We all thought he would die when he came home from the goldfields, but my Aunt Meg was determined he wouldn't, and neither he did. Well, not for a long while, anyway. He bought 'Riverdell' and it hasn't really altered since they bought it. They bred wonderful horses on that place. They were always horsey people. I remember the huge Clydesdales that they had there. I am sure we have lost something by not using horses as we used to, now that everyone is riding around in these new-fangled autos and using tractors on the farms instead of horses. I think they miss a lot. Everyone thinks machines nowadays. They even fought the war from aeroplanes. I suppose one day they will expect people to fly in them from place to place. Well, it won't be in my time, thank goodness. Where was I? Uncle Alec used to be pushed around in a sort of pram thing and while he could, he still ran that farm and he knew just what was going on there until the day he died. Young Ian started off a bit wild and married a no-good girl, but she died when their first child was born. I think it was a bit of a relief to Aunt Meg. She didn't get to like her much. Anyway, she died and left Ian with little Peter and as you know, he was a great fellow. Aunt Meg brought him up until Ian married again and that's where your Aunt Beatrice came into the family. After that, things went well. They still breed the best horses in the district, but not Clydesdales, as you know."

"Tell me about the family in Sydney now, Granda. What about the MacKenzies?" Jane snuggled down in one of the big leather chairs that were in this part of the living room. "They were your mother's relatives, weren't they?"

"Yes, Uncle Fergus was Mother's brother. He stopped in Sydney and worked for Mr. Trent. His children married into the Trent family and I cannot remember now who married which one. Your Granny would know, wouldn't you, dear?"

"Well, yes, I do, but they would only be names to you Janey. I will show it to you on the family tree."

"Have you written it all down, Granny? Do show me sometimes, please."

"I must admit I didn't, dear. Granda's mother was a great one for writing things down and her diaries are here somewhere. Where do you keep them, Duncan? Are they with yours?"

"Yes, my dear, they are. They are safely kept there in my cedar cabinet. Would you like to look at them, Jane? Perhaps, if you are interested I may give you them to look after when I am gone."

"I hope that won't be for a long time, Granda. But yes I would love to read them. Did your mother always keep a diary?"

"No, not at first. But after we moved here she kept a tally of all that went on here and all of the family's doings. I imagine that your grand children would regard them as bits of Australian history. Perhaps they should be carefully kept for such a time. Can you imagine what your grandchildren, sixty years from now in 1980, would think of it all?"

"If I ever have any, Granda," laughed Jane.

"Well, I shall get the diaries out for you tomorrow. They will take quite a lot of reading, so be prepared to start a marathon."

"I will look forward to that. Anyway, back to Uncle Fergus,"

"Well, my Uncle Fergus became quite a businessman and ended up with the stores you now see in Sydney. Big department stores, as you know. He certainly had a knack for selling things. Mr. Trent's son, Hugh, was never really interested in the business and so Uncle Fergus and his son, Hamish, bought him out of the business when Mr. Trent died. From there on they spread like mushrooms and had branches everywhere. There always seemed to have enough boys in the family to carry on in the same way. My branch of the family is the only one that runs short of boys and we started late, didn't we, Cattie?"

"Yes, dear, but I think we go in for quality, not quantity. What do you think, Janey?"

Jane laughed, "I hope Colin marries Linda and has lots of boys for you, and quite quickly, too, so you can enjoy them. Incidentally, Granny, if they do get married soon, do you think I could move upstairs with you and Granda and let Colin and Linda have the downstairs?"

"By all means, dear. That is what we would expect to happen.

This will always be your home. It is already in our wills, isn't it, Duncan?"

"Yes, my dear, there will be room for you in this nest and one day it will be yours. Probably not too far in the future."

"Well, I don't want you to go for quite a while yet, Granda," said Jane, adding wistfully, "but maybe I will spend my old age in that chair, too, looking at Great Grandmother's picture."

Chapter 27: *Epilogue 2*

Jane Macdonald now sat in the old leather chair looking through the picture window. What a difference. The dust from the quarry on the next property was drifting over the old orchard in clouds. On days of wind like this you could almost feel the grit on the trees. No tree could withstand such an onslaught. No wonder Colin had lost interest and she could not blame his boys for giving up on it. Colin was an old man now and had moved up to the Avoca Beach on the Central Coast of New South Wales to get away from the devastation that the old woman looked out at now.

"Are you awake, Aunty?"

"Yes, Sally, I'm awake. I have just been sitting here looking at it all."

"I wish you wouldn't, Aunty. You cannot do anything about it, so please just shut it out. We still have this wonderful house to live in and we must be thankful about that."

"Yes, and I am thankful that you and Bill are happy here with me."

"Don't worry, Aunty, when Daddy moved away I was only too pleased for us to come back to the old house. I had a very happy childhood here and I love it so. Bill and Chris do, too. It is handy for Bill to go to his practice in Penrith and now that Chris is at Hawkesbury College, it is close for him too."

"Just fancy your Chris following the old tradition of agriculture. I thought he would be a doctor like his father."

"Well, he isn't and we are both very glad about it. You never know, if they stop crushing gravel right on our doorstep, he may be able to use the farm again. It would be good to see. It would please you, wouldn't it Aunty?"

"I was just sitting here wondering what will become of it all, Sally. It has been in the family for so long that I couldn't imagine it not being a farm."

"It must really hurt you, Aunty, to see it so."

"Yes, it does, but I daresay I will not live long enough for that to be a trouble to anyone."

"Tell me about the family in the old days, Aunty. As a matter of fact, Bill and I were talking about it at breakfast. I think I would like to write it all down while I can. You have some old diaries, haven't you, that your grandmother or someone wrote? Would you let me have them for a while so I could do that?"

"Sally, that is such a good idea, I had always meant to write about them myself. I can fill you in on lots of things, too. You'd better do it before I die. It will give me something to do. You are right about the diaries. My great Grandmother started them and then my Grandfather carried on and I carried on after he died. They are rather wonderful bits of Australian history. It is really 'Nerrigundah' history, as great Grandmother started them when they came here, but she told quite a lot of their leaving Scotland and the voyage out here, their first years here until they bought 'Nerrigundah'. I love reading them and I would be happy for you to read them and use the information in them for a story. Would you really do it, dear?"

"Yes, Aunty, I would like to do that."

"Well, no time like the present. Let us go and get them now. Bring the tray-mobile, Sally. We will need it as there are a lot of them."

"Goodness, I thought there would be only one or two."

"No, there are lots of them. Come on."

Sally helped her old Aunt to get out of the old deep leather chair that had sat in front of the window for generations. Jane stood still for a moment until her legs straightened, took her niece's arm and they went into the front bedroom of the house to a lovely old cedar chest of drawers.

"Bring that chair over here, dear, where I can sit down. I find it hard to open these big drawers now and so I leave the bottom drawer open a little. I can get the diaries out by leaving it open that much. Open it up."

"Aunty! There are a lot. I had no idea. What a feast of information."

"I think I am a bit cold here, Sally, so put them on the tray-mobile and let's take them into the front room near the fire. I can't believe it's been about 60 years since I first read these. Granda was still writing his."

Sally soon had them piled up on the trolley and they went back to her aunt's favourite chair.

"The blue ones are Mary Macdonald's diaries, Sally, and all the others are Granda's. Mary, my great Grandmother, was a neat, orderly person, I take it, and liked her diaries to be the same and so there is quite a set of them. They are in very good order really, aren't they? Granda started writing his in any old book, then later, as he grew up, he bought the same kind of book and so made another set."

"What lovely writing Mary had! I see that the first is the story of their coming here, as you said, Aunty."

Jane leaned over and picked up one of her grandfather's red books. She leafed through one, put it down, picked up another and put it down, picked up a third and leaned back, leafing through the pages and signing a little.

"What is wrong, Aunty?"

"Nothing, dear, I just found the place where he writes about my Father and Mother dying. He was very sick just after this happened and he didn't write for quite a time. I remember him sitting here, just like I am at this moment, on a day during his convalescence and telling me about these diaries. It was the first time I took any notice of them. I always knew he kept a diary and I suppose I knew about Mary's too, but it wasn't until that day when he was so weak from the 'flu that we talked about them at length. He had been very ill. We nearly lost him, and he was so stunned by my parents' death, that I think Granny and I just wanted to keep him amused and so I asked him about the family history. It certainly started something, because I have been interested in it ever since. I am so pleased that you are too, Sally."

"Well, it was something that Chris said this morning that started me thinking about it. Aunty, I am sure that the young ones of today do not understand what the old people put into this country to make it the pleasant place it is to live in. That is why I thought I would put it together so that people like Chris would read it and know."

"It is a good thought, dear. I wonder though, whether the young are interested in what happened so long ago. They are always going at such a pace that they don't seem to have time for the past, anyway?"

"Well, dear, I suppose you cannot live in the past. Daddy always tells me that every generation thinks that the greatest change came in their lifetime, but I cannot help feeling that most has come in this last generation. Since the Second World War. You must feel that. What was it like after the First World War, Aunty?"

"There was much change then, Sally. My parents died just after that war and, of course, that meant a great change for me, for all of us. Then Stephen was killed in that first war and I never found anyone else I wanted to marry. It was that war that started the real machinery age, I think. When I was a little girl we went everywhere either on horseback or in a horse-drawn vehicle of some kind. After the war we were all car mad and horses became rather a thing of the past. It hit the Fraser family hard and that is when they sold 'Riverdell' and the family was dispersed. Come to think of it. I don't think I know the whereabouts of one of the Frasers.

"I still write to Jenny Fraser, Aunty. We were very close at school and we keep in touch. She lives in Adelaide now and her daughter has just had her first grandchild. I keep in contact via phone."

"Grandmothers seem to be getting younger every year! Well, after that war everything began to speed up, but there was still value in life. I think life has lost some of its glow. No, don't look at me like that. I don't only mean that life has lost its glory for me, but for the younger people. Life isn't as simple as it was. People make their lives so complicated. My Grandfather just wouldn't have imagined that anything could disturb life on 'Nerrigundah'. One tilled the soil, working very hard, one saw the results of one's effort, with God's help, and you kept doing this until your children took over from you. It's not the same anymore."

"No, I can see that. Of course, the younger ones cannot see that they should follow in father's footsteps just because he did a certain thing, that is furtherest from their minds. I daresay values are just different."

The old lady turned and looked at her niece. "Sally, what will become of 'Nerrigundah'? What will happen to it?"

"Aunty, I don't know. I cannot say, but you realise, as I do, that it will never be the same again. Why don't you think up some wonderful scheme for it, in case Chris doesn't come back to it, or the gravel dust gets worse and we can not use it for agriculture."

"I don't suppose your brothers will ever want it. I was so pleased when Uncle Malcolm's Grandsons, Dick and John did Agriculture at Hawkesbury College. I thought that it would be a continuity of Macdonalds again, but look where they are sitting at city desks, being, what do you call them? Rural scientists."

"Yes, dear. You cannot expect them to come back here. Their wives are city girls anyway."

They fell to musing again and looking through the diaries.

"What a tragedy it all is," the old lady thought. "But is it? What right have I to want to tell these young people how to live their lives. Maybe life is changing, but look at the age Australia is. So ancient that one couldn't take it in. What terrible upheavals have happened in its long history. I suppose white men came here, the Aboriginal people thought that life was finished too. It was for some, but it goes on and on. Well now the story has been written for our future generations! Thank you Sally for helping me."

"What was it Granda used to say? 'God is in his Heaven and all's right with the world'. I'm sure he was right!"

Jane lay back in the big leather chair and slept.

FAMILY TREE OF EMIGRANT FAMILIES & AGES

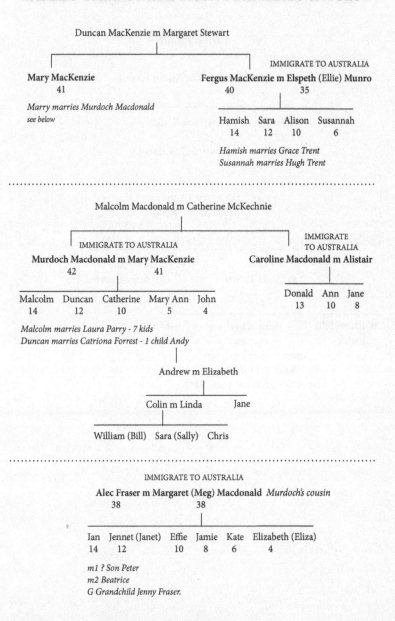

Duncan MacKenzie m Margaret Stewart

Mary MacKenzie
41

Marry marries Murdoch Macdonald
see below

IMMIGRATE TO AUSTRALIA
Fergus MacKenzie m Elspeth (Ellie) Munro
40   35

Hamish	Sara	Alison	Susannah
14	12	10	6

Hamish marries Grace Trent
Susannah marries Hugh Trent

....

Malcolm Macdonald m Catherine McKechnie

IMMIGRATE TO AUSTRALIA
Murdoch Macdonald m Mary MacKenzie
42   41

Malcolm	Duncan	Catherine	Mary Ann	John
14	12	10	5	4

Malcolm marries Laura Parry - 7 kids
Duncan marries Catriona Forrest - 1 child Andy

IMMIGRATE
TO AUSTRALIA
Caroline Macdonald m Alistair

Donald	Ann	Jane
13	10	8

Andrew m Elizabeth

Colin m Linda   Jane

William (Bill)   Sara (Sally)   Chris

....

IMMIGRATE TO AUSTRALIA
Alec Fraser m Margaret (Meg) Macdonald *Murdoch's cousin*
38   38

Ian	Jennet (Janet)	Effie	Jamie	Kate	Elizabeth (Eliza)
14	12	10	8	6	4

m1 ? Son Peter
m2 Beatrice
G Grandchild Jenny Fraser.

HAWKESBURY FAMILY THAT HIRES MACDONALD

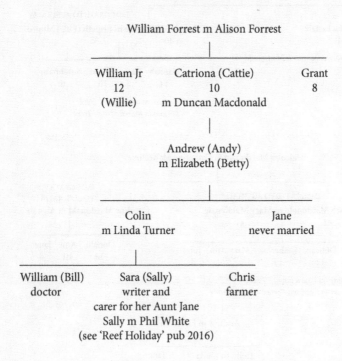

Forrest Family

William Forrest m Alison Forrest

William Jr	Catriona (Cattie)	Grant
12	10	8
(Willie)	m Duncan Macdonald	

Andrew (Andy)
m Elizabeth (Betty)

| Colin | Jane |
| m Linda Turner | never married |

William (Bill)	Sara (Sally)	Chris
doctor	writer and	farmer
	carer for her Aunt Jane	
	Sally m Phil White	
	(see 'Reef Holiday' pub 2016)	

OTHER FAMILIES IN THE STORY

Hawkesbury Family

Charles Parry m Isabelle Parry

Sophia	Laura	Charles Jr	Diana
10	8	6	4

Laura married Malcolm Macdonald and had 7 Children

. . . .

Sydney Businessman - hires Fergus

John Trent m Emma Trent

Hugh	Grace	Philip
6	4	born later

Hugh married Susannah MacKenzie
Grace married Hamish MacKenzie

ABOUT THE AUTHOR
Sheila Hunter
1924–2002

Sheila Hunter was passionate about her family and loved to research their history. This story is gleaned from a mix of both her husbands and her own Scottish families and their settlement and contribution to our country. Her Father was the grandson of Scottish immigrants and he was both born and brought up on the Victorian goldfields as was her mother. Sheila's husbands family were also from Scotland (McLeans) and came out as described in the book, only they were of the illiterate class (speaking only Gaelic) from the Isle of Mull. Life was hard for them and they were helped to learn and settle in the new colony by John Dunmore Lang and his wife. They were taught to cut trees, farm, milk cows, make cheese and they learnt with gusto turning these skills into what later became Norco Dairy Co-Op in Northern New South Wales.

Sheila was born in New Zealand to Australian parents, Murdoch and Mabel McDonald (or Macdonald as they were known before they went to New Zealand) moved back to Melbourne Australia with her family when only 4 years old. She was a nurse by training, but an adventurer in her life! A wife and mother she was a great story teller, often making up very long stories for both her children and grandchildren. They would listen enwrapped within the stories of her telling.

In 1999 Sheila was awarded one of 20 Federal Recipients of the Year of the Senior Citizen Awards. She was an amazing woman! Life was tough - growing up during WW II in a single parent family (her dad had left them to beck to the two children in New Zealand, from his first marriage). They lived on the docks in Melbourne in a family Service Station. She went to school during the day and worked in the Service Station after school, weekends and at nights. She won a full 'Cello scholarship about this time but it was during the war and on arriving home one day found that her mother had sold her 'Cello to help pay the household bills! Yes life was hard! On leaving school she enrolled in Nursing only to be the butt of jokes from her family, but she not only succeeded but excelled at this caring role, ending up as acting Matron of "Roma" Private Hospital in East Gosford NSW.

Sheila, married Norman M Hunter in 1955 and they lived in Avoca Beach all their married life and had two children, Norman Jnr and Sara. Norman and Sheila were a well known couple on the Central Coast NSW with Norman a well know Real Estate Agent also owned and operated Avoca Beach Picture Theatre in Avoca, as well as amassing an amazing Natural History Collection that was known and studied world wide and together they were part of many groups and associations in the area. It was soon after their marriage that they faced the loss of Normans orchard on the Nepean River at Birds Eye Corner, Castlereagh, due to dust from the Gravel pit from the next door farm at Castlereagh, near Penrith NSW. This same orchard was the first farm in the area in 1801 at 'Jacksons Ford' or 'Birds Eye Corner' at Castlereagh (known in the book as Riverbend). It was this that inspired the writing of this book.

In 2000, her beloved husband and fellow adventurer, Norman, died from Dementia and she unfortunately followed only two years later from Cancer.

Sara Powter 2018

See
www.sheilahunter.com.au

ALSO BY THIS AUTHOR

Part of the *Australian Trilogy*

"MATTIE - Coming of age in Convict Australia"

Woodslane/Hand in Hand Publications
ISBN: 9780994578204
by Sheila Hunter

Mattie aged 12 is convicted for petty theft, given the sentence of 7 years and is sent to Australia. She meets another convict woman who at her death gives Mattie a chance for a new life. Mattie makes the most of everything that comes her way. She earns her freedom, falls in love, marries and becomes a mother. Life is not kind to her. She meets bushrangers, moves to the Gold Fields in Bathurst, and starts a store. Mattie is the kind of woman that made Australia what it is today.

Child Convict, Wife, Bushrangers, Widow,
Bathurst Gold Fields, Shop Keeper, Town Builder ...
A remarkable woman!

Originally published on Amazon as
"Mattie" - the Story of an Australian Convict Child
ISBN: 1533458537
Large Print ISBN: 1533458537

Also available on Amazon/Kindle under the name of
MATTIE, The story of an Australian Convict Child
Kindle ASIN: B00TTEDBT0

***

ALSO BY THIS AUTHOR

Part of the *Australian Trilogy*

"RICKY - A boy in Colonial Australia"

Pacific Wanderland Publications
ISBN-13: 978-0-9945782-1-1
by Sheila Hunter

Ricky and his mother immigrate from England to join his father in the new Colony of Sydney. On arrival there is no sign of his dad. Ricky's mum uses the tiny amount of money they brought with them to get lodgings in a run down building. Things go from bad to worse when his mother dies and he is thrown out of the lodgings and all their possessions are confiscated by the caretakers.

Ricky finds himself living on the streets of Sydney Town as a street waif. Ricky finds safe places to sleep and befriends freed convicts who can help him survive. One day he finds another lost child and he helps reunite her with her family. These people try to help him but by his stubbornness he insists of doing things his way, but he has found a mentor and confidante. The story follows him through his life. He survives and turns his life around also helping others along way, some of whom he 'adopts'.

OTHER EDITIONS
Kindle ASIN: B00MLYN6IG
Amazon: ISBN-10: 1500770574
                               ISBN-13: 978-1500770570
Amazon Large Print: ISBN-10: 1533472742
                               ISBN-13: 978-1533472748

***

ALSO BY THIS AUTHOR

"REEF HOLIDAY"

Great Barrier Reef adventures in Queensland

Amazon ISBN: 1503298078
By Sheila Hunter

Sue White, aged 13, is excited that her parents are to take her on a holiday to the Barrier Reef. Her friend Alison advises her to speak to another girl in their school who lives on a Great Barrier Reef island, for tips about life in such a place. They are surprised to find that the White family is actually planning to holiday on the very island where Jess Carey and her family live.

The Whites, Phil, Sally & Sue, Jess Carey and her brother Lewis all travel to the reef together and so begins a great adventure for Sue and her new found friends. The Carey's are Alan and Bob, brothers, and their wives, Barbara and Win. Bob's son, Paul, is quite a skilled amateur naturalist and is most helpful and instructive when he takes parties of guests on to the reef.

The Carey youngsters and their extended family know their reef well and this holiday proves to be a learning experience for all at the resort. All the children get along well and have many adventures, including meeting some pirates.

This is a great introduction for kids to learn about life on the Great Barrier Reef in Queensland.

While this is not part of the Australia Colonial Trilogy you can trace the family to the end of 'The Heather to the Hawkesbury'. Sally, Sue's mother is a great great great granddaughter of the Macdonalds who arrived from Scotland in 1850's.

Available on Amazon/Kindle
Amazon: ISBN 1503298078
Kindle ASIN: B01LY8L6GT

***

COMING SOON

"AUTOBIOGRAPHY"

ANOTHER BLOOMING SHEILA! - the Early Years

VOL 1
by Sheila Hunter

Sheila Hunter (née Macdonald), spent her first years growing up in Ngakawau, a timber town on the North West Coast of the South Island of New Zealand.

Her beloved father, Murdoch Macdonald, although belittled by his wife Mabel, was a brilliant Engineer and built all sorts of mining and Timber equipment, including converting a tractor to a Locomotive and developing and Patenting a guy rope, pulley system to access tall trees in very steep valleys with minimal destruction. This system was used world wide, may still be, and was able to deliver full trees to the mill on the floor of the valley with safety and ease.

This takes the story through The Depression, her parents separation and divorce, and up to the beginning of the adventures that started with her marriage.

Sheila is the Author of an Australian Colonial Trilogy and a children's adventure story set on the Great Barrier Reef.

Co-Winner of *1999 NSW Senior Citizen of the Year* in the Year of the Senior Citizen.

VOL 2 LIFE WITH NORMAN
    - the Adventures begins

VOL 3 THE ECLECTIC ECCENTRIC COLLECTOR
    - the Museum Story

***

amazon REVIEWS FOR
THE HEATHER TO THE HAWKESBURY

5 stars ☆☆☆☆☆
Mary Wheelright on JANUARY 18, 2018
Format: Kindle Edition

Wonderful in every way!!!! Mary W

*"I could not get enough of Sheila's stories. They were great
and made me want to read more after I had read one I had
to keep going. This is a great story of people wanting a better
life in a new world. The way she tells it is amazing. I could
not stop and kept reading it until I got to the end. I loved all
her book and would recommend them to all."*

***

4 stars ☆☆☆☆☆
Jan Rouse on OCTOBER 30, 2016
Format: Kindle Edition

"Just loved it."

***

5 stars ☆☆☆☆☆
Ronnale on APRIL 25, 2016
Format: Kindle Edition

"It was amazing"
*Lovely end to a series of books on the life and times of a large
Scottish family of immigrants who come to Australia due to
the "Clearance" of Scotland."*

***